THE
CASTLE
OF 1000 DOORS

TOROTH-GOL BOOK I

KENNY GOULD

The Castle of 1,000 Doors (Toroth-Gol Book I)

Copyright © 2023 Kenny Gould

BOOKS BY KENNY GOULD

<u>**Toroth-Gol Series**</u>

The Castle of 1,000 Doors

Dungeon School

Prey House

The War of Fangs

<u>**The School Beneath the City Series**</u>

The Potionmaster

<u>**Other Work**</u>

The Midnight Carnival

Monster Summer Camp

This one is dedicated to you, dear reader.
That's right—you. The kooky cats who inspire me to write.

Thank you for reading.
Stay crispy!

THE EMPIRE

The Wastes
Peakskill
Brigadoon
Portside
Cort
Argoston
Oriel
Spiderhead
Helios
Bourdoux
Steel City
The Great Basin
Ironwood
Bellablanco
Velda
Vrich
The Crescent
Sanmar
Palmer's Pavilion
Atlantis
Barrier's Pavilion
Takura
Crystal Keep
Reo
Red Hills
Aramel
Binti
Irbo Jamrain
The Sea of Paradise
Arid Dominion
Hub
Lobster Isles
Shining Dunes
Fain

PROLOGUE

Lucca Bert, Captain of the Steel City Guard, stood before the double doors to the highest room in the city's tallest tower and waited to be summoned by a monster.

Why did I take this promotion? Lucca thought as his heart thumped. *I'd rather be anywhere except here. I don't even need to be at the Stadia. I could be on patrol. I could—*

"Come in."

Lucca's thoughts were interrupted by a voice from inside the room, low and masculine, with a timbre that raised goosebumps on his arms. He pushed inside. The room was airy and spacious, with a marble floor and three unadorned walls of strange gray metal. The far wall was made entirely of windows. Through them, Lucca could see the glittering lights of the city he called home. From this vantage point, he could see all the way to the city's edge and farther still, out to the harbor where the wealthy docked their boats in anticipation of the evening's lightball match.

But the strangest feature of the room was a six-foot-square box made from the same gray metal as the walls. It was perfectly smooth except for a thin rectangle of mirrored glass that sat level with Lucca's eyes.

the doors behind Lucca shut with a loud *boom*. Lucca dropped to one knee, his head bowed, his eyes on the tips of his standard-issue boots.

"Lucca Bert." Jaguar's voice came from the box. "My brave captain. You brought what I requested? Rise, and show me what you've found."

Lucca stood, and though he kept his eyes down, he reached under his arm for the photographs he'd kept there. Before him, the mirrored glass on the face of the box slid to one side.

Don't look in, Lucca thought, trying to suppress an involuntary shiver as he held out the photographs. *You don't want to see Jaguar's face. For the love of the Empire, don't look at what's inside the box.*

And for once... Lucca's traitorous body complied. There was a slight pressure on the photos, and then they were gone, drawn into the box by the monster that lived inside. The piece of mirrored glass slid shut.

Lucca stepped back, his heart hammering, and adopted the waiting position of the Steel City Guard.

For several seconds, the only sounds were Lucca's pounding heart and the soft whisper of paper against paper as Jaguar flipped through the photographs.

"So Valentine has tipped his hand," Jaguar finally said. "You caught him as he exposed his rotten core."

"Yes, my... my lo—my lord," Lucca stammered. He forced saliva down his too-dry throat. "In the first five photos, you see Valentine being greeted by the Thuins. The next set feature the laboratory where Valentine met with our enemies. I fear the Thuins got wind of our investigation, as much of the lab had been stripped before our arrival. But the pictures speak for themselves, and my men have already traced the lab's funding back to Valentine's accounts."

"Pictures can be doctored," Jaguar said. "Stories invented. But a trail of dirty money never lies. Well done, Lucca. You captured the Thuins who worked in this lab?"

"Of course, my lord. As soon as Valentine left. They were arrested and interrogated. Their hands are being dyed as we speak."

"Good. And Valentine?"

"He…" Lucca licked his lips. "We let him go, my lord. Valentine is… well-loved by the people. Some say he might replace August Morgan. We wanted to hear your orders before we made a move."

"Ah." Lucca couldn't tell whether Jaguar was pleased or disappointed. He hoped he'd made the right move. According to whispered rumors, Lucca's predecessor had done *something* to displease Jaguar, and now he was gone, disappeared one night as if he'd never existed.

"I'm going to ask you a question, Lucca, and I want you to answer me honestly," Jaguar said. "And tell me the truth—I'll know if you don't. Yes?"

A bead of sweat dripped down Lucca's neck. *This isn't fair,* he thought, his eyes still on the tips of his boots. *I worked through the ranks. I did everything right. So why are my men down at the Stadia while I'm talking to Jaguar?*

But he only said, "Of course, my lord."

"Do you think we should have magic in civilized society?"

The question surprised Lucca. "No, my lord! I've seen the Thuins do some… interesting things with magic. Powerful things that would be, ah, nice to replicate. But no. No! Magic has no place in the Empire. I couldn't begin to imagine such a travesty."

"A smart answer. Do you know why I hate magic?"

Again, Lucca hadn't anticipated the question. *What if I say the wrong thing? Will I end up like Dario? Gone without a hint I'd ever existed?*

Lucca shook his head. "I wouldn't presume to guess, my lord."

"To create something stable, you need a solid foundation. But magic is unpredictable, which makes it anathema to the Empire. The very nature of magic is diametrically opposed to the world I'm trying to build." Jaguar paused, and when he spoke again, his voice was harder: "Magic must be kept in check, at all costs. That's why we can't let the Thuins continue to run wild. That's why we need to pull the Heart of the World from its fortress."

"Of course, my lord." More than anything else, Lucca wanted to get out of that strange room with his life, and he'd do or say whatever it took to make that happen. "We can't have magic in a stable Empire. It wouldn't do."

"We need a message to those who might think of betraying us." Jaguar continued as if Lucca hadn't spoken. "Tomorrow is Empire Day, is it not? When the Sledgehammers finish playing the Serpents, arrest Valentine—and his mongrel son. Dye their hands as ones who have betrayed the Empire and send them into Toroth-Gol. The day after tomorrow, make their treason the stunning headline of the day."

Lucca felt his heart skip. "My… my lord? I…" He trailed off. It was folly to mention his fears. Not here, not before the altar of fear itself.

"Speak your mind."

Another bead of sweat dripped down the nape of Lucca's neck. "Valentine is one thing, but there may be some trouble if we arrest King Crow, my lord. We have no proof of any wrongdoing from him. And if the Sledgehammers win, then…" He didn't finish the sentence. "I have no doubt the son is as guilty as the father, of course, though bringing both of them to justice will likely cause some unrest."

Jaguar was silent, and Lucca closed his eyes, certain the creature inside the box would end him with a thought.

You had to speak up, didn't you? You gave your opinions to the most dangerous creature in the Empire and now you'll pay the price.

Finally, Jaguar spoke. "You address me with honesty and courage, and in service of the Empire, so you have nothing to worry about from me. My brave, loyal son. Captain of my guard. You should be rewarded."

The words were so comforting that Lucca couldn't stop a nervous giggle from escaping his throat.

You idiot. Why would you laugh *in front of Jaguar?*

"But I need you to act *decisively*," Jaguar continued. "Show our people the cost of betraying the Empire. We must make an example of Valentine, and taking the only other person he loves will encourage those who might betray us to think twice. I wish Valentine's late wife were still with us, so we could send all three to the Hunt, but she was a fly we swatted years ago."

Lucca nodded. It was folly, but he wouldn't say anything else. Not when he was this close to escaping. Lady Violet Valentine had been even more popular than her husband, especially among those who lived in the Dregs, and her death had nearly been the end of the Empire. If she were still alive and they sent *her* into Toroth-Gol, Lucca would've had to deal with a full-blown rebellion.

It wasn't an issue. "I will make the arrangements you've requested, my lord," Lucca said. "Valentine and King Crow will go to the Hunt and fight their way through Toroth-Gol. Long live the Empire."

"Long may you live, Lucca Bert."

Sensing he was dismissed, Lucca bowed and turned to leave, but Jaguar's low voice stopped him: "Start your preparations tomorrow, Lucca. For tonight, enjoy the exhibition."

"My lord?" Lucca blinked. Was Jaguar telling him to *go out*? To join his men at the Stadia?

"The Sledgehammers' match," Jaguar said, and Lucca realized that's *exactly* what Jaguar was telling him to do. "It would behoove our people to have you present there."

"Thank you, my lord!"

"You make the Empire proud, Lucca. Go with my gratitude."

Saluting crisply, Lucca turned and marched out the doors. As they closed behind him, he couldn't help but feel like he was on the cusp of something great. And half an hour later, as he entered the Stadia and heard the cheers of the crowd, he was already half-drunk in celebration. He was still wearing his uniform, and in that moment, Lucca Bert felt like a hero.

1

The Steel City Stadia was a marvel of modern engineering, a multi-purpose stadium built opposite the Spire at one end of the city's Pleasure Gardens. Commissioned by the city's sixteenth Prime Minister, the Stadia was made of the same white marble and glass as the other buildings on the highest of the city's three levels, though the Stadia also had a retractable roof for open-air games and events. Inside, it boasted a wide array of shops and restaurants, making it a full-fledged entertainment hub. From the Stadia's east side, it was a short walk across the skybridge to the casino.

Depending on one's proclivities, many said that the best view in the house was from the Prime Minister's box, with its wide balcony that offered a sweeping view of the pitch from the fifty-yard line. Others preferred the top-down view of the Atrium, the museum dedicated to Steel City's past victories where one could watch the game through a glass floor. Still another group preferred the private rooms with walls of one-way mirrors where one could sip ice wine and take in the events while remaining invisible to the rabble below.

Whatever one's preference, I maintain the best view in the house was from the twenty-yard line of the pitch itself, when your team was tied with your biggest rivals during the exhibition match before Empire Day, eighteen seconds remained on the clock, and thirty thousand fans chanted your name.

King Crow! King Crow! King Crow!

I was sweaty and tired, my right shoulder aching from a dirty hit I'd taken in the third period. The lightball hovered above my left palm, and I thought about the best way to get it into the goal. A second passed, and then another. I had enough time to make a single play.

King Crow! King Crow! King Crow!

The hulking brute who guarded me was named Magnus Croyden. He was the son of Helios nobleman Julien Croyden, one of my father's political rivals. Whereas my lightball game relied on strategy and tact, Magnus was all about power. He had about six inches and seventy pounds on me, and he was the one responsible for my throbbing shoulder.

"Daddy can't save you now," Magnus spat as the clock ticked down to ten seconds. Did I mention Magnus *hated* me? Many years ago, a nobleman named Sal Valentine had adopted me from the Dregs, Steel City's lowest level. Valentine was a hero to the common man, and many said he might become the next Prime Minister. That rubbed purists like the Croydens the wrong way. Magnus had grown up with a silver spoon, his family mansion even bigger than my father's.

Something to exploit? Yes. That should do nicely. I took a deep breath. *This is going to hurt.* Eight seconds left.

I winked at Croyden. "Saw your mother last week. Amazing how someone as handsome as you came from someone as ugly as her."

I *almost* felt bad about how easy it was to manipulate Magnus. The idiot roared and charged me, leaving his position to dole out some measure of petty revenge. Five seconds remained on the clock.

As Magnus barreled toward me, my teammate Zorba took up a more advantageous position along the goal crease. Four seconds. I shot the lightball to my teammate Kenzo, who passed it to the wide-open Zorba. *Three. Two.* The keeper lunged at her, his fan flashing, but Zorba didn't miss from the doorstep. With a second left on the clock,

Zorba faked high and shot low, burying the lightball into the back of the net.

The crowd erupted. I could hardly hear the cheers over the airhorn and the sound of my own blood beating in my ears—and Magnus cursing my name.

"King Crow!" the audience shouted. "King Crow! King Crow!"

Magnus wailed on me with his fists, screaming obscenities, but I didn't care.

We won! I smiled through a mouthful of bloody teeth. *Take that, Helios. The Steel City Sledgehammers earned another win.*

My teammates pulled Magnus away, and a huge pair of hands lifted me from the ground. I looked up into the smiling face of Frederic Ortega, my team's star enforcer.

"The boy wonder comes through again!" he rumbled, pulling me into a sweaty hug. "Well done, Crow. We did it!"

No sooner had Ortega let me go than my other teammates had me in their arms. They laughed, slapping me on the back, the sweat on their foreheads glistening under the Stadia's bright lights. From his team's bench, Magnus glared at me with murder in his eyes. I blew him a kiss. He stepped toward me, but his coach grabbed his shoulder and I didn't spare the man another thought as I was pressed against Zorba. I hugged her, shouting words of thanks into her ear that were lost in the Stadia's roar. Around us, the referees blew their whistles, trying to restore order. Technically, there was still a second left in the game.

When everything settled down and our team was back on our side of the pitch, the shooters lined up along the middle line and the enforcers took spots in their circles near our goal. Zorba and Frederic stood outside the center circle and I crouched inside it, the Serpents' center on the line before me and the lightball on the ground between us. The game was as good as over: I'd won three out of every four face-offs against the Serpents' center, and even if he got the ball, a second wasn't enough time to do anything. Not against the Sledge-hammers.

Not against me.

The referee signaled for the face-off and I slipped under my opponent's arm, scooping up the ball and launching it into the air. It was a showy move, a way of rubbing salt into the wound, and I wouldn't have done it against anyone but Helios—well, anyone but Magnus. As the lightball shot toward the sky, I caught the look on Magnus' distant face, and I would've paid 10,000 Empire marks to have it captured in a picture.

Before the ball started falling, the game whistles blew, cementing our victory: Helios Serpents, 26. Steel City Sledgehammers, 27.

The crowd cheered and fireworks exploded. Frederic grabbed me from behind, lifting me into the air, and then my teammates were around him and I found myself carried on their shoulders. They set me down amidst a sea of flashing cameras.

"King Crow!" A microphone was shoved into my face. I recognized the person who held it, a handsome man in a crisp blue suit. He was good-looking in a traditional way, with a square jaw and thick, brown eyebrows. His teeth were white and perfect. His chin was dimpled, and his salt-and-pepper hair was slicked away from his broad forehead.

In a city that thrived on entertainment, Elvis Madden was the de facto master of ceremonies.

"Undefeated on the season and now a stunning victory over your rivals, the Helios Serpents," Madden continued as he placed a hand on my shoulder. "Tell us: what was going through your head on that last play?"

More flashing lights. Another round of fireworks. I peered past the cameraman, searching the rows behind him for my father. His usual spot was empty.

Still in Ironwood.

Madden registered my distraction and wiggled the microphone expectantly.

"Uh, it was good," I said. Madden surreptitiously prodded my foot with the tip of his snakeskin boot, indicating that I hadn't actually answered his question. "Sorry! Big victory and all. It's just… a lot! I'm excited. And distracted."

"And who can blame you? But tell us—how did you get the best of Magnus Croyden? He's the best enforcer in the league, and when he lined up against you at the end there, I thought for sure the game would end in a tie. Was there something you said to him? He seemed quite upset!"

I gave up searching for my father and turned to face Madden. "Helios has a great team this year, but I felt like I owed something to our fans. I knew Magnus was expecting me to take the shot, so I wanted to throw him off his game. I simply told him we were going to win. I have complete trust in my teammates and it was awesome to see them pull through."

"That's great," Madden said, his head moving up and down like one of those King Crow dolls that had springs in their necks. Somehow, amidst all the activity, I heard the voiceover from the commercial: *'Only fifteen Empire marks at the Sledgehammers official team store!'* Again, Madden prodded me with his boot.

"Speaking of Croyden, I've heard rumors of a rivalry between you and the Helios enforcer. Can you tell us more about that?"

I shook my head. "If there's any rivalry, it's coming from his end. I don't hold anything against him. I respect what Julien Croyden is doing in our fight against the Thuins and I think Magnus is a terrific player."

Madden flashed a smile at me, his perfect teeth shining under the Stadia's lights. "One last question: as you know, the Hunt starts tomorrow. Any guesses as to how far the prisoners will get this year?"

Now it was my turn to smile. "I don't watch the Hunt. I think lightball is better entertainment. But I'm sure this is the year someone will bring the Heart of the World from Toroth-Gol's depths."

Madden squeezed my shoulder. "King Crow, captain of the Steel City Sledgehammers, thank you for your time."

"Thank you," I replied, but Madden was already walking away. The noise of the Stadia rushed back to meet me. My teammates were around me again, all of them pushing me toward the tunnel that led to the locker rooms. I let them guide me, ignoring the lesser reporters and screaming fans that vied for my attention, but before I disappeared into the darkness of the tunnel, I turned to face the crowd and lifted my hand in the Steel City salute.

The crowd went absolutely nuts.

2

S everal hours after the game, once the interviews were over and
the game ball had been awarded—and after I'd confirmed that,
yes, I was able to get a picture of Magnus Croyden's face in that
perfect moment—I let myself into the Salvador Valentine Center for
Athletics.

The Center wasn't technically part of my adoptive father's estate,
but it was close enough, connected by a tunnel for which only two
people had keys: Sal Valentine and me. After big wins, when my teammates were out at the casino and the public was out with them, I liked
it here. The casino was fine. An empty practice field at midnight was
better.

The halogens warmed with a slow click as the containment field
shimmered to life around the pitch. I dragged a wheeled case of practice flyers behind me and cracked it open at center field. Three dozen
flyers nestled in gray foam, sized from my head down to an Empire
mark. I pulled out the lightball and rolled it across my palm.

"Let's see if I can beat my personal record," I told the case, tapping
through the modules. I picked one called Forsyth's Revenge. The
flyers rose, slowly rotating, each glowing the color of its shell.

"Welcome, King Crow," the case said. "Module initializing. Speed set at two hundred percent."

"Wait. What?"

"Module starting in three. Two. One."

A blue flyer the size of an apple shot through the space my head had been. I ducked, swore, and rolled.

"Computer, set speed at forty percent. Forty!"

"Request denied."

"Stop the module!"

"Request denied. You must tag all the flyers to end the module."

"By the Dregs," I hissed.

On a normal agility run, the flyers played coy, drifting away to make me give chase. These ones swarmed me like aggressive birds. I glanced the wrong way and the smallest flyer hit me in the chest before darting back behind the red one, which hovered over it protectively.

Only one way out of this.

I shifted my head, quick as a striking cobra, and a blue flyer zipped past my ear. At the same time I raised my left palm and triggered my glove. The lightball rocketed forward. With a *crack*, the blue flyer's glow winked out, and it dropped to the pitch, dim and inert.

"Not so tough now, are you?"

The remaining flyers seemed to disagree. They came at me in a cloud, and I worked through them: pulling the lightball back, sending it out again, kicking a downed red flyer into the path of an orange one to interrupt its trajectory. With each shot, the case's voice ticked off another tag.

The hardest one was the smallest. It took three tries to drop the purple flyer, and by then I was breathing like I'd played a third overtime.

"Run ended at one minute and twenty-three seconds."

"That felt... way longer," I gasped. "Now tell me... how I ended up... with the speed set at two hundred percent?"

"Practice makes perfect, eh my boy?"

My father stood in the doorway. Then everything made sense.

"I should've known it was you," I said. "Why would you put me through so much pain only an hour after a game against Helios? We won, by the way."

Sal Valentine was dressed in one of the blue suits that were his habit. He leaned on his cane, which was a thin piece of black wood with a golden head in the shape of a duck.

"I caught the feed on the way back from Ironwood," he said. "You looked slow. Consider that I'm doing you a favor. Oh, and quite the deep cunning, using Magnus' emotions against him. If you didn't catch the look on his face..." He trailed off, kissing his fingers. "A thing of beauty. It won't ingratiate me with Julien at all, but I hate the man. I'm quite proud of you."

I wanted to be mad at my father, though his charm made it difficult. I flashed him a smile and turned off my battery pack.

"I've almost beaten your win record, old man," I said as I walked toward him, my arms held in a wide embrace. "How was the trip? Did you have a nice time in Ironwood?"

My father pushed himself off the doorway and dipped around me, trying to avoid my sweaty hug. Although age had stripped away much of his muscle, and his right hip often bothered him from an old light-ball injury, he was still a powerful physical presence. I caught him before he got too far, one hand on his shoulder. Without dropping his cane, he grappled my wrists, keeping me at a distance as I attempted to pull him close.

"Get off me, you oaf," he spluttered. "I should send you back to the Dregs. Have some respect for your father."

I settled for a wet, smacking kiss on his forehead. He stepped back to wipe at the glistening smudge, and I rocked on my heels, grinning at him. "Nah, you'd miss me too much," I said. "Just as I've missed you!"

My father grunted. Then he sighed, running a hand through his hair. He looked... tired. For the first time, I noticed that the sides of his head were shot with more gray than black.

When had that happened?

"The trip was productive," he said, the final word delivered with a shrug of his wide shoulders. "Conditions in the mines were much better than they were at this time last year. I can't say Samson was happy, but the results speak for themselves. Efficiency is up twenty percent since he introduced the new measures, and that means we should hit our quotas without a problem. As long as the Empire gets the raw materials for their war machines, they'll be happy."

"Gratitude is the attitude," I said, repeating a phrase I'd often heard him say. My father had spent the last month touring the mines of Ironwood, an area to the south of Steel City that provided most of the ore for his warehouses. Samson was his foreman. Privately, I suspected he had another reason for taking that trip. As to what it was, I couldn't begin to guess. Especially of late, my father had grown secretive, agreeing to private meetings at odd hours and disappearing on long work trips. It was something I'd been planning to ask about.

My father nodded. "Quite. I think that—"

Whatever my father had been about to say was interrupted by a loud crash that echoed around the pitch. I met my father's eyes and then both of us were moving. My father's hip pain was clearly forgotten as he pressed his back to the wall beside the door. He pulled on the head of his cane, and the tip crackled with electricity.

I crouched behind a practice case that sat against the wall on the other side of the doorway. *You idiot*, I thought, chiding myself for leaving my own collapsible baton in the pocket of my pants in the changing room. *How many times has father told you to keep a weapon on hand?* I wasn't naïve enough to believe that my fame or my father's standing would protect me from enemies, especially not in the viper's nest of politics that was noble life in Steel City. Both of us were targets—even more so now that my father's drives toward reform had caught on among other nobles.

From the atrium came the sound of muffled voices and booted footsteps. I glanced over the top of the practice case, catching my father's eye. He held up his baton, his question obvious. I shook my head. My father rolled his eyes, then inclined his head toward the pitch. I glanced over. *What is he trying to tell me?* There was nothing to see except for the downed flyers and empty practice case. I looked back at him.

'Lightball,' he mouthed. 'Duh.'

Of course. I was still wearing my gloves and I was a better shot than anyone in the Empire. I found the silver ball on the pitch where I'd dropped it, then held up my left palm to draw it toward me—only to realize that my battery pack wasn't on.

Breathe. Calm. Panic won't help you.

I took a deep breath. The shouts from outside the room were getting closer. With one hand, I flipped on my battery pack. At the same time, I reached to the panel above me, disabling the containment field. Then I pulled the lightball toward me and exhaled with relief as the familiar weight smacked into my palm.

Now anyone who attacks us is in trouble.

No sooner had I settled back behind the case than a dozen members of the Steel City Guard streamed through the doorway. They wore the white and gold of the Empire, rifles in their hands and batons at their waists. They spread out as they entered, lining up along the boundary of the pitch. They were followed by Lucca Bert, captain of the Steel City Guard, who strode into the room like he owned the place.

"Not here, eh?" Lucca sneered. "They couldn't have gone far. Find them."

The guards hadn't seen us. I looked over at my father. We could still make something happen. I sized up my opponents as he'd taught me, planning out the moves in my head. Twelve against two, one of whom was well past his prime. *Bad odds.* The guards clearly weren't here for fun, and the last thing I wanted was to go down without a fight.

My father gave an almost imperceptible shake of his head. 'Trust me,' he mouthed. What was he planning? I didn't know, but I trusted Sal Valentine more than anyone, even more than my teammates. He disabled his baton. The electricity flickered out, and he dropped the foot-and-a-half-long piece of metal at his feet.

"We're here, Lucca," he said, stepping away from the wall and holding up his hands. "Easy, now. We don't want any trouble."

The guards whirled, their guns raised. Lucca turned with them.

"Sal Valentine." Lucca's voice was nasal and grating. He saw me, the lightball still in my hand, and his eyes widened slightly. "And King Crow. You don't want any trouble, eh? Drop the ball. Hold out your wrists and we won't have problems."

My father did as Lucca requested, and I did the same. At a signal from Lucca, two of the guards stepped toward my father and another two walked toward me. They approached cautiously, as if we were caged animals.

I suppose that's exactly what we are.

One of the guards slapped a pair of shackles around my wrists.

"Is there a reason we're being accosted in the facility that bears my name?" my father asked as Lucca's guards gave him the same treatment.

Lucca offered a smug smile, then said, "Sal Valentine and Nathaniel Valentine, by the authority vested in me and in accordance with the rules of the Empire, you're both under arrest for high treason."

Trust for my father or not, I fought. But the guards were ready. I only managed to break a single nose before I felt a sting in my neck and found myself slipping into the quiet dark of unconsciousness.

3

A day later, I was shackled to the hard bench of a rail car with the Empire's most notorious criminals.

For the thousandth time, I ran through the events of the previous evening, trying to recall every detail. Thanks to whatever chemical the guards had jabbed into my neck, everything was a blur. But I remembered enough: I'd been pulled into the Spire, separated from my father, and given a guilty verdict. Before I could protest, the guards had dragged me into the Tomato Bin, bundled me into an extra-large orange jumpsuit, and dyed my hands a pure, obsidian black from the tips of my fingers to my wrists.

The Tomato Bin was the colloquial title for Steel City's prison, so named for the vats of multi-colored dye that the Empire used to mark their criminals. Yellow for theft, blue for piracy, green for assault, red for murder, and black for treason. Black was the worst. Usually, the Empire didn't mess around with dyeing your hands black—they killed you.

I guess I got lucky. At least I was still alive. But I wasn't unscathed: the Empire had taken my right eye and replaced it with an ocular implant. Thankfully, I wasn't awake when it'd happened, though the skin around my eye still felt crusty, and there was a dull throb inside my skull.

I was being sent into Toroth-Gol. I was joining the Hunt.

I blinked. I *still* didn't know what crime I'd committed. Well, I knew I was in for treason, but that didn't make sense. I was a loyal son of the Empire. I stood before games when they played the anthem, shouted, "Rah! Rah!" at all the right times, dedicated my wins to August Morgan, Steel City, and the might of our great union.

Is this Croyden's revenge? Or did my arrest have something to do with my father?

For the hundredth time since our arrest, I remembered the look on his face in the Athletic Center, the pleading in his eyes as he mouthed the words: *Trust me.*

I'd trusted Sal Valentine, but could Sal Valentine trust the Empire?

Since my arrest, I hadn't seen my father. I'd looked for him at the rail station and had continued to look for him, leaning as far as my chains would allow to try and catch the familiar curve of his nose or the black of his hair, but I hadn't seen him, so I had a feeling he wasn't on my train. That didn't mean much, as there were at least a hundred other people in my car and dozens of cars both ahead of and behind us, but it pained me not to know his fate. Was he suffering like me? Or did the Empire have other plans for Sal Valentine?

Even with my eye taken and the dye on my hands, I kept waiting for someone to pop out, tell me this was a joke, give me a plate of oysters and a bottle of cold champagne, and load me in a copter back to Steel City. As the landscape outside the rail car's massive side windows changed from pleasant field to grim forest, that possibility seemed less and less likely.

So what else could I do? I shifted from cheek to cheek with the other prisoners, trying and failing to find a comfortable position on the plastic bench.

The first few hours of our ride passed uneventfully. A few of the criminals around me traded quiet stories about their crimes. I didn't speak until about five hours into the trip after the Thuin next to me had finally piped up.

"What'd you do to get here, *pacho*? What put you in Toroth-Gol? Anything fun?"

The Thuins came from Thua, one of the cities perpetually at war with the Empire. A few years ago, the Empire had labeled Thuins as public enemies and shipped every one they could catch to the camps between Steel City and Helios. At one point, we'd had a Thuin keeper on the Sledgehammers. He'd been the one to teach me that *pacho* was the Thuin word for *friend*.

I grunted. "I don't want to talk about it."

"Treason, then. Got that much from your hands." He held up his own palms. At least, he tried. With the shackles, he could only get them up to his stomach, but I still saw the red dye that marked him as a murderer. "I killed the man who called out my sister in the street. In Thua, everyone would do this. Not in the camps, though, I guess."

Great. I'm sitting next to a murderer.

"Yeah. They tend to frown on that."

The Thuin's smile tightened. "Well. You ever watch the Hunt?"

I shook my head. Other than lightball, the Empire's greatest entertainment came in the form of the Hunt, a once-a-year event where the Empire sent their worst criminals into a desert dungeon called Toroth-Gol. No one knew who'd built Toroth-Gol, or why it existed, but it was the only place within a thousand miles of Empire borders that still ran thick with magic. Monsters existed in Toroth-Gol. Monsters, traps, and treasures. Supposedly, the dungeon had ten levels, though they changed every year. If a prisoner made it through all ten levels, they'd find a chamber containing a jewel called the Heart of the World. Bring the Heart of the World to the Empire and you went free.

I'd never heard of anyone going free.

"You're big, *pacho*, so you have an advantage," the Thuin continued. "Unless we end up in small tunnels. Then you'll get stuck in place until *pinotes* strip your flesh."

Pinotes. Monsters. I sighed.

"I've seen it," the Thuin said. "Even though televised death is not the Thuin way." The Thuin cocked his head at me. "Say, you look familiar, *pacho*. Have we met?"

I shook my head, which made my chains rattle. From the moment I'd realized I was heading to the Hunt, I'd decided to keep my identity a secret. I didn't want to attract unnecessary attention. Yes, I'm six feet tall with a recognizable scar down my right cheek—and sure, my face is plastered on half the posters across the Empire. But people never see the obvious if they aren't expecting it.

"Doubt it, *majoré*." *Majoré* also meant friend, though it was only used as a response to *pacho*. "My friends say I look like that lightball player. The big one from the Sledgehammers? Maybe that's it. But we wouldn't have met. You look dangerous. As a matter of habit, I avoid people who look like they could take me out in a fight."

The Thuin smiled. "Name is Jocko, *pacho*. Wherever you go, may your efforts yield water."

He was polite, at least. "Same to you, *majoré*," I said. "But I'd be obliged if you didn't mention water. I'm not sure if they're stopping this car any time soon and I really have to pee."

We sat in silence as the landscape on either side of the car turned to desert. At one point, I thought I saw a hare, but I blinked and it was gone. Then there was nothing, not even a shrub. Only miles and miles of sand and heat-blasted rock.

I swallowed, barely managing enough spit to coat my dry throat. If I'd had any water to spare, I might've cried.

Why am I here? And where is my father?

The desert gave me no answers.

Over the course of the journey, I fell asleep and woke. Fell asleep again. The rail car kept rolling. At some point, someone behind me started screaming about stopping for the bathroom and how they were innocent and this and that. Maybe they were innocent, but we were all in the same stifling, stinking prison car. The screaming lasted until the screamer's neighbor got tired of listening to him yell. Then there was a *crack* and the yelling stopped. When I turned around, the screamer's neighbor flashed me a self-satisfied smile. The screamer himself was slumped over his wrists, his head resting on the bench in front of him. I couldn't tell if he was unconscious or dead.

I must've fallen asleep a third time, because I awoke to someone yelling, "There it is! I see it!"

I blinked away my daze and stared out the rail car's windows. Trenches had been dug into the sand, lined with barricades and barbed wire. This was the edge of the Empire, a place where magic ran wild and the only protection between chaos and civilization were the fortifications and gun emplacements. Two long barrels stuck out from the cover of a sand dune. A mech stood nearby, its armored shell covered with patches of brown and green fabric to keep it camouflaged.

In the distance lay the end of the line.

From the front row of the car, three southerners started humming. It was a deep, eerie hum, a tone only available to those who naturally spoke an octave lower than any northerner. Around me, people wept and whispered hushed prayers. A reptilian two rows in front of me started banging its scaled head against its shackled wrists.

"It was nice knowing you, *pacho*," Jocko said from beside me. "I'd like to think I won't scream when I die. If you make it out, find my sister. She lives outside Thua. Her name is Rafsa. Tell her that I loved her. Anyone you want me to find for you if I make it?"

I thought about it for a minute before I said, "Don't worry about it."

I didn't have anyone, and it didn't matter, anyway.

Neither of us would make it out alive.

4

The door to the rail car slid open and I saw someone silhouetted against the sunlight. I blinked, trying to make my eyes adjust to the brightness. The figure looked familiar, and it took me another second to realize that it was Lucca Bert.

But what is he doing here?

"Welcome to the big time," Lucca said. "I have the pleasure of giving an orientation to you ingrates. I suppose you all know why you're here. But let me tell you how this will go down. As soon as I finish, your ocular implants will activate. Those are the cameras in your eyes." He tapped his forehead above his right eye. "For those of you who have never used one—which should be all of you—these are what allow the Empire to communicate with you while you're in the dungeon. They'll also be used to identify helpful information. These implants are on loan from the Empire. Any attempt to tamper with them will—"

What happened next was as awesome as it was stupid. There was a woman by the door—at least, I assumed it was a woman from her cascading dreadlocks—who, after several hours, finally moved. Her head lifted and she hocked a loogie that struck Lucca right on the cheek. I swear, it hit with such force that I heard it smack.

Lucca stood there, his mouth open in shock, and then he raised a hand to his cheek. He wiped it away and looked at his hand as if he expected blood. While he was looking, the woman hit him with *another* loogie, not as powerful as the first but this one landed directly in his eye.

Lucca stumbled backward. "Figure out the system on your own," he snarled, catching himself against the door. He looked to the side and said, "Release them—except for that one." He pointed at the woman.

Several guards filled in around him. They followed Lucca's finger, noted the dreadlocked woman, and then moved through the car, bending down to unlock the first prisoners.

Jocko must've seen the look in my eyes, because he shook his head, his chains rattling as he nudged me with his knee. "Beware that one, *pacho*. Not the guard. The woman. Don't go to bat on her behalf. She can handle herself."

"Drama makes good television," I growled. "Besides, this is personal."

"Trust me, *pacho*. You're gonna die if you get involved. She knows what she's doing. Leave her alone."

"Hey, Lucca," I said, calling to the captain of the Steel City Guard. "We have some unfinished business, you and I. How about I stay here with you, and you let her go? I think we could have some fun together."

"*Faesala*," Jocko said from beside me. I won't tell you what that means.

At the sound of his name, Lucca looked up. His gaze wandered over the prisoners until he found me. When he did, his eyes glowed with the malevolence of someone who got their daily kicks from shooting at kittens with a nail gun. When he narrowed his eyes at me, I knew I was in trouble.

"You. I knew you'd cause trouble. You're lucky to be alive."

"I'm a loyal citizen of the Empire. Where's my father?"

Lucca shook his head. "You'll join him soon enough. Guards, keep moving. I want—"

Whatever Lucca was about to say was interrupted by yours truly. I'd been arrested for treason, bundled into a jumpsuit, and had my eye forcibly replaced. All this for one of the Empire's most famous sons? It didn't make any sense.

"Why am I here?" I shouted, straining against my chains. "Where's my father? Where's my father, Lucca?"

I knew I was causing a scene. Jocko attempted to calm me down, but I couldn't be tamed. I screamed, spit, and shook my restraints like a wild animal, my outburst stoked by the hint of fear in Lucca's eyes.

When I wouldn't stop screaming, Lucca signaled his guards. "Let her go down," he said, gesturing to the woman near the door. He pointed toward me. "He stays with us."

It took the guards ten minutes to release everyone. They undid the prisoners one at a time, letting their shackles fall to the floor and leading them onto the platform before coming back for the others. The whole time, I didn't stop screaming. I yelled myself hoarse, my wrists being scraped as raw as my throat as I pulled against my chains. When the guards finally came for Jocko, he glanced at me with sympathy.

"I figured out who you are," he whispered from the side of his mouth. "I know your father. If you survive, come find me. Dark City. Meet me at the fortress there."

If there was anything that could've stopped me from screaming, it was those words. But before I could ask Jocko any questions, the guards were upon us. My short-term friend smiled at me as they freed him. I tried anyway.

"What do you know that I don't?" I said, searching his face for answers.

The guards led him off the train. As soon as they turned their backs to me, I lunged, hoping to sink my teeth into them. I couldn't, of course; the restraints were designed to prevent exactly that.

"Come face me, you cowards," I shouted, straining against metal links that cut into my wrists. "Guards! Lucca! Come here and face me!"

But Lucca had left without me noticing, moving onto another car or to take care of whatever business the Empire had assigned him. Once I was the last person on the train car, a half-dozen of the guards approached me.

"Well," one of them said, his hands on his hips. "This is going to be fun."

I'd like to say I put up a fight. But I was shackled at the wrists and ankles and the guards weren't. Over the years, I've taken quite a few hits on the field, but I've never suffered the type of unrelenting beat-down I got on that rail car over the next several minutes.

When the guards were done, they unlocked my chains and left me shivering on the bench. I lay sideways, my cheek pressed against the sticky plastic, though I didn't remember stretching out. It must've been at least an hour before I pushed myself upright, reopening a half-dozen recently closed cuts in the process. Sometime after that, I crawled from the train car, leaving a trail of dripping blood behind me. Lucca and the guards were gone. Everyone was gone. I stood alone on a platform in the middle of the desert.

Despite my injured state, I remembered the oppressive heat and sulfur scent of the surrounding air. I suppose I could've run, but there was nowhere to go. There was nothing around us but oppressive heat and soldiers.

There was only one direction to go.

At the far end of the platform sat the entrance to Toroth-Gol. Growing up in a society where its yearly explorations were regarded as the pinnacle of entertainment, I had some familiarity with the dungeon. I'd seen pictures of the entrance, though I hadn't expected it to be so small. It was little more than a crypt, like the kind you'd see in the average cemetery. A sandstone monolith in the middle of the desert.

Somewhere beneath my feet were treasures, traps, and monsters so fierce that they scared even those who ran the Empire. Beneath my feet was *magic*.

A rivulet of blood ran down my cheek. I was loopy. I swayed on my feet, staring at the entrance to Toroth-Gol on the far side of the platform. A message appeared in my vision.

Toroth-Gol (Entrance)

Anyone reading this should get inside ASAP or they'll be stuck outside. If you're inside, you'll have a fighting chance. If you're outside, you'll be shot by the guards. Or maybe tortured and then shot. Who knows? The guards aren't very nice.

"Huh?" I said. "What's that?" I waved a hand in front of my face. As my hand passed in front of me, a new message popped up.

Human (King Crow)

An orphan and human native of Steel City, King Crow worked his way up from the Dregs to become one of the most celebrated lightball centers ever to play the game. Known across the Empire for his speed and brute strength on the field, as well as his quick wit during press conferences, King Crow was a perennial favorite of Sledgehammers' fans before he was sentenced to Toroth-Gol for treason.

"What's going on here?" I said to no one in particular. But I already knew: the ocular implant. It not only provided a livestream of every-thing I saw to the Empire but presented me with key information about the dungeon.

In the top right of my field of vision, I noticed a countdown timer. Nine minutes and fifty-three seconds. The numbers were red. I blinked, but they stayed where they were, changing only as time ticked past. Nine minutes and fifty-two seconds. Fifty-one. I wondered what would happen when they got to zero. When I moved my head, the numbers moved with me.

As I stared at the numbers, I noticed that several other items now overlaid my vision. Where my eyes met the horizon, I saw what could only be described as buttons. The first said "Inventory" and a second said "Map."

Since I'd been inside a haptic pod several times before, I knew how to use the buttons. *Inventory*. A translucent image appeared in front of me. It showed a grid that was ten squares across and ten down, each square empty. Text above the grid showed my current carrying capacity, which was 443 pounds. I had no clue how that was calculated.

Map. The image changed to a blank screen with a red "X" over it. That was all it displayed. Perhaps the Map hadn't been unlocked, or maybe the features wouldn't be activated until I entered the dungeon. I turned around, hoping to make something change, and the screen followed, yet still showed the X.

As my eyes fell on the train car, the image in my vision shifted again. Where the red X had been, I now saw text.

Rail Car (Single)

It's a rail car. The floor is covered in urine. Also, there's plenty of human blood from a big shot who couldn't keep his mouth shut. Type O+.

"Ha," I said. I wondered who was writing the descriptions. They seemed oddly personal.

My legs aching, I walked to the dungeon's entrance. Beyond the threshold, a stone staircase descended into the earth, the way lit by lanterns affixed to the walls. But I didn't enter immediately. Instead, I glanced behind me, taking a final look at the platform, the railway, and the surrounding desert. Anything that meant I was still alive and breathing with two feet on the surface of the Earth. I looked back at the crypt and got the same message as I had earlier.

Now that I stood before the entrance, I noticed details that hadn't been visible from farther away. There were words carved above the doorway: *Nich la'min fortante*. Whatever that meant. Beneath the words sat a creature, something massive and gelatinous with a single eye and hundreds of barbed tentacles that ran along the top of the door and down the sides of the frame. Near the bottom of the door, at the end of each tentacle, were tiny human forms. They clutched small tools like shovels and picks. One held a wheelbarrow. Perhaps most disturbing was that each miniature face displayed an expression of pure agony.

The blood loss made me feel lightheaded. "Whatever's inside, I'm going to beat it," I said, patting the stone doorframe. "I'm going to tear this dungeon apart from the inside out. Lucca will fall. The Empire will fall. And I'm going to find my father."

Yup. Definitely lightheaded.

I walked through the door. The countdown timer froze at eight minutes and two seconds. I didn't flinch as a giant slab of stone crashed to the ground behind me.

5

I'm underground without a light in a magic dungeon, I thought, as I stood inside the entry to Toroth-Gol. It was pitch black. The only thing I could see was the countdown timer in the upper right-hand corner of my vision, which had started counting down from sixty minutes.

Before me was a spiral staircase made from brown stone. At even intervals along the walls were sconces filled with purple flame.

"I guess I'm supposed to head down this creepy staircase before the timer runs out?" I said aloud. I didn't expect anyone to answer, and no one did. Gingerly, I touched my ribs where I'd taken the hardest kick from the guards upstairs. I winced as pain lanced through my side.

This is going to be a challenge. Good thing I haven't recently been beaten to a pulp.

It took me twenty-one minutes and thirty-seven seconds to reach the bottom of the staircase. Each step was agony. Back on the field, other players had complained about their knees, but I'd never felt that pain. I'd always made fun of them, calling them old and making jokes about arthritis. But now, my ribs and knees ached with a pain similar to the growing pains I'd had as a child.

I leaned against the stone wall. *That wasn't so bad*, I told myself as I surveyed the room. I stood in the entrance to a chamber that was about the size of a lightball field.

At least it's cooler here than on the platform. Twenty degrees, if not more.

Toroth-Gol (Entry)

We've got good news and bad news. Which would you like first?

Sorry. It turns out the snacks we put in here for the enjoyment of all new hunters have already been eaten. So just bad news.

The bad news: you're in the dungeon now. This is where hunters choose their loadouts.

Loadouts remaining: 1

Like the stairway, this room was illuminated by purple flames, though the ones in this room were considerably larger. They sat in the hands of bronze statues that lined the walls.

To my surprise, that was hardly the strangest thing about the room. No, that was the hundreds of mannequins filling the center of the room, each arranged in neat, orderly rows.

Of course. Mannequins.

As I turned in a circle, text popped up and spun like life had turned into a slot machine. I slowed my gaze, trying to catch a static image. Sure enough, when I focused on a single mannequin, an image populated the left side of my vision and text appeared on the right. The image showed a leopard skin in the shape of a cape, with two buckles at the neck, as well as a pair of floating claws, which had three blades each. While the image stayed still, the text moved as I read, almost like it knew what line I was on.

Leopard-kin Loadout

To those who consider themselves the best at what they do (even if what they do isn't very nice), Toroth-Gol presents these claws and cape. What this loadout lacks in defensive prowess, it makes up for in agility. It comes with a set of three-bladed claws that extend and retract upon the wearer's command. You also get a cape which improves reaction time by a flat twenty percent. How terrifying!

This loadout comes with a special skill called Mammalian Fury. This skill increases speed and attack by thirty percent for thirty seconds. This skill can be used once, and then goes on cooldown for twelve hours afterward.

Confirm? Yes or No.

The "Yes" button was grayed out so that I couldn't click on it. Not that I would've taken the first option without at least checking a few more. *Or are they all the same?* My eyes found another mannequin and I read the text that appeared in my vision.

Polite Pyromaniac's Loadout

The items in this set once belonged to Bradley F. Smith, gentleman arsonist. Turns out the "F" in "Bradley F. Smith" didn't stand for "Frank," but "Fire."

After Smith was captured and hanged for burning down an elementary school, this set became available to the dungeon. The leather tunic and pants provide protection against burning while the flamethrower shoots fire in a concentrated fifteen-foot-long jet.

Confirm? Yes or No.

That answered that question. But once again, the "Yes" and "No" buttons were grayed out.

I wonder if it was first-come, first-served. Maybe these loadouts already got chosen. And then: *Is this the only opportunity I'll have in ten levels for an upgrade, or will there be other chances deeper down?*

I didn't know—and since that was the case, it was best to assume this would be my only chance. *Prepare for the worst, and let yourself be surprised if things turn out better. I might as well choose the loadout that makes me as powerful as possible. Assuming I can find one that hasn't been taken yet.*

It was strange to be alone with that immobile army. I walked down the rows and read the descriptions for three dozen loadouts. I found a few combinations of weapons, armor, and magic I thought would serve me, but the "Yes" buttons were grayed out, even on the loadouts I didn't want to take.

As I walked through the strange room, I spotted movement out of the corner of my eye. I turned, squinting across the sea of mannequins, and saw a person behind a table on the far side of the room.

"Hello?" I yelled, then kicked myself.

This is Toroth-Gol, you idiot. You might not know much about the dungeon, but you know it's dangerous. What if that's a monster that wants to eat your brains?

When nothing moved to eviscerate me, I cautiously made my way across the room.

A man stood behind the table, and I recognized him immediately. It was my father. I ran toward him, a shout of joy on my lips, but skidded to a halt.

My father was translucent. I could see straight through him. *A monster, then?* My heart pounded as I ducked behind the nearest mannequin.

I peered over the mannequin's shoulder and watched as he folded orange jumpsuits and placed them in neat piles on one side of the table. I could hear him humming softly to himself. His familiar cane leaned against the wall behind him.

What did they do to you? Unless this isn't really you.

No sooner had the thought crossed my mind than the apparition waved at me. "Hello, my son," it said in my father's voice. "I was wondering when you'd get here."

You're not going to trick me that easily.

Even though the apparition had already seen me, I bent down behind the mannequin so as to put *something* between us. The plastic mannequin wasn't much, but some cover was better than nothing.

"Prove to me that you're my father," I shouted. I didn't know what I'd do if the apparition was a monster, but that was a problem for later. "What did I say the first time I saw my new room in your mansion?"

Although I couldn't see the apparition, its voice rang through the room: "You said, 'How many people share this one?' It was very cute. When I told you that you had the room to yourself, you said, 'I think I'm going to like it here.' Don't get me wrong, Crow—I'm not your father. I'm here to help you all the same. Now come out here and let's talk like adults."

I poked my head out from behind the mannequin. That *was* what I'd said the first time I'd seen my new home. Although the apparition hadn't moved from behind the table, he had stopped folding the jumpsuits. When he saw me, he motioned me toward him.

"I'm not going to hurt you. I promise."

I sighed. *Here goes nothing.*

I walked toward him.

Gatekeeper (Sal Valentine)

Like any self-respecting dungeon, Toroth-Gol has a kindly figure to guide you through your Choosing and explain the terrible horrors that lie ahead. The Gatekeeper appears as a different person for each hunter who sees it.

I groaned. I supposed it had been too much to hope that I'd find my actual father.

"You see?" Gatekeeper Valentine said as he noticed my reaction. "I'm not him. But I'm here to help."

I stopped in front of the table. Other than the fact that I could see through Gatekeeper Valentine, he was the spitting image of my father.

"Do you know where I can find him?" I asked. I refused to believe that my real father was no longer alive.

Gatekeeper Valentine smiled sadly. "I can't tell you anything about the real Sal Valentine."

By the Dregs. So much for that idea.

"What can you tell me?"

Gatekeeper Valentine tapped the table before him. "You know the rules of this place, yes? Ten levels to earn your freedom?"

"Sure."

"You haven't reached the first level yet," he continued. "Consider this the lobby before you head into the main building. Everyone starts their journey here, in the Entry. If you'd gotten here earlier, you would've had a choice of loadouts. But they're awarded on a first-come, first-served basis, and no two hunters get the same loadout. At this point, there's only one left."

I felt numb. I still didn't know my father's fate and soon I would be headed into the world's most dangerous place with a set of equipment that had been rejected by several hundred other people.

"Don't be too upset," Gatekeeper Valentine added. "I think you'll like what I've got for you. It's over there, second row in, sixteen from the back. Shall we go see it?"

What other choice do I have?

Gatekeeper Valentine grabbed his cane from where it leaned against the wall and I followed him down a row of mannequins.

"It's strange how this worked out, but some things are for the best," he said as we walked.

"What do you mean by that?"

"You'll see. Here we are. This one."

I stared at the plastic doll that he patted on the shoulder. It wore a leather belt. A small pouch hung from the belt, as did a pair of gloves.

Lightball Loadout — Potato Theme

"You're not just a fighter—you're a food fighter!" That's the infamous line from the cult classic movie, *Galaxy of the Potato Hunters*. If you saw it, you might recognize this set of gloves, which were worn on set by actor James "Crispy Skin" Mallorie.

With the leather lightball gloves and battery pack included in this set, you'll be able to bat away cakes and pies with ease. You'll also be able to shoot around the other piece of this set, an electromagnetically charged potato that comes in its very own custom leather pouch.

Clip the pouch to your belt and the electromagnetically charged potato will never, ever leave your side! "What if it breaks?" you ask. "What if a monster eats it?" Well, who could blame the monster? Your electromagnetically charged potato is at least a dozen times tastier than a regular one. But fear not, intrepid hunter, if you lose your electromagnetically charged potato. Simply wait twenty-four hours and a new one will appear in your custom leather pouch.

Confirm? Yes or No.

This time, the "Yes" button wasn't grayed out. I read the text several more times before I spoke: "Is this a joke?"

Gatekeeper Valentine smiled. "Maybe. You made some powerful people very angry. But lucky for you, drama makes good television. And you do know how to use a pair of lightball gloves."

That's when it hit me: I was going to die. I was going to be slaughtered, probably in gruesome fashion, on live television.

"I can't survive if I'm using lightball gloves to shoot a potato at my enemies," I said. I ran a hand over my head, feeling the bristle of stubble.

I guess hair grows back when you don't have a hygiene crew to shave and oil your scalp twice a day.

"You'll have to try," Gatekeeper Valentine said.

"Try?"

"What other option do you have? Unless you've got a very neat trick up your sleeve, I don't see you walking out of here anytime soon."

I sighed. Then, because there really wasn't anything *else* to do, I hit "Yes."

Nothing happened. "You'll receive the items and bonuses from your loadout when you enter the real first level of the dungeon," Gatekeeper Valentine said, apparently noticing my questioning look. "Remember, this is only the Entry. A word of advice: when you do get into the dungeon, you'll want to equip everything as soon as possible."

Of course. Don't want to let anyone get too comfortable with their new gear before they're thrown into a murderous dungeon.

"Is there anything else you can tell me?" I asked. "Anything that might help me survive?"

"Hmm." Gatekeeper Valentine looked thoughtful. "The dungeon doesn't admire restraint or playing it safe. Go big or go home. You were always strong, Crow. Double down on what you've got."

I nodded. Even if Gatekeeper Valentine was a piece of my imagination, it felt good to hear the compliment said in my father's voice.

"Do you know how to use your Map?" Gatekeeper Valentine asked. "It should be active. You can use a mental command to open it. For now, what you see is what you get, but you should have upgrade opportunities as you move deeper into the dungeon."

With a thought, I pulled up my Map again and was surprised to see that detail had been added since I'd tried the same move on the train platform. Instead of a red X, there was the outline of the room in which we stood. There was also the next room, which looked like a long hallway, and a building beyond that.

"Oh! One more thing," Gatekeeper Valentine said. "You see that countdown timer in the upper right-hand corner of your vision?"

I found the timer, which showed twenty minutes and forty-three seconds. "I see it."

"That timer tells you how long you have to complete each level before the Purge. It's there to keep you moving. If you fail to clear the first floor before the timer runs out, you'll find yourself pursued by a wave of living flame. Take too long on the second and face a horde of flesh-eating cicadas. And so on. Make sure you find the door to the next level before time runs out."

I shook my head in disbelief. *As if things weren't already difficult enough. But I suppose there's no use complaining about reality.*

"I think that's everything," Gatekeeper Valentine said. "Unless you have other questions? I can't promise I'll be able to answer them, but I can try."

I racked my brain. *I still have another twenty minutes. What would be helpful to know?* Jocko's words came to me, then: "If you survive, come find me. Dark City. Meet me at the fortress there."

"Do you know what the Dark City is?" I asked.

Gatekeeper Valentine shook his head. "I can't say anything about that. You'll have to figure it out for yourself. Anything else?"

I wanted to use my time with Gatekeeper Valentine as wisely as possible, but I couldn't think of anything else to ask.

"No. Might as well get on with it."

Gatekeeper Valentine nodded and I followed him to a door in the wall at the far side of the room. It wasn't anything special: just a wooden door with a brass knob.

Toroth-Gol: Promenade of the Condemned

"You're gonna be fine, Crow," Gatekeeper Valentine said as he put his hand on the knob. "I believe in you."

I stared into Gatekeeper Valentine's eyes. *Father's eyes.* I wasn't sure, though I thought I could see the real Sal Valentine behind them.

"This isn't going to be fun, is it?" I asked.

Gatekeeper Valentine shook his head. "No. But you'll get through it. Beat the levels. Retrieve the Heart of the World. Good luck, Crow."

He opened the door. Behind it was a shimmering blue portal. Without another word, I stepped through.

6

For over a decade, I'd been one of the best lightball players in the world. You don't maintain that position by slacking. A standard Sledgehammers' workout consisted of a ten-mile run, two hours of weight training, and almost an hour of dynamic stretching. And that was before the extra workouts my father gave me.

Still, when I walked through the door behind Gatekeeper Valentine and found a pair of lightball gloves in my Inventory, my stomach felt queasy. Toroth-Gol was a place where I could find myself pursued by a wall of living flame or flesh-eating cicadas. I glanced at the countdown timer in the corner of my vision, which had reset to give me sixty minutes.

Sixty minutes until the Purge. How the heck am I going to survive by shooting a potato?

When I focused on the image of the lightball gloves in my Inventory, I was presented with the text:

Equip? Yes or No.

Mentally, I selected "Yes" and the items appeared in the air in front of me.

"By the Dregs!" I moaned after trying and failing to catch the items before they fell to the ground.

I groaned in pain as I bent down. I was still in bad shape from the beating I'd taken on the train. My lip was split and my ribs ached from where I'd taken repeated kicks from a steel-toed boot. I still felt an ache in my skull from where the Empire had pulled out my eye.

If I don't find a way to heal myself, I'm going to be in trouble. It'd be nice if there were a magic potion or something that could patch me up. I wonder if that exists down here?

Until then, the only thing I knew that could heal me was a good rest, but I was racing against the clock. The countdown timer hung ominously in the upper right-hand corner of my vision, a grim reminder of what would happen if I didn't complete the level in time.

I picked up the lightball gloves. Technically, they weren't full gloves, as the leather ended at the knuckles. Other than that, they were exactly like the ones I had at home: thin leather turned dark with sweat, velcro straps at the wrist. I slipped them on, and they fit perfectly.

The portable battery pack was about the size of a paperback book. It sat inside a leather case with a hole cut out near the power switch so I could turn it on and off. The battery appeared to be one of the newer training models, which used an ambient charging technology to suck power from the air. It was a slow, inefficient process, but as long as I remembered to turn off the battery when I wasn't using it, I wouldn't have to worry about running out of charge.

The case that held the battery pack had two loops in the back, and I used them to connect the pack to my belt. Then I lifted the leather pouch. It was really quite handsome, with the image of a crow embossed on the front flap. The pouch snapped closed with a brass button, which I undid to reveal the contents. Sure enough, it contained a potato. The round vegetable fit snugly in the palm of my hand.

I sighed. Somewhere in the Empire, millions of viewers were dying with laughter. I slipped the potato back into the pouch, closed the flap, and then slipped the pouch onto my belt with the battery pack. I wouldn't win any fashion awards, but the entire set-up was quite functional. And now, at least, I wasn't defenseless.

Only once I'd equipped the battery pack and pouch did I take a minute to look around. I stood at one end of a long hallway that made me think I was in a museum, or perhaps an old library. The floors were marble, patterned with diamonds and chevrons, and the walls held bookshelves filled with musty tomes. Those must've accounted for the smell, which was something between wet dog and old leather.

Secret Area of the Beaten Unfortunate (Hallway)

Yay! You've found a secret area. Every once in a while, the dungeon takes its most pitiable denizens and gives them a little boost. As you're the last to come through from the Reliquary, we're going to assume that you're either weak, dumb, or both. Perhaps you waited too long, hoping someone might come to save you. Or perhaps you mouthed off to the wrong guards and they kicked your butt. Who knows? Either way, you're a heck of a long way behind the others. Here's your opportunity to get a fighting chance. Walk down this hallway to learn more.

"Thanks a ton," I muttered.

Per the dungeon's instructions, I limped down the hallway. Cobwebs clung to the eaves and piles of ash gathered in the corners. I studied the books on the shelves, but none of the spines were legible. Against my better judgment, I pulled one out and opened it, but it was written in some pictographic text I didn't recognize. I slid it back and tried another.

Same thing. Not getting any information from that.

Before the doorway on the far side of the hallway sat a machine I recognized from every street corner in Gomindor. It was a chest-high wooden box with a small keypad and a peephole window built into its top. The Kinetoscope II, it was called, after a similar device from another era. While the original Kinetoscope played a short film when one looked through the peephole, the new version was used to make video calls. Simply look through the hole, punch in a number on the keypad, and *bam*! The Kinetoscope II would connect you to your desired contact.

Which you could do with a phone, I thought, which was pretty much the thought I had every time I saw one of the bulky devices around the city. So why did you need a Kinetoscope to make a call? The answer was simple: you didn't. But phones didn't invoke nostalgia. They weren't *cool*.

Despite my disdain for the silly device, it was quite clear what the dungeon wanted me to do. I stopped in front of the Kinetoscope and lowered my eyes to the window. Inside was a screen.

Confirming... Live on *Elvis Madden's Hunter Talk* in 3... 2... 1...

"Nope," I said. I wanted to back away but found myself unable to move my head. *It's my eye. There must be a magnet in my ocular implant that's holding me here.*

So perhaps the Kinetoscope hadn't been put there by the dungeon. *The Empire, then.* That was surprising. Previously, I'd thought of the Empire and Toroth-Gol as two distinct and potentially even oppositional entities. Although Toroth-Gol did the Empire's dirty work by killing prisoners, I considered it to be wild. Feral. Unaffiliated with anything but its own unknown objectives. Now, it looked like I needed to reconsider that point of view. Because clearly, the Empire had *some* sway over what happened in the dungeon.

Once again, I attempted to move my head. It remained stuck. A second later, the screen in front of me flashed and I found myself staring at Elvis Madden. Although it'd only been two days since he'd interviewed me after my big game against the Helios Serpents, it felt like I hadn't seen him for weeks. He sat behind a desk, his hands folded on the wood in front of him.

"Crow," he said politely. The word came through a speaker built into the side of the Kinetoscope. "Good to see you."

"Wish I could say the same," I muttered.

"Hmm." For the first time since we'd met, Madden was at a

genuine loss for words, though he recovered. "Answer the questions and you'll be back to the dungeon. My producer doesn't want to hold you here any longer than necessary."

"Scene 3B, take one," someone yelled from offscreen before I could respond. "Action!"

A "Live" icon appeared in the bottom right-hand corner of my screen.

"Hello, King Crow," Madden said as if we hadn't already been speaking. "You know, a lot of people were wondering whether that was really you, myself included. We won't get into the sad and disturbing circumstances that brought you here, but we will reassure viewers that this is indeed King Crow, former center with the Steel City Sledgehammers. So, King Crow, tell us. What do…"

I stopped listening. *Do I test the Empire's sway over the dungeon? If I push back and they can't do anything other than hold me here, I'll know I don't need to worry about their influence. Of course, if the Empire does actually have control over the Kinetoscope, they could always hold me here until I starve. But would they? I doubt it. I'm the highest-profile prisoner they've had in the dungeon for years. I'm too important to their ratings.*

It was worth a shot. "Actually, I'd very much like to get into the circumstances that brought me here," I said in my most annoying voice, interrupting Madden. "I'd like that quite a bit. Can you tell me what's going on, Elvis? I'd like to know why a proud citizen of the Empire was sent to Toroth-Gol. Or can you tell me where to find my father?"

Madden held up a hand. "Cut!" The "Live" icon disappeared from the bottom of my screen.

So we're not actually live. Another lie from the Empire. That tells me something, at least.

Madden tapped his fingers on the desk. "Crow, I like you, man. You've been a great asset to the Empire. But my producer is telling me that we can't get into the reason you're here, and we're not going to talk about your father. You're only in the entry to the dungeon. The Empire can still reach you. Get it? The Empire might not control Toroth-Gol, but until you get deeper, they've still got ways of making your life difficult. I'm a big fan of the Sledgehammers, man. You had an awesome career. There wasn't a better player going. So, I'd like to see you live to fight another day. Yes?"

Is Madden intentionally giving me the information I need? I wasn't sure. But either way, he'd told me exactly what I'd wanted to know.

The Empire doesn't control events down here, but they still have some influence until I get deeper. Sounds like I need to go deeper.

Madden took my silence as acceptance. "Look," he said. "I know you won't want to use another Kinetoscope again, and there's nothing forcing you to look through the viewfinder, but on my love for the Sledgehammers, I promise you this: the next time you see one of these dumb, bulky devices, look through it and I'll help you." He glanced over his shoulder as if worried that someone might overhear him and get him in trouble. "Even if you don't trust me, you can trust that the Empire wants to keep people distracted. Right? We both work in entertainment. We can level with each other. And what's a better distraction than the world's best lightball player fighting his way through Toroth-Gol? They want you to survive, man. So help me help you. Okay?"

I nodded. I'd gotten what I needed. "Yeah. Fine. Thanks."

"Cool." Madden nodded. "Let's try again. Boys?"

A voice from offscreen said, "Scene 3B, take two. Action!"

A surprisingly convincing fake smile appeared on Madden's face. "So, King Crow, tell us: what do you think your chances are at reaching the Heart of the World?"

I knew how to handle the media. "Same as my chances were of winning Player of the Year," I said. "At least, before I wound up in Toroth-Gol."

"And what are those?"

I matched his smile. "One hundred percent."

Madden threw back his head and laughed like I'd said the funniest thing in the world. "Confidence! I *love* that. Well, Crow, I'm sure this won't be the last we see of you. Ladies and gentlemen, if you're just joining us, you've heard it here first: that is indeed King Crow, former star of the Steel City Sledgehammers, who is sure to be a fan favorite this season. King Crow, thank you for your time."

Madden winked at me. 'Thank you,' he mouthed. Then he disappeared.

Something clicked inside the Kinetoscope, and I was released. Because of my size, standing at the viewfinder for too long was uncomfortable. I stepped away from the machine and cracked my neck.

That was strangely helpful, I thought as I continued through the door at the end of the hallway. I found myself in a circular vestibule with a stool at its center. There was a new smell to this room, something airy and refreshing. It wasn't anything specific, though it was a stark contrast to the musty hallway, like moving from the Dregs to a higher level of the city. On either side of the room were two stained-glass windows that filtered colorful light into the room. In deep grays, blues, yellows, and blacks, the windows showed a castle sitting on a hill. Beyond the castle, the black sky seemed almost sickly.

The strangest thing about the vestibule was the oil painting that hung in a gold frame on the wall across from me, directly between the two stained-glass windows. The painting, which was about the size of my torso, depicted three balloons against a black background: one red, one green, and one blue. That was it. Three rubber balloons, each trailing a string, their cheerfulness incongruous in the dungeon.

Secret Area of the Beaten Unfortunate (Prize Room)

You've found the Prize Room! To unlock your chance at a prize, you must answer a riddle. Failure to answer the riddle within the allotted time will result in certain death.

When you know the answer, speak it out loud. You may guess as many times as you'd like before time runs out. Ready?

Yes.

There wasn't another choice. I took a deep breath. *Yes.* A riddle appeared on my screen.

Given away
On random days
That some call arbitrary
Or in the first month of the year
For births in January.

Good luck!

A timer appeared in the center of my vision. It was different than the Purge timer in that the foot-high red numbers showed I had thirty minutes to make my guesses. A beat later, the "30:00" changed to "00:29."

"Gah!" I didn't have thirty minutes. I had thirty seconds.

I tried to dissect the riddle, but it was hard to concentrate when I was that close to oblivion.

What was given away on random days?

"Soup," I yelled. "Socks! Money!"

They were random guesses, and it didn't surprise me when the timer didn't stop. I thought about the next part of the riddle. *What would you get in January if you were born in January? That was also given away?*

"A gift. A present!"

The timer stopped at fourteen seconds. I looked at the rhyme again, considering the question. *Huh. That actually makes sense.* You could give a gift or a present at any time, though it was customary for birthdays.

As I stood there, trying to catch my breath, a dusty box appeared on the stool. When I say "appeared," I mean that one second the stool was empty; the next, a box sat atop it. I hadn't even noticed how it'd gotten there.

Was that magic? I didn't believe the Empire's propaganda about magic being the most destructive force in the universe, but growing up in Steel City *had* given me an innate mistrust of anything that couldn't be explained through science. Cautiously, I approached the box and blew off the dust, revealing the glint of something metallic. Another blow revealed purple wrapping paper. I used my hands to brush off the rest of the dust.

Present of the Beaten Unfortunate

Congratulations on correctly answering the riddle. Here's a present. What could it contain?

"I guess I'm supposed to open this?" I said aloud to the room. When nothing happened, I ripped off the paper, revealing a cardboard box. I jumped backward immediately, worried that something might pop out and bite me, but nothing did. I gave the box an experimental poke with the tip of my boot. When nothing bad happened, I lifted the box's lid. Inside, I found a rectangular contraption about the size of my fist. Embedded in its surface was a single red button.

Contraption of the Beaten Unfortunate

Press this button.

"Here goes nothing," I said, then pressed the button.

Two things happened at once: first, my ribs felt cold, as if someone pressed against them with a hunk of ice—from the *inside*. The cold radiated down my legs and into my aching knees. The same freezing crept into my split lip and behind my ocular implant. The feeling was kind of soothing, more strange than uncomfortable.

That's definitely magic. I didn't know what else it could be. I forced myself to take slow, calming breaths.

As the freezing feeling spread through my body, there was a loud *bang* and the painting of the three balloons fell off the wall, revealing a miniature version of a gambler's wheel. I wasn't a big gambler, so I didn't have much experience with the wheel, but I'd seen them in the casino. To play the game, the participant made a bet and spun the wheel, which was divided into several segments with something different written on each slice. Most of the slices on the normal version in the casino said bad things, like, "Lose Your Bet" or "Lose Half Your Bet," but a select few contained good ones, which I guess was why people played. There was a little arrow at the top of the wheel, and when the wheel stopped, you got whatever was written on the slice highlighted by the arrow.

This wheel was smaller than the one in the casino, which took up the entire center of the fourth floor, though the multi-colored segments were unmistakable. Similar to the larger wheel, there was text written on each segment, only instead of "Double Your Bet" or "Win a Vacation Home," the slices were more dungeon-appropriate.

The smallest segment said, "Invincibility Potion." That seemed too good to be true, so it made sense why it was the smallest chance. There was a slightly larger segment that said, "Greater weapon upgrade." Two equally sized segments said, "Lesser weapon upgrade." Then there was "Cake" and "Confetti."

The three largest segments said, "Certain Death."

Once again, I could only shake my head in disbelief. I'd solved the riddle and beaten certain death only to find myself spinning a wheel where several of the options were, once again, certain death.

Even as the dungeon offered a new threat, it also gave me a boon. As quickly as the freezing feeling had started, it subsided. So did my aches and pains. Without thinking too much about it, I brought my hand to my side and prodded the spot where one of the guards had kicked me. Surprisingly, my ribs were no longer bruised. I rubbed a finger over my lips and the blood flaked away, leaving nothing but smooth skin.

Would the dungeon really heal me if I was about to die? There's got to be another way out. I pressed on the glass windows, which didn't budge, and walked back through the hallway, looking for any alternative exit. But the walls were made of cold stone and there was nothing behind the books. I tried pushing and pulling on everything, hoping to trigger some type of hidden lever. Again, nothing.

"I suppose I don't get a choice on whether or not I want to spin this?" I said, though I already knew the answer.

The hard is in the doing. Might as well get on with it.

I stepped to the wheel and gave it a mighty spin. The wheel turned to a multi-colored blur as it moved, clicking every time the arrow passed over a segment.

Please let me survive this. I closed my eyes, but thought better of it and opened them again. The colors of the wheel's many segments became more defined as it slowed. *This can't be how my story ends. I need to find my father. I have to get revenge on whoever put me here.*

My stomach dropped as I understood where the wheel would land. Perhaps I should've taken more time to find peace with my gods. The wheel moved from "Cake!" to "Confetti!" to "Certain Death." *Just* when I thought it would stop, it gave another click, and the arrow settled on "Lesser weapon upgrade."

I got confetti anyway. It blew out from behind the bookshelf, making me jump. To be fair, I had a right to be jumpy; I'd almost died before I'd even entered the actual dungeon. One of the windows slid to one side, revealing a door.

You beat the odds! That means you've earned a lesser weapon upgrade, which allows you to upgrade a weapon of your choice to its next tier of rarity. Lesser weapon upgrade can't be stored.

You have one eligible weapon. Upgrade your Ball Launcher - Potato Theme from Uncommon to Rare?

Confirm? Yes or No.

I didn't see the downside, so I selected "Yes." A new message popped up.

Your Ball Launcher - Potato Theme has been upgraded to Potato Gun. Check it out in your Inventory!

I opened my Inventory and scanned the stats of my new weapon.

Potato Gun

Forget the regular ol' potato! This weapon comes with a *sapient* electromagnetically charged potato. As in, your potato can now talk.

Have fun!

"Um, what?" I said.

But my thoughts were interrupted by a noise from the pouch at my waist. "Hey! Hello?" it said. "It's hot down here. Can you let me out?"

7

I froze. *I don't want to seem ungrateful for any type of weapon upgrade. And I didn't land on certain death, which was nice. But a* talking *potato?*

"Hello?" the voice said from my pouch. "I know you're up there. I can hear you breathing. Please. I'm baking in here. Like, I might be dying. I don't know what to do."

I undid the flap. Inside my pouch sat the potato. With trembling fingers, I took it out.

"Hey there!" the potato said. It had two eyes, a wide mouth, and full, fleshy lips that framed a mouthful of perfect, white teeth. Wispy hairs sprouted from the top of its head.

"By the Dregs!" I let the potato drop. It hit the ground with a stream of expletives and rotated around to face me.

"What are you doing, man?" the potato said. "We're supposed to be working together."

At the time, the only magic I'd ever experienced was in stories. Everyone in the Empire knew magic existed, but the Empire defined itself in opposition to magic. Saying anything otherwise earned you a one-way ticket to Toroth-Gol.

"Buddy? You okay? I'm not getting much out of you here."

"I…" Nope. I still didn't know what to say.

"You can call me Spud, by the way. What's your name? And are we gonna explore this dungeon or not?"

I'll ignore it. That's the solution. The potato would serve the same function as a lightball: nothing more, nothing less. I picked it up and stuffed it into my pouch, ignoring Spud's cries of protest. *Think of it as a lightball. You can deal with that.*

With the potato in my pouch, I opened the door that had appeared behind the window and stepped onto a promenade similar to something one might see in the Pleasure Gardens—*if* the Pleasure Gardens had been built by giants. Stained-glass windows as tall as the pillars cast the room in a soft, multi-colored twilight. Pillars as wide as the ones that supported Steel City's higher levels stretched to the ceiling hundreds of feet overhead.

Toroth-Gol: Promenade of the Condemned

Congratulations, fighter! Or should we say *food* fighter? You've crossed the threshold of the ordinary world and taken your first steps into the unknown. What could lie ahead? Tests? Allies? Enemies? A meeting with a goddess? We wouldn't be that predictable. Or would we? You'll have to find out for yourself.

This is the first true room in Toroth-Gol. We wanted to get you excited, so hopefully you're impressed. Anyway, it's time to take your little potato down the promenade. And that's NOT a euphemism.

The timer in the upper right-hand corner of my vision had reset to sixty minutes. *Sixty minutes to find the next door.* I took a few tentative steps down the promenade. On either side of me, marble pillars rose to the ceiling.

I'm a big guy with an even bigger wingspan. Even if a half-dozen people my size all held hands, I'm not sure we could've reached around a single one of those monoliths.

Which made me feel small. It was a shocking feeling. I hadn't felt small since my days in the Dregs.

I'd stopped to marvel at the size and scope of the room when I received a new message:

WARNING: Spicing things up in 3... 2... 1...

Yipping echoed across the promenade, and four dogs came bounding around a pillar about a hundred yards distant. Despite my lingering shock at finding myself incarcerated and sent into a magical dungeon, my reaction was swift and decisive. I could thank my father for that; he'd known the threat that his position posed and had insisted I learn how to defend myself. A big part of that training was simply learning how to stay calm under pressure.

With one hand, I flipped on my battery pack. With the other, I drew Spud from his pouch.

"What's the big idea?" he said as I set him to hover above my left palm. As the description of the potato gun promised, he worked like a lightball. One of the hyenas yipped again and Spud rotated to face them. "Oh no," he said as he caught sight of the snarling, slavering animals. "Put me back. Put me back!"

But I couldn't do that. Freaky or not, Spud was my only weapon. And given the situation, he was a good one.

Death Hyena

Found in groups of four to eight, death hyenas aren't very smart or interesting. But if you're not prepared to handle an enraged group of charging pack animals, these angry canines will really mess up your day.

The description didn't give me much in the way of helpful info, but the image on the left side of my vision showed a rotating image of the charging death hyena. I found a weak point almost immediately: their *huge* crimson eyes. It wasn't just their irises that were red, but the pupils and sclera as well. It was like the creatures had two massive targets built right into their heads—and if there was one thing I was good at, it was hitting targets.

"Don't shoot me at those things!" Spud said. "Please!"

I stepped to one side of the promenade, putting a pillar at my back. The pillar was hard. Stolid. I'd always thought "stolid" was a mix of "stoic" and "solid," and I don't think that's actually the etymology, though it did mean "impassive" or "dependable." Which was pretty much a mix between stoic and solid—exactly what I wanted behind me while four death hyenas charged toward me.

"Get ready," I told Spud.

"Ready?" he moaned. "Don't do it!"

I sighted down my left arm and aligned Spud with the lead hyena some seventy yards away. With the fingers of my right hand, I activated the electromagnet in my glove and pushed. Spud crossed the distance between my glove and the lead hyena at a hundred miles per hour. *Thwack.* The sapient potato entered the creature's eye with the wet, bone-cracking sound of an egg hitting pavement. The creature stumbled immediately. Using my other glove, I locked my cone of magnetism onto Spud and pulled. In a lightball game, there would've been competition over the ball, with varying degrees of force coming from several different angles. But in the Promenade of the Condemned, there was no one to compete with my pull. Spud met the bones of the death hyena's skull.

Crack. The side of the hyena's face exploded. The potato hurtled back toward me, blood and bits of bone sloughing off him.

"Ugh," Spud gasped. "Not again."

I ignored him. *He doesn't want to get shot at death hyenas? Well, I don't want to fight for my life in a magic dungeon, but here I am. Looks like everyone is disappointed today.*

"One down," I growled. I pushed again, sending Spud at the second hyena.

The hyenas must've possessed a decent awareness and great reaction times, because the second hyena refused to go down like the first. As it saw Spud leave my hand, the muscles in its shoulders bunched and it dodged to one side. Spud shot past it, and I was left with barely enough time to grab him with my cone of magnetism before he left my range. I pulled him back and took a second shot, but again, the hyena jumped to one side. Spud sailed past it, striking a third hyena in the ribcage, but it didn't disable the creature; if anything, it only served to anger it. The hyena howled in pain and snapped at Spud, and only a quick pull kept him from becoming dog food. The creature's jaws settled around empty air, snapping closed with an audible *click*, and Spud smacked into my waiting palm.

"Please, no more," he gasped. "My whole mouth tastes like blood and dog meat."

I bared my teeth at the charging hyenas. In my training, I'd worked with multiple targets. But this was no longer a sniper's game; the only way to solve this challenge was with hand-to-hand combat. I gave Spud his wish, letting the potato drop to the ground.

"Thank the god of all that's fried and crispy," Spud said, rolling around the other side of the pillar. "I'm getting out of here."

Worry about him later. For now, deal with the dogs. The first lunged from five yards out, so it was my turn to dodge. I stepped toward the second hyena as the first soared over my head and crashed into the pillar behind me. The second hyena had also jumped, and its red eyes widened slightly in surprise as I moved toward it. More than likely, it hadn't expected its prey to go on the offensive.

But I *wasn't* prey. I punched it straight in the nose, throwing it off course and feeling its sharp teeth scrape against my knuckles, then turned to meet the hyena that had gotten behind me so I could lash out with a vicious roundhouse kick. As luck would have it, the first hyena had recovered from its collision with the pillar and predictably launched itself at my unprotected back. My shin connected with its muscular side and something cracked—hopefully in it, not me. The hyena flew through the air and I turned again, getting my right forearm up in time to keep the third hyena from biting into my neck. It clamped onto my arm. Pain radiated through the bone. I grit my teeth and pushed through it.

It's only pain. With the pointer and middle finger of my left hand, I dug into the creature's eye. It was gross and gooey, but this was a fight to the death. I dug deeper. The hyena howled and released my forearm, but I wouldn't let it go. Screaming in both pain and rage, I hooked my fingers around the bone that made up the underside of the hyena's eye socket, yanking it this way and that to avoid the creature's snapping jaws.

The second hyena, the one I'd punched, lunged yet again. I turned, pivoting my hips and hands to place the one-eyed creature between us. The second hyena bounced off the one I held, backing away with its head down and its hackles raised, then growled as it circled for a better position. The first hyena also circled, trying to catch me off guard. My kick hadn't taken it out of commission, but I could see that it moved tentatively.

Need to tip the scales. My hands were slick with blood and I was losing feeling in my right arm. With a jab from my right hand, I poked out the third hyena's other eye. As I did, my left hand slipped and I lost my grip, but that was okay—after I'd poked out the creature's other eye, it went limp. I let it fall to the ground.

"Two down," I said, dropping into a low stance and placing the pillar at my back once more.

My whole right arm had gone numb and the two remaining hyenas had seen my tricks. Even if one of them was injured, they knew what I could do. I had a feeling they wouldn't underestimate me again. The first hyena circled right and the second went left; as soon as I went for one, the other would pounce. And that would be the end of King Crow.

"Um, excuse me?" A voice rang across the promenade. "A penny for your tots? Ha. Get it? Because I'm a potato!"

Spud sat on the ground behind and between the hyenas. *He must've rolled around while I was fighting.* He was diminutive already, and even more so in the massive hall, but his voice was clear enough. The hyenas glanced backward only for a second, but that was enough. Like a viper, I darted toward the first hyena, the one I'd caught with my kick, and caught it in a headlock. The hyena tried to slip from my grip, its snapping jaws inches from my nose and its hot, reeking breath in my face, but I brought a knee into its side, the same side I'd hit with my kick. Something cracked a second time. The hyena yelped and went limp, so I dropped it to catch the other hyena, which had jumped for my back.

Once again, I held up my right forearm as the sacrifice, but the hyena had seen what had happened to its now-eyeless brother, which still whimpered as it bled out only a few feet away, and refused to take the bait.

That was its mistake. I caught it by the throat, hooking my right elbow over the top of its head. I no longer had the strength in my right hand to create any leverage, but with my elbow forming a strong hook, I twisted my entire body. A second later, the hyena's neck snapped.

"Three. Four," I gasped. I let the hyena fall, stumbling over to the beast whose ribs I'd pushed into its lungs. It stared up at me through red eyes as I brought a boot down against its skull. I repeated the treatment for the hyena whose eyes I'd taken.

"I think I'm going to be sick," Spud said from the ground beside me. "That squelching has got to be the *worst* noise I've ever heard."

You've killed a death hyena (x4).

Nice work! You not only survived your first battle in Toroth-Gol but have also learned the meaning of haste. Although the Promenade of the Condemned technically isn't a timed area of the dungeon, you'll want to keep your eye on the timer in the upper right-hand corner of your vision.

Continue to the other side of the Promenade of the Condemned to claim your reward. Need we remind you to do it quickly?

Spud spun in a quick circle, shedding blood and gore. "Hey," he said. "That was bonkers. Hot diggity dogeroonee. You can fight beside me any day. You mind if I ride on your shoulder?"

I couldn't think straight. My right arm was bleeding freely from the bite wounds and the sleeve of my jumpsuit had turned into a wet mess.

He saved your life. *Might as well give him what he wants before you pass out.*

It was a silly thought. Shock and blood loss will do that. I couldn't have moved my injured right arm if my life depended on it, but with my left glove, I brought Spud from the ground into my hand, his round body smacking into my palm. Then I set him on my shoulder, where he squealed with delight.

"Great view from up here. *Way* better than in the pouch. And way better than rolling. When I do that, I have to keep my mouth shut or my teeth click against the stone. Say, you look familiar. You never told me your name. Did you ever go to summer camp?"

I started walking.

"Nah, that's not it," Spud continued. "You didn't attend Camp Green Lake, did you? No, that's probably not it, either. But I *swear* I've seen you somewhere..."

8

By the time we reached the end of the Promenade of the Condemned, I'd grown loopy from blood loss. I'd used my belt as a makeshift tourniquet, but the holes punched into the leather didn't allow me to cinch it tightly. My only other option was to hold the belt tight with my left hand, but I couldn't get the angle I needed to do a really effective job. I grew weaker by the second.

At the end of the promenade was a fountain, a multi-tiered affair with a wide stone base that came up to my waist. A tray of gold coins sat on the fountain's edge, each of them round and about the size of an Empire mark. In the center of the fountain was a series of bowls that grew smaller the higher up they were, each adorned with carvings of boar heads that shot water from their mouths.

"I love some good boar art," Spud said from my shoulder, nodding appraisingly at the carvings. "Someone did a stellar job with those tusks."

Behind the fountain were two massive doors, each as tall as one of the pillars from the Promenade. I don't know how much force it would've taken to move them, but one of them was opened a crack so that a person my size could slip through. I had a feeling that they'd close as soon as I stepped between them, like the door at the entrance to the Crypt.

But what really caught my eye was a body lying next to the fountain, a dead man stripped to his boxers with an arm thrown lazily across his chest. If his eyes hadn't been open, I might've assumed he was simply asleep.

Deceased Human

It looks dead. Poke it with a stick!

Loot? Yes or No.

The buttons were grayed out. The body must've been scavenged before I got there. But getting new loot seemed like the least of my worries.

As I looked at the fountain, I got another message.

Promenade of the Condemned: Fountain of Wishes

What's cooler than a fountain? Uh, nothing. EXCEPT A FOUNTAIN THAT HEALS YOUR PAINS AND GIVES YOU UPGRADES! That's right: we took the coolest way to turn any random plaza from "blah" to "yeah!" and put it right here.

You'll find one Fountain of Wishes on each level of Toroth-Gol. Drink the water of the Fountain of Wishes to heal your pains. Throw a gold coin into the Fountain of Wishes to claim your upgrade.

I didn't need any additional invitation. Setting Spud on the rim of the fountain, I practically threw myself over the edge, hanging on precariously while I pressed my dry lips to the cool black waters. I'd never tasted anything so delicious in my life.

"Ah," I gasped as I came up for air, wiping my mouth with the back of my right hand. Once again, I could feel my right arm. I pulled off the tourniquet and rolled up my sleeve, looking down at my forearm. Where there had previously been bloody puncture wounds, there was only smooth skin.

Magic.

From the edge of the fountain, Spud clicked his tongue. *"Finally,"* he said. "I was waiting for you to stop bleeding everywhere. That definitely improves our chances of survival. By the way, you never told me your name. What should I call you?"

Now that I wasn't facing an imminent threat or actively dying from blood loss, I focused on my companion. *He's definitely a loudmouth. But he's cheerful. And funny. I think I like him.*

"I'm King Crow," I said.

Spud raised an eyebrow. "Is that a nickname?"

"Yeah. Before I came into the dungeon, I played professional lightball. And I had a habit of always being near the ball. It's said that crows are attracted to shiny objects, so one of the announcers started calling me 'the crow.' Later that year, I won the King's Cup, which the league gives to the most impressive rookie, so my nickname changed to 'the king crow.' And that morphed into a proper noun—King Crow —and the name stuck."

"Huh. Interesting. Speaking of shiny objects, you probably want to take one of those coins from the tray next to me."

I shifted my gaze to the tray.

Gold Coin (x43)

See those coins there? Yes, those ones. You hereby have permission to take ONE. Eat it, stomp on it, cover it in blue paint and use it for an art project. It's your choice! But if we're being real, you should probably throw it into a Fountain of Wishes.

"Make sure you follow the directions and only take *one*," Spud said as I finished reading.

I pulled the text back up. "Wait a minute," I said. "You can see that?"

"Of course. The dungeon texts appear for me like they do for you. I also have a countdown timer in the upper right-hand corner of my vision. You have that too, right?"

I nodded. *So he doesn't see what I see, but what another hunter would see. Interesting.*

"I'm not sure how much you know about Toroth-Gol, but the dungeon is famous for its tests," Spud continued. "And I bet this is a test to see whether or not you can follow directions. What would happen if you broke the rules? Oh! I bet that if you try to take more than one coin, the coins turn into metal spiders that bite your hand. The spiders are called *Spirilla Suprema*. Their venom makes your blood boil inside your veins. You'll be dead in seconds."

"Is that a real creature?"

"Nah. I went through a phase where I got a kick out of inventing new species. But I still wouldn't recommend taking more than one coin."

I stepped to the tray and picked up a single coin, rubbing my thumb over the ridged edge. It was surprisingly heavy for such a small item. One side featured a boar and the same words I'd seen carved into the dungeon's entrance: *Nich la'min fortante*. I still didn't know what that meant. The other side showed a castle.

"Let's see what happens," I said. I tossed the coin into the fountain and watched as it sank, glinting beneath the frothy water.

"Here we go!" Spud said.

You've been granted one upgrade by the Fountain of Wishes. Choose wisely.

Armor Upgrades.
Weapon Upgrades.
Misc. Upgrades.

"Yes!" Spud said. "Weapon upgrades, Crow! Weapons, weapons, weapons!"

I wasn't opposed to choosing a weapon upgrade, but at the same time I wanted to make sure I understood my choices. But when I clicked into the armor upgrades screen, I got an error message.

Error. No available armor to upgrade. No armor upgrades available at this time.

Hmm. Nice to know that it's possible to get armor, even if I don't have any right now. Maybe armor could've protected me against the hyenas.

Feeling self-conscious about the scant protection offered by my ripped and bloodied jumpsuit, I backed out of "Armor Upgrades" and clicked "Weapon Upgrades."

"Here we go," Spud said. "Get ready to choose something awesome."

This time, the text showed three options, each with its own description.

Waffle Fry (Spud Beauregard Spuddington)

What do you get when you quarter-turn a potato before each pass over the corrugated blade of a mandoline? Increased surface area relative to volume! I.e., more room for water vapor to escape! I.e., increased Maillard reaction during the cooking process! Not ringing a bell? Okay, we'll make it simple—you get a waffle fry. Admired across the Empire for its distinctive shape and tastiness, the esteemed waffle fry creates a lattice from each slice of a potato. With this upgrade, your sapient, electromagnetically charged potato gains the ability to mimic this lattice, converting into a 4-foot-by-4-foot net that can be used to ensnare or trip opponents.

The description was interesting, though something else had caught my eye. "Your full name is Spud Beauregard Spuddington?" I asked.

Spud ignored me. "Bless my lucky starch," Spud whispered reverently. "This is the best day of my life."

"Right," I said. "Well, I don't think we should make a choice until we look at all the options."

I pulled up the description for the next upgrade.

Potato Pancake (Spud Beauregard Spuddington)

Clap your hands and stomp your feet... your enemies are about to eat... potato! With this *wildly* awesome upgrade, your sapient, electromagnetically charged potato is able to flatten itself into a three-foot-by-three-foot shield. Sure, it's smaller than the net you get from the Waffle Fry upgrade, but that baby can't stop bullets. This upgrade can block a wide variety of projectiles, fists, claws, and teeth. Pretty cool, eh?

That's even better.
"I like it!" Spud said. "What's the final choice?"
I continued reading.

Hot Potato (Spud Beauregard Spuddington)

Light my fire. Ring of fire. Set fire to the rain. Or dip this spud in hot oil AND GET YOURSELF A FLAMING HOT SAPIENT, ELECTROMAGNETICALLY CHARGED POTATO.

For the pyromaniacs among you, this is the obvious choice. Ever hear a potato scream? Better get used to it. Every use of this weapon upgrade causes your sapient, electromagnetically charged potato to holler at eighty decibels or more.

But those aren't screams of pain. They're screams of joy. Most likely.

"Hot Potato, Hot Potato, Hot Potato," Spud said, bouncing up and down on the fountain's edge. "That's the one. Trust me! We'll be unstoppable with that one. Imagine the fight that just happened, but with fire!"

I thought about it. Honestly, I couldn't decide whether it would've been cool or terrible.

"Did you see the part about the screaming?" I asked.

"That's only to scare us," Spud said. "I mean, think about lighting yourself on fire. Sure, it'll hurt a little, but it'll also feel so *good*. I'm telling you, Crow. You want Hot Potato."

Clearly, Spud and I had different definitions of "good." Still, I wasn't opposed to Hot Potato. In my opinion, it probably *was* the best of the three weapon upgrades, but I wanted more information. I backed out of "Weapon Upgrades."

"Um, no," Spud said. "What are you doing? You should be selecting Hot Potato. Crow? Crow? Crowwwwwww!"

Don't let his enthusiasm force you into making a snap decision. Now that you have some time to think, set yourself up for the best possible chance of survival.

"I want to see what's available," I said. "Give me a second."

I clicked into the final set of upgrades. The new text showed only two upgrade options, each labeled with the somewhat mouthy header of "Ophthalmic Augmentation." As I scanned the descriptions, I realized that each upgrade affected the implant in my right eye.

Ophthalmic Augmentation: Lights, Camera, Action

Let there be light! This upgrade gives the implant in your eye the power to emit a distracting burst of light within the portion of the electromagnetic spectrum visible to the human eye. Capable of one blast every six hours. Extremely powerful against the undead. Does not work against robots, elves, or creatures without eyes.

"That's neat, I guess," Spud said as I finished reading. "But I don't understand why you wouldn't take what's clearly the best upgrade. Imagine it. Imagine me. On fire!" When I didn't respond, Spud said,

"Really, Crow. I mean it. Take the fiery version of me. Set me on the path to unlocking my true form."

True form? I couldn't tell if Spud was being serious or being... Spud.

"What's your true form?" I asked.

Spud smiled. "I'm so glad you mentioned that. It's called Satanic Spud. It allows me to channel power from the hell I visit when I die."

"Wait. What?"

"Yeah! In the twenty-four-hour period between when I die and when I reappear in your handsome leather pouch, I go to Potato Hell. There's a bunch of other potatoes down there who definitely aren't as nice as me. They call me names and poke me with sharp weapons. It's terrible. But imagine if *I* was the one doing the poking!"

I didn't know if Spud was joking or not, so I decided to continue reading, jumping down to the description of the second option.

Ophthalmic Augmentation: Cut the Cord

Imagine you're a hunter. You're prancing along, you get thirsty, you spot a little brook, you put your little hunter lips down to the cool clear water... BAM! You accidentally trigger a trap that blows you into bloody pieces! That's a major bummer.

With this augmentation, you'll have the opportunity to break traps down into their component pieces. Upgrade triggers within a ten-foot radius of traps.

Even as I read, I knew Spud was going to say something critical. Sure enough, as I finished reading, he said, "Traps, shmaps. Triggering traps is a critical part of the Toroth-Gol experience. I think. I don't have too many memories from before our time together. But you don't want this, Crow. Trust me on that."

Is he saying that because it's actually a bad upgrade? Or because he wants me to choose Hot Potato?

I considered the options. There was potential value in "Lights,

Camera, Action," but I still didn't know what we'd face. What if I got deeper into the dungeon and every enemy was a robot? Or an elf? Cut the Cord definitely seemed useful, but I also didn't know anything about traps.

I wonder if traps are a common thing. Are they easy to avoid, or are they something I can only get around with the Cut the Cord upgrade?

I didn't know, and I needed something that would help *now*. Plus, there wasn't a price I'd put on sanity. If I didn't choose Hot Potato, I knew I'd never hear the end of it. Even as I ran through my options, Spud bounced along the side of the fountain and shouted for his preferred upgrade.

"Hot Potato!" he said. "Hot Potato! Hot and crispy! You know you want it! Hot Potato!"

I made my choice.

9

"Light me up, baby," Spud said. "Let's try my new power!"

It was a good suggestion. *Better we figure this out now than in the thick of a battle.* I took Spud off my shoulder and set him to hover over my palm.

"Do you know how this works?" I asked. "Do I need to press something, or can I think, *Fire...*"

As soon as the thought crossed my mind, Spud burst into flame. I felt the heat through my glove, but it wasn't unbearable.

At least, it wasn't unbearable for me.

"*Agggghhhhhh*," Spud screamed. He'd been covered in dried blood from the death hyenas, but as soon as he caught ablaze, it crackled like hot bacon and sloughed away, turning to ash that sprinkled the ground at my feet. *Go out!* As quickly as the flames had appeared, they stopped.

Spud breathed heavily. "Why'd you turn it off? That felt *incredible*. My god, Crow, the power! I'm drunk with it. Starting now, the Spud Squad will be *unstoppable*. That's pretty good, right? Spud Squad? Light me up again and leave me burning."

Fire, I thought, and the flames reappeared around Spud.

"Oh, yes!" he screamed. "Yeah, baby! *Agggghhhhhh*, it burns so good."

"Nice to know how the power works," I said. "I'm turning you off for a second. I want to get my bearings."

With a thought, I turned off the fire. Then I looked around the room. After the wide expanse of the promenade, it felt relatively claustrophobic. Half a dozen human bodies lay around a well in the room's center. The well was stone and circular, with a peaked roof supported by four wooden pillars.

Promenade of the Condemned: Well of Ascension

Did you ever read the longitudinal study about the kids who were offered one marshmallow now or two later? The ones who waited were shown to be more successful later in their lives than the greedy ones.

Congratulations! If you still have your coin, you were probably the type of kid who would've waited for two marshmallows. Drop your coin down the Well of Ascension and receive a new special skill.

I didn't know what a special skill was, though it was too late for regret. I'd gotten a pretty sweet upgrade, and I was happy with it. If I wanted a special skill, I'd have to hope I found more coins—and another Well of Ascension—in the future.

"Whatever we got from the well probably wouldn't have been as good as the weapon upgrade," Spud said, his voice cheerful and reassuring. "I mean, you saw me when I was burning. How cool was that?"

His enthusiasm was infectious. Still, with the number of bodies that surrounded the well, I couldn't help but feel a sense of grim solemnity. I studied the corpses more closely. Unlike the single body near the fountain, these ones were in bad shape. All of them were stripped to their undergarments, and they were covered in a variety of grievous physical wounds. Two of the bodies were missing limbs. One was even missing its head. Scorch marks and slashes marred the floor where it wasn't covered in blood, bone, and viscera.

"What do you think happened?" I asked Spud as new text appeared in my vision. It was the same text as I'd seen when I looked at the earlier corpse: *Deceased Human. It looks dead. Poke it with a stick. Loot? Yes or No.* Once again, the options were grayed out. "Do you think this was another test from the dungeon?" I continued. "Or some sort of in-fighting?"

"I don't know," Spud said, "but I think we should keep moving. This room doesn't smell great, and I doubt there's anything for us in here."

I couldn't argue. On the far side of the room was another door, so I walked toward it, with Spud held at the ready.

Toroth-Gol: Level One (The Castle of 1,000 Doors)

Ready for your adventure, hunter?

"Ah, the big time!" Spud said. "Fire me up, Crow. Let's do this!"

My heartbeat quickened. *This is it. Until now, I've been in the lobby of the dungeon, but once I go through this door, I'll be in the dungeon proper.*

Before I could lose my nerve, I turned on Spud's flames and pushed through the door. Immediately, the timer in the upper right-hand corner of my vision changed from twenty-eight minutes and a handful of seconds to twenty-four hours.

Twenty-four hours until the Purge. So another twenty-four hours of life. Assuming I survive whatever comes next.

The room in which I stood was set up like a dining hall, but sized for giants. The long, empty tables were at least thirty feet high. At the far end of the room was a dais with a high table, also empty, and in the wall behind that table were three massive doors. On either side of the room, tall archways opened to long hallways. I picked up on a unique smell, and after I sniffed a few more times, I realized the whole room smelled like roasted chicken.

The Castle of 1,000 Doors (Feasting Hall of the Giants)

The journey of a thousand miles starts with a single step. And your journey into Toroth-Gol starts with the Castle of 1,000 Doors. Right now, you're standing in the feasting hall of a castle with a thousand different doors, each of which opens to a different landscape. All of those landscapes contain their own geography, enemies, challenges, and treasure. Which door should you choose? How do you know what's behind them? Good luck!

When it didn't look like anything would attack us immediately, I turned off Spud's flames. There didn't appear to be a limit to his power, but the heat—and his moaning—were distracting. For whatever reason, he didn't complain.

"There's definitely a game here," he said. "Walk closer to those doors on the other side of the room. I want to see what info we can get."

"Good idea," I said. Sure enough, as I approached the doors, new text appeared.

Ghost Ship.
Candy Land.
Random Forest.

But those words were the only information I received. Nothing else.

"I bet that's the name of the world behind each door," Spud said. "Isn't that what the text said? That each door opens into a different landscape?"

I nodded. *A thousand doors, each opening to its own geography, enemies, challenges, and treasure. And we need to choose one. Our first real test as hunters.*

I knew which one to choose. "We're looking for a door called Dark City," I said, repeating Jocko's words from the rail car. I opened my Map. The castle was shaped like the letter H, with two wings and a central hall between them. There were at least twenty rooms on this level alone, ranging in size from a closet to the grand room that spanned the middle part of the "H" between the wings. The rooms were unlabeled.

"What's so special about that one?" Spud asked as I closed the Map. I told him about my experience with Jocko, but he didn't look convinced. "We're supposed to trust some criminal you met on a train?" he said. "If we're acting all gullible, I know a *great* way to double your income by working from home. Or, if you're looking to make a real estate investment, I can get you in on the ground floor of a project on the moon. Building rights, drilling rights, you name it!"

I tuned him out. I didn't know *what* we'd face in the Dark City, or why Jocko had told us to meet him there, but I've always considered myself a good judge of character.

Jocko was a good man. He wasn't telling me everything, but I trust him.

Still, I recognized that it was important to maintain the team dynamic. "Do you have a better course of action?"

"Not at all," Spud said. "I just like talking."

I rolled my eyes. *True enough.* I walked toward one of the arches, past a suit of armor that reached halfway to the ceiling. As we did, a spider scurried across the floor and disappeared into a crack between two armored plates. It poked a glossy foreleg from the crack and wiggled it as if testing the air.

I shivered, quickening my pace and crossing under the archway. A tapestry hung on the wall beside another massive door. It depicted a pale woman in flowing gossamer robes. With one hand, she clutched a thick leather book to her chest. With the other, she held the hand of a small boy dressed in the traditional garb of an Empire page: a black velvet tunic with gold embroidery above black trousers, all tied with rope. In the far distance was a castle, though the woman and the boy were walking away, heading into the depths of a forest.

"Oh, that's nice," Spud said. "She's leading him through the forest. I bet if we went through this door, we'd find a woman like that. Maybe she's a guide construct or something."

As I studied the tapestry, I realized something wasn't quite right.

From a distance, the trees appeared innocuous enough. When I focused on them, I saw that what I'd thought were knotholes were actually bodies embedded in the wood. What I'd mistaken for roots were thorny, blood-spattered vines.

Wait a minute. Why is the woman leading the boy away from the castle and into the forest? Already, vines hovered near the boy's boots, looking ready to ensnare him.

"Ah, maybe," I said. "I'm not so sure."

From there, we followed the Map to another hallway, each as high and wide as the Promenade of the Condemned. These hallways were dotted with doors, and their text flashed across my vision as we walked past.

Wayward Timberland.
Plateau of the Scorched.
Halcyon Wetlands.
Crooked Stepstones.

I didn't spend too long on any of them, as I already knew where we needed to go. Still, I remained on high alert. At any second, I expected another pack of death hyenas to round the corner and charge down the hall, their eyes blazing and foam on their lips.

Or maybe something else will appear. Something worse. Who knows what inhabits the castle depths?

I was scaring myself for no good reason. I forced myself to think of happier thoughts. Like reuniting with my father. *I wonder where he is. I hope he's okay.*

Spud interrupted my thoughts. "I've made a brave decision," he said, after a spider scuttled over my boots for at least the fourth time in a twenty-minute period. "I think you should send me after the spiders."

That is *a brave decision.* Then again, I hated spiders. Did Spud hate them, too? Or was there an ulterior motive behind his suggestion?

Before I could probe, Spud said, "I hate creepy crawlies as much as the next potato, but if we're going to work together, we should practice as much as possible. You can activate my flames, and then we can see how effective they are at lighting stuff on fire."

I considered the idea. "With the way you scream, I don't think we should use the flames—not until we know if it'd attract unwanted attention. However, you're right about getting in some practice. I'm game for a little hunting."

The next time we saw a spider, I sent Spud shooting after it. There was a *crunch* as Spud crushed the arachnid between his body and the wall.

"It's crunch time!" Spud said after I'd pulled him back into my palm. "Just promise you'll wipe off the guts. Ew, I think I got them in my mouth."

By the time we reached the end of the hall, I was eleven for twelve. The one I'd missed must've had some kind of sixth sense, because it had darted into a crack between two stones as soon as Spud had left my hand. Or maybe it'd gotten lucky.

I could use a little luck myself, I thought as I pushed through a doorway and into the room beyond.

10

We passed through a doorway into a human-sized kitchen: sinks along the far wall, an island of ranges in the middle.

The Castle of 1,000 Doors (Sammy's Kitchen)

In the hierarchy of enslaved people who served the giants in the Castle of 1,000 Doors, few stood higher than Head Chef Sammy. A wizard at cooking roasted flesh and gelatinous desserts, she had her helpers whipped into shape before the end of their first shift— literally. Mind your corners and keep your station clean, else you might find yourself in the pot.

I turned my attention to what I might be able to scavenge. *Nothing.* After cautiously opening cabinets and drawers, I realized that Sammy's Kitchen was as picked over as the Feasting Hall of the Giants had been. If I'd been in the market for ladles or wooden spoons, it was a gold mine. But in terms of anything I could use as a melee weapon, or anything to eat, Sammy's Kitchen was sadly empty.

"There are sinks, at least," Spud said. "I think you flesh-bodies need water to survive. Right? Or is it just food and soil? Food and air? I know it's food, but I can't remember what else."

I followed Spud's gaze to one of the sinks, suddenly realizing I was thirsty. I was hungry, too—being in the kitchen made my stomach rumble.

When did I last eat? Some oatmeal before they took out my eye. That felt like years ago.

It'd be good to stay hydrated. But when I turned on the sink, nothing happened. I gave the handle a few more twists and was about to close the tap when I heard the *thunk, thunk, thunk* of something making its way through the pipes.

"There we go," I said.

A stream of brown slime sputtered from the faucet, filling the room with the putrid smell of dead animal boiled with the skins of other dead animals.

"Turn it off!" Spud said, retching at the scent. I hadn't known potatoes could retch. I tried turning the handle, but the slime wouldn't stop. "Let's get out of here, then. Oh my god, that's terrible. That's worse than the underwear of a week-old corpse. That's worse than anything in Potato Hell."

I wanted to ask Spud if he *actually* knew what the underwear of a week-old corpse smelled like, but it wasn't the time. The scent was too all-consuming. I'd just pulled my jumpsuit over my nose and had started looking for the exit when the first slime slipped out of the faucet.

I say "slime" and not "maggot" or "grub," because that's what the text that appeared in my vision told me. It looked like a white balloon, but then it dropped from the faucet and landed with a plop in the dirty brown goo that had gathered in the base of the sink.

"What's that?" I asked as another white balloon dripped from the faucet. The first slime slipped over the side of the sink, landing on the floor with a wet *plop*. That's when I realized it was alive. And coming toward us.

Common White Slime

Often found in basements or old pipes, the common white slime differs from other types of slimes by its color and the numbing acids it secretes to dissolve its prey. Given their slow rate of movement, the common white slime doesn't present much of a threat. Unless you're trapped in a kitchen with hundreds of them.

"Run!" Spud said. But it was too late to move. With a *bang*, the kitchen door slammed closed. Another *bang* and the door on the far side of the room also snapped shut.

"Now we're in for it," Spud said. "Great job, Crow. As if the smell wasn't a hint. Note to future Crow: when you smell something like that, or see a ghost or a sexy potato with a pitchfork and fangs, you run."

I ignored him. Since the kitchen door was closer, I tried that one first. It would be just my luck to discover later that it wasn't locked.

The door *was* locked. So was the one on the far side of the room.

"Any idea how to fight these things?" I asked, watching from one side of the island as more slimes slipped into the sink and then from the sink to the floor. There were about ten of them now, all moving across the tile in short, jerking motions.

They seemed to be following us.

"No idea. Don't shoot me at them. Please. They have numbing acid."

Just to see what would happen, I grabbed a wooden spoon from where it lay next to the stove and tossed it into the middle of the slimes. The result was like throwing a lightball into a group of children. As the spoon clattered to the floor, all of the slimes moved toward it.

"They're attracted to sound, I think," I said—which was a dumb thing to do, because as soon as I'd spoken, the slimes turned back toward us.

More slimes slipped from the faucet. The sink was full of them now, so whenever a new slime dripped out, it landed on a bed of white goo. One of the slimes rolled over the spoon, and the cutlery appeared a second later, floating inside the slime's translucent body. I imagine it would hover there for days or weeks or however long it took for the "numbing acids" inside the slime to dissolve the wood.

"Do you think they're flammable?"

"What?"

"Do you think we can light them on fire?"

"I think you can light anything on fire. But don't shoot me at them. *They're* not flammable. Definitely not. Green slimes, maybe, but not white ones. No way. Crow, don't make me touch them!"

But that wasn't my plan. I'd seen what the slime had done to the spoon, so I had no desire to launch Spud into something which could absorb him into its body. Instead, I moved toward the far door. While it was locked, it was also made of wood. And I wasn't only a professional athlete—I was a *strong* professional athlete.

"Here we go," I said. I lifted a booted foot and slammed it into the lockset. The door shuddered but didn't open. I tried again, then again. On my fourth kick, I was rewarded with a crack and the door flew open.

"Great work, Crow! Now let's get out of here. Wait, where are you going? Wrong way, Crow! Wrong way!"

With the door open, I ran back to the stoves at the center of the room and opened the burners. Years of disuse might've caused the water pipes to dry, but it hadn't done anything to the gas. My actions were rewarded with a pleasant hiss and the smell of natural gas.

"You're crazy. I know what you're doing, Crow, and this is a bad plan. You got the door open. Let's get out of here. Oh my god, Crow. They're coming. They're right on top of us!"

The slimes had gotten close, but I'd accomplished my goal. "Taters gonna tate," I said as I ran back toward the open door. I grabbed Spud off my shoulder and set him to hover above my hand. *Fire*, I thought, and the potato exploded in flames.

"*Agggghhhhhh*," Spud screamed. "Your pun was terrible!" I ducked behind the door as Spud continued yelling: "Close it, close it, close it!"

"Not yet," I said. "I need more time."

"Close it, Crow!" Spud begged. "You're playing with fire!"

I was. But I wasn't worried: I'd made more difficult shots at least a hundred times before. *Calm, cool, and collected,* I thought as I took aim. As the first slimes reached the door, I sent Spud shooting toward the burners. There was the *whoosh* of gas and the room lit white with flame. I could feel the heat singeing my eyebrows, but I couldn't stop. In one clean motion, I pulled the screaming Spud back toward me with my left hand and closed the door with my right, slamming it shut just after the howling potato slid through the crack between the door and the frame. Then I stumbled backward while patting out the fire that danced along my jumpsuit.

Spud's momentum was arrested by the glass jars that lined the shelves along the far wall. He bounced off them and fell to the ground, hitting the floor with a little gasp. Mentally, I extinguished his flames.

"In the name of all that's crispy," he said as the last flames crackled and died against his blackened skin. "That was *awesome.*" His eyes were wide. "What a thrill. What a rush! You really made them peel the burn."

I laughed, half from the pun and half from the realization that I'd survived yet another brush with death. "That was pretty wild."

Spud spun in a circle. "Put me on your shoulder again, buddy. There's nothing that can stop us." I pulled him into my hand and set him on my shoulder, where he danced a little jig. "I can't wait to do that again. Spud Squad!"

We stood in a pantry. The shelves along the walls were stacked with jars of pickled vegetables: cucumbers, peppers, onions, and beets. There was a trapdoor in the floor, which I opened to reveal a dark hole. A ladder disappeared into the darkness. My thoughts were corroborated when text popped into my vision.

The Castle of 1,000 Doors (Sammy's Larder)

Cucumbers, beets, and meats, oh my! In Sammy's Kitchen, Head Chef Sammy and her crew of chefs de partie prepared meals for the giants who inhabited the Castle of 1,000 Doors. The giants ate human flesh but Head Chef Sammy kept herself fed with provi-

sions from this larder. One day, she hoped to use these provisions to make her escape. Spoiler: she never made her escape.

"Jackpot, baby!" Spud said. "You follow me and see where you get. As a sapient, electromagnetically charged potato, I don't need to eat to live, but I know your fleshy body has its needs."

Another message flashed across my vision.

You've killed a Common White Slime.

It disappeared, replaced by another message.

You've killed a Common White Slime.

The same message appeared again, again, and again. *That fire in the kitchen must really be burning. Burn, baby, burn!*

It took quite a while for the messages to fade from my vision. There had been a lot of slimes. When they finally did, I examined the jars. I'd half expected to see an ear floating in the brine, or perhaps a set of teeth, though it looked like solid produce. I opened a jar of pickles and gave it a sniff.

"Smell like poison?" Spud asked.

"Not sure." I bit into the pickle. It was a dill pickle, perfectly salty but with a nice hint of the fresh, springy namesake. When I didn't immediately keel over, I ate the entire thing.

"Slow down there, Mr. Chonk. Don't you want to see how they'll affect you?"

In all honesty, I didn't care. I was hungry. And thirsty. As Spud berated me, I finished my second pickle and ate a third. When I was done, I wiped my hands on my jumpsuit and took a long sip of the juice. For many years, Valentine had touted pickle juice as one of the world's greatest forms of refreshment, as it contained a healthy mix of water, electrolytes, and good bacteria. It made my eyes water, but I had to admit that it was refreshing, especially after fighting my way through several rooms of Toroth-Gol.

"That's good," I said, screwing the lid back onto the jar. "I'm taking as many of these as I can carry."

I grabbed a couple of each type of vegetable and put them in my Inventory. When I pulled up the Inventory, I noticed that each type had been grouped together. Even though I had ten jars of pickles, they didn't take up ten squares; instead, they took up a single square, with a little "10" in the bottom right-hand corner. Same with the peppers, onions, and beets.

Since they hardly made a dent in my total carrying capacity, I took *all* of them. The weight brought me a good portion of the way to my capacity, though I could always jettison them if necessary.

When everything was done, I had seventy-nine jars of pickled cucumbers, forty-two jars of peppers, thirty-eight jars of onions, and twenty-nine jars of beets. At the back of the larder, I also found seven untouched hams. I put those in my Inventory, too.

"That should keep me fed for a while," I said. "Ready to get out of here?"

I nodded to a nearby trapdoor, and Spud stared at it dubiously. "It looks dark down there. If only you had, oh, I don't know, a flaming potato you could shoot into the darkness to light the way. So let me answer your question with a question, my hungry friend: are you ready for this?"

Before I could stop him, Spud rolled off my shoulder and into the hole.

He screamed all the way down.

11

"Spud?" I said, shouting into the hole. "Are you okay?"

About a second and a half later, a *thud* came up from the hole, followed by a flash of white light—strange, because I hadn't turned on Spud's flames.

"*Agggghhhhhh!*" Spud shouted from far below. "I'm all good, Crow! It's about a thirty-foot drop. The room here is filled with barrels. Oh baby, I'm *so* hot. Come on down!"

A short while later, I stood beside a flaming Spud in a wide, low-ceilinged room. The room was filled with neat rows of barrels stacked three high with wooden pallets between them. I also saw massive single barrels that stood vertically, their tops nearly brushing the stone ceiling.

"Can you activate your flames by yourself?" I asked. "Because you're currently on fire and I hadn't activated anything."

"Oh, yeah. I can do that."

"That's good to know. But next time, maybe wait until I'm ready before jumping into a mysterious hole?"

"Sure. You got it. *Agggghhhh!* The Spud Squad makes its decisions as a unit. Say, did you also know that I can moderate my heat? Oh, it burns!"

As I watched, Spud glowed more brightly, the flames on his skin jumping higher. Then he brought them down to a smoldering glow and his screams became a low, fairly disturbing moan.

"Ah, no," I said. "I didn't know that."

I glanced around the room.

The Castle of 1,000 Doors (Sammy's Cellar)

Just as artists have studios and engineers have workshops, Sammy had this cellar. It's where she did all her experimentation, creating new treats for the giants as well as her almost-patented Spider-Killing Solvent. Because if you haven't noticed by now, the Castle of 1,000 Doors has a spider problem. A big one. That was the case even before the Insanity took the giants.

What's the Insanity? Another question without an answer.

"*Agggghhhh!*" Spud shouted as he blazed with flame, interrupting my thoughts. "What's your stance on bold reds?" He jumped atop a barrel and rolled from one side to the other.

"Spud, watch out!" I said. From my time in the Dregs, I'd learned many things, but few lessons were more important than keeping fire away from mysterious barrels. When you worked in a warehouse on the lowest level of Steel City, it was a lesson that came hard and fast. I activated my glove, falling backward even as the blazing potato shot toward me. Then I held my breath, hoping I'd caught him in time.

"*Agggghhhh!* Let me go, you great oaf," Spud said. He strained against the force that held him above my left palm. "So hot! So hot! This skin might look crispy, but it contains a temple. My body, my rules. This is an outrage!"

After a few seconds, when there was no explosion, I released my breath. I could hear my heart beating in my chest: *thump thump. Thump thump.* That was good, at least. It meant I was alive.

"Turn down your flames," I said. "Let's see what's in that barrel before you roll atop it while on fire."

I stared at the barrel.

Sammy's Spider-Killing Solvent

One part bifenthrin, one part deltamethrin, one part vinegar. All parts death… to spiders, at least. Still, you wouldn't want to get this on your delicate human skin.

WARNING: HIGHLY FLAMMABLE.

There was a pause in which I could tell that Spud was reading, too. Then his flames dulled to a low smolder that provided just enough light for me to see my surroundings.

"Oh," he said. "That might've been bad. Well, sir, I'll give you this one. If we'd been blown into a million pieces, that would've been on me. You heard that correctly. I'm big enough to admit when I'm wrong. That *definitely* would've been my fault. Say, way to think on your feet, Crow. I'm proud of you. Great instincts. That's why you're an important and valued member of the Spud Squad."

I continued staring at the barrel. Even if it wasn't wine, I could see how it might come in handy. Cautiously, I set Spud back on the ground and walked around it, trying to gauge how hard it might be to lift. When the examination didn't reveal anything untoward, I pulled the bung and wafted some air toward my nose. I choked almost immediately. It was a good thing I hadn't brought my nose to the hole, as even that brief whiff had singed the hairs in my nostrils.

"That's powerful," I gasped. "Okay, let's try and take one. This place is full of spiders, and it would be just our luck to run across a giant one."

I replaced the bung, smacking it down tightly to make sure it wouldn't pop out and spill solvent down my chest. When it was secure, I wrapped my arms around the wood and heaved.

The barrel was heavy. Like, stupidly heavy. As I attempted to put it in my Inventory, a message flashed across my vision.

Error. Item exceeds current carrying capacity. Unable to place item in Inventory.

"Get rid of some of those jars," Spud said. "Why do you have so many? And eighty-three *pounds* of ham? That's indulgent."

So began the arduous process of pulling things out of my Inventory, lifting the barrel, trying to place it in my Inventory, getting an error message, and starting over. When I finally succeeded, sweat glistened on my forehead. I'd had to remove several items: all my beets, for one, but I'd never liked beets. Too earthy. Losing several jars of onions was a blow, and I'd needed to lose all but two of the hams, but in the end, I'd stored the barrel of Spider-Killing Solvent.

"That weighs almost four hundred pounds," I said, wiping my brow.

"Sure, but that's the kind of item you want in a pinch. Say, this meat is great. What did you call it? Ham? Dig in, Crow. Eat as much as you can. You don't want any of this going to waste."

I joined Spud on the ground near our pile of abandoned food, where I downed a quarter of a ham and an entire jar of pickled onions. Just for kicks, I tried a beet, but it tasted exactly like I remembered, so I spit it out and went back to the onions. When I'd eaten my fill, I washed everything down with a few sips of brine. The salty vinegar burned my throat and made my eyes water, but Sal Valentine had rarely steered me wrong. And I needed the hydration. Other than the Fountain of Wishes, I hadn't seen another source of water since I entered the dungeon. Until we found one, I'd need to keep drinking pickle juice.

When we were done, I stood and wiped my mouth with the back of my glove. It hurt to leave so much good food, but I had a feeling we'd want the solvent. Then I opened my Map.

"Looks like we need to go that way," I said, pointing in the direction of the star.

"Lead on. Say, can you do that pulling thing on me? And leave me hovering above your glove like you did before?"

"Like this?" I asked. I activated my glove, pulling Spud into the air. I clicked my fingers so that the electromagnet in the glove generated a stable field, and Spud hovered over my palm.

"That's it! Here, look. If I make myself a little brighter, you'll have your own flashlight. Not bright enough for me to start screaming, but —oh! Oh, baby! That feels *so* good!"

He moaned as he brightened. It was creepy, to say the least. I was about to tell him to stop but the light had utility. If I could put up with a little moaning, I had my own torch.

"That's pretty cool?" I said. I still wasn't entirely sure what I thought about it.

"Oh yeah, baby. Yes, yes, yes. Told you to choose Hot Potato."

I ignored him and walked deeper into the cellar.

12

At some point in our exploration of the Castle of 1,000 Doors, we started seeing signs. Literally. We found them in groups of ten or twenty, each about two feet long and printed with the names of different landscapes. It was only a matter of time before we found the one we wanted.

"Dark City," I said as I noticed a sign with an arrow that pointed to our destination. "All right!"

We heard the fellow hunters before we saw them. As we walked down a hall, there came multiple gunshots and a screech from the room at the other end. Then what sounded like human voices.

"Oh, baby. That sounded like gunfire," Spud said, his words followed by a soft moan. "Did that sound like something getting shot to you?"

I nodded. "Turn off your flames." The hallway went dark. Pressing myself against the wall, I inched forward, Spud held at the ready. Before we crossed into the next room, I lifted Spud toward my head and whispered, "I'm going to peek inside. Hopefully we find friends, but you never know. Just be ready for action."

"I don't think that's the best idea, Crow," Spud said. "You're not exactly the stealthiest individual. If I need someone to open a pickle jar—or, you know, eat all of the pickles before anyone else has a chance to try them—you're the one I'd call. But this is cloak-and-dagger stuff. Why not use me? I'm small, sneaky, and the last thing anyone in there would expect to see."

The idea had merit. *That's surprisingly intelligent. No one would expect to get spied on by a sapient potato.*

"Can you keep quiet?" I asked him. In response, Spud nodded.

So he is capable of keeping his mouth shut. But can I trust him not to blow our cover or set the room on fire?

Spud must've guessed my thoughts. "Trust me," he said. "I've got this. I'll scout and report back. That's it."

I sighed. Then I nodded. *I suppose we've got to believe in each other at some point.* I turned off my glove and let him drop into my palm. His skin was warm to the touch.

"Good luck," I whispered as I set him on the ground.

"Luck is my middle name."

"I thought it was…? Never mind."

As Spud rolled away, I was surprised to feel a little pang of… something. I didn't know exactly what it was. It felt a bit like homesickness combined with fear. But not fear for myself—fear for Spud.

We hadn't known each other long, but I already missed that little guy.

Perhaps a minute later, Spud rolled back through the doorway, and I helped him along by pulling him into my hand. After the explosions and the screech, and the low murmur of human voices, I hadn't heard any sounds from the room beyond. And while he'd been gone, I hadn't seen any flashes of text across my vision. It wasn't reciprocal: Spud could see the messages delivered by my ocular implant, but if he received any, I couldn't see them.

I lifted the potato. "What'd you see?"

"Those noises we heard were *definitely* gunfire. The room beyond is a ballroom, but it's, like, sized for giants. Kind of like that first dining room. Except this is so much nicer. There are these chandeliers, and beautiful carvings of angels along the walls, and a whole second level that looks down onto the first. High up on the walls, you've got these incredible blue drapes. It's really terrific fabric. I can't remember the last time I've seen that quality of craftsmanship."

Count on Spud to get distracted by fabric.

"Are there any hunters in there? Any dangers? Any signs that point to the Dark City?"

Spud rolled his eyes. "Yeah, well, I'm getting to that. There were signs, and one of them pointed to the Dark City. So that's good. But there's also a creature bleeding out on the floor. I'm not sure if it's a hunter or something that came from the dungeon. I have no clue what you'd call it. It's the same size as you—well, not the same size, because you're freakin' huge—but it's roughly the same size, and it's the same shape, too. Only, the creature has a tail. And scales? It was kind of like a lizard."

I recognized the description. "A reptilian," I said. That was the only creature I knew that would fit the bill. I didn't know much about the mysterious creatures, but I'd occasionally seen them in private boxes at my games. I remembered the first time I saw one. After growing up in the Dregs, where the only humanoids I ever saw were just sweaty, sooty humans, it was quite a shock to learn that we weren't the only sapient creatures in the Empire.

I needed to be certain. "Did it have gills?"

"I didn't get that close. Just saw the hole blown through its gut. I also saw who did it: three hunters in pirate costumes."

I raised an eyebrow. "Pirate costumes?"

"Well, they might not have been costumes," Spud continued. "Maybe they were actually pirates. You know, that makes sense. The text that popped up said something about them being pirates even before they entered Toroth-Gol."

I shook my head in disbelief. "You didn't read it?"

"I read it! I just wasn't paying that much attention. It was scary in there, Crow! Big ballroom, dead body, pirates. And to be honest, I was quite distracted by that fabric."

Keep him moving. If he thinks you're blaming him for something, he'll start getting defensive.

I motioned for him to continue. "Tell me more."

"Now we're talking! So the fabric really was *quite* sensational. The only blue I've ever seen with the same depth came from this super rare type of sea snail. You'd need to kill an entire colony to make the dye for a single square inch."

I sighed. "Tell me about the pirates."

"Oh!" Spud's face fell. "So there was this one guy with flowing gray hair and one of those eye patches. His name was Skiv or Skeev or something. He was quite dashing. The only thing I remember about the text I got was that he'd served as first mate on a ship called the *Rancid Pearl*. Does that name mean anything to you?"

I racked my brain, but I'd never heard of a ship by that name. I shook my head.

"Sounds kind of gross though, right?" Spud asked. "The *Rancid Pearl*? Anyway, that dashing pirate had two big pistols hanging from a leather belt. Now that I'm thinking about it, he was a bit like you. Not the dashing part—just that he was kind of a hulking brute."

Is that what he thinks of me? I was a little hurt, but before I could ask about it, Spud continued.

"He also looked *angry*. Like, really mad. He was sort of standing off to the side with his arms crossed. Then there was another guy, though this one had red eyes. Just the pupils, mind you. Glowing red, like the bad guys in Potato Hell. This pirate's name was Marland and he served on the *Rancid Pearl* as the quartermaster. He was crouched down by that lizard's body. And he carried a violin. I think it was some type of weapon. Though, now that I'm considering it, I don't see how that's a weapon, unless he's really bad at playing it. Maybe the music is so bad that he scares away monsters? Anyway, he had this little red dot floating near his head, and at first I thought it was my imagination, but I really squinted and realized that it was a tiny lady with wings. How cool is that? I think she saw me."

My eyes shot to the door of the ballroom. "She saw you?"

"Yes, that's what I'm telling you. Don't freak out about it. They're not going to bother us. They're gone."

Despite Spud's assurances, I couldn't help but worry. "What do you mean?"

Spud huffed in frustration. "Can I please finish my report?"

I took a deep breath. *Calm. Stay cool. He's trying his best. And if he's telling the truth, you're not in immediate danger. Stay alert, keep him on track, and let him finish. Then you can make your decision.*

I nodded, though I didn't take my eyes from the door to the ballroom. "Sure. Go on."

"Thank you. The tiny flying lady saw me and must've said something to that Marland character because he stared right at me. Then he got to his feet and said something to the third member of the group. That was Cara Thorne, captain of the *Rancid Pearl*. That's right —the captain was a woman. Pretty progressive, right? Wavy dark hair, kind of like Skeev, and full, perfect lips. Cheekbones that could slice your hand. I thought I had a crush on Skeev but I'll tell you what—I'd let Cara Thorne cover me with pepper and eat me up any day of the week."

Stay calm. Deep breaths.

"She was looting the body, but when Marland said something to her, she stopped. She had this saber at her waist, and she went to draw it, but Skeev said something to her and she didn't. I didn't hear what she said back to him, but then the three of them went through this door right in the middle of the fireplace. Did I tell you about the fireplace? Carvings of angels all along the mantel and this beautiful blue fabric that—"

I couldn't let him start talking about the fabric again. "But they're gone," I said. "That's what you're saying, right? They've left?"

"What? Oh yeah. Went through a door marked 'High Seas' and closed it behind them. Now it's just an empty ballroom with a dead lizard on the floor."

I nodded. That was all I needed to hear. Before he could get off track again, I stepped through the doorway. The scene was exactly as Spud had described: massive two-story ballroom, chandeliers, blue drapes. Fireplace with a door in the middle.

The Castle of 1,000 Doors (Contessa Georgia's Ballroom)

What does a party look like when you're a giant? Just ask Contessa Georgia. Born to entertain, Contessa Georgia threw myriad events in this room, hosting famous musicians and entertainers from around the world. As the years passed and the giants succumbed to the Insanity, this room became better known for Smash, a game in which giants competed to make the biggest mess by mashing two human prisoners together.

The room was silent. I shivered as I imagined the twisted game the giants had played.

There was a dead reptilian on the floor, and I walked over to it. As I said, I hadn't spent much time around the strange, semi-aquatic race, but I knew enough about their biology to recognize one. The reptilian was female, with burnished red scales, almost brown.

Deceased Reptilian

It looks dead. Poke it with a stick!

Loot? Yes or No.

The buttons were grayed out, but I'd already expected that. The pirates had been there before me.

As I read the text, something moved in the corner of my eye. I whirled around to see a pair of yellow eyes staring at me from the shadows of a nearby doorway. As soon as I'd spotted them, they were gone. There wasn't even enough time for the text to trigger in my vision.

"What the heck was that?"

It was a rhetorical question, but a voice rang out across the ballroom in response. "That was a very naughty reptilian named Geeta," it said. "Quick. Vengeful. Made weak by virtue. The quintessential outlaw, raging against an unjust system and sure to be even more fanatical now that we've killed her willful partner."

I turned back around and saw a woman standing before the

doorway in the fireplace. Where had she come from? She was dressed in black britches and a trench coat made from brown fabric. Beneath the coat, she had a billowing white blouse with frills on the cuffs.

And wavy hair. And full lips. And cheekbones that could cut your hand. Even before the text popped up, I knew who she was.

Charming Captain (Cara Thorne)

Beware, landsmen! Beneath a traditionally beautiful exterior sits a heart blacker than the depths and blood that runs colder than the frigid Northern Seas. If Cara Thorne had a mother, she died long before the infamous pirate Nile "Whitemane" Thorne raised his children aboard the *Rancid Pearl*. When Whitemane died, Cara took over the *Rancid Pearl* as captain. She was captured with her crew and sentenced to Toroth-Gol for piracy.

"Cara Thorne, I presume?" To Spud, I whispered, "I thought you said all three of them had gone through the door?"

"Two of them, at least. I got kinda scared when they saw me and came back to you. Maybe, uh, all of them hadn't gone through."

The pirate captain bowed, one gloved hand on the hilt of her sword. "My reputation precedes me," she said. "And you..." The woman wagged a thin finger at me. "Your reputation precedes you as well. I recognize you. You're the one who got beaten up by the guards. You look like that famous lightball player, you know that? Especially with those gloves."

"I am that famous lightball player."

"Really?" Cara looked me up and down. "Perhaps you are. What are you doing down here, then? Black hands for treason, I see. You get too popular and make a powerful enemy? Or were you actually plotting against the Empire?"

"Take a guess."

Cara swept a hand through her wavy brown hair. I couldn't help but imagine what it would be like to run my hands through those tresses. "Before I was captured, I ran a pirate crew. We sailed the Southern Seas, and our ship was called the *Rancid Pearl*. Heard of her?"

"No."

Cara shrugged. "No matter. I also made some powerful enemies. It took six Empire galleons to bring me in. Managed to sink four of 'em. But here we are together, eh?" She spread her arms, finally taking a hand off the hilt of her sword. "Cara Thorne and King Crow. A match made in Hell." She threw back her head and laughed. I'm ashamed to admit that it was a beautiful sound, deep and husky, made all the more appealing by the view of her collarbones. But what she said next withered my attraction.

"To be honest, I *was* going to run you through and steal your valuables, like we did to Silvana." She pointed at the reptilian's body with her sword, which had found its way into her hand. I hadn't even seen it leave the scabbard. "But I've seen you on the field, Crow. I might root for the Serpents, but I always liked the Sledgehammers. Always liked you. And it was noble of you to stick up for that woman on the train. As much as it pains me, I'll let you go. This time."

Cara saluted me with her sword and drove it back into its scabbard. Then, turning on her heel, she placed one hand on the doorknob and blew me a kiss.

"So long, Crow. Follow me, if you want. I think we could burn cities together."

Then, she was gone.

13

Thanks to the signs, I knew where to go. However, a large part of me wanted to follow Cara Thorne instead. The dungeon had warned me that Cara had a heart blacker than the depths and blood that ran colder than the frigid Northern Seas. Still, I almost followed Cara through the door.

It was Spud who pulled me back to reality as I started to walk toward the door she'd just entered. "Get a hold of yourself, you moon-eyed baby. You disgust me. Didn't you hear a word she said? She killed that poor lizard thing. And she was going to kill you. Snap out of it! That woman would gut you without a second thought."

I shook my head, a fog lifting from my mind. *Had Cara possessed some sort of charm magic? Probably. That's a decent explanation for why I'd want to start following a murderer.*

"This room gives me the creeps," I said, eyeing the body of the dead reptilian. "Let's get out of here."

We left Contessa Georgia's Ballroom through a human-sized door, Spud's light guiding the way as we walked down a long corridor. For a while, we were silent. I thought about the doors and what might be behind them. If there were a thousand doors, it was likely that most of the prisoners would head to different destinations. Would we all meet up again deeper in the dungeon? Or was the train the last time we'd see our fellow convicts?

Truth be told, I was also still thinking about Cara Thorne—rather, I was thinking about what she represented. Growing up in the Dregs, I'd stolen my share of kisses from girls who cycled through the warehouse, but my father had rescued me before I considered going steady with any of them. During my young adulthood, I was too busy with practice for dating. Once I became famous, there was no shortage of attention, yet I always felt that it came for the wrong reasons. People wanted me because of my name, my talent, or my money. Or they knew I was from the Dregs and wanted to experience something dangerous. Throughout my life, I'd never felt that any of my partners actually *saw* me.

And unless I survived Toroth-Gol, they never would.

It was just another reason to escape the dungeon. I needed to get out so I could find out why I'd been sentenced to the dungeon in the first place. But I also wanted to experience love. Not the momentary lust I'd experienced when I found myself desired by someone attractive, or that had just come from a pirate's charm magic, but the type of love that the poets wrote about. The type I'd heard about from my father when he spoke of his late wife. I'd never met Violet Valentine, but there was a picture of her above the mantel in my father's office. Brown hair, green eyes. The painter had captured the glow of her porcelain skin. I could see why my father had fallen for her. Yet it wasn't her looks that had made him stay, he'd said, but her personality. My father had said that before he'd met Violet, he'd been a noble like the others, enjoying the pleasures of Gomindor without a thought to those who labored in the depths of the city. It was Violet who'd made him think about his actions. Violet who'd made him want to be a better person. He always said that he wouldn't have been able to change if he hadn't already possessed the capacity for kindness, but it was Violet who'd unlocked those doors of compassion and empathy in his heart.

I wanted a love like that.

We turned a corner and walked down another corridor. "Here's what I don't understand," Spud said, interrupting my thoughts. "All of you are prisoners, right? You're all here at the whim of this Empire. And yet, the second you get down here, you all try to kill each other. Wouldn't it make more sense to team up?"

Poor, naïve Spud. "You'd think so, wouldn't you? But that's not how it goes. My old coach had a saying: you don't learn about a person until the going gets tough. At the beginning of every season, when we got our new players, he'd arrange for difficult situations or hardships to occur, just to see how people reacted. If someone was selfish, it came out under stress, and then he'd bench them until he could trade them off the team. A good egg can learn how to play light-ball, he said. But a rotten egg is always a rotten egg. And rotten eggs stink."

"I didn't think Cara smelled *that* bad, but if it's a metaphor, I see the point."

"It's a metaphor."

"Ah. I think I would've liked that guy. Your coach, I mean."

We passed several more doors before coming to an open chamber. Pillars ran along the center of the room, holding up an arched ceiling with decorative molding. At even intervals along the ceiling were chandeliers that burned with white candles. Candelabras at the base of each pillar also held the burning white candles.

The Castle of 1,000 Doors (Reception Room #3)

What do you do when you have a stupid number of resources and nothing so pressing to do with them? You buy stupid stuff! Cars, boats, watches—really anything to tell your stupid rich neighbors, "Hey, I've got way more money than you." And what happens when you buy those sweet flexes and still have a stupid number of resources? You help those less fortunate than you. Just kidding! At that point, you flex even harder by building rooms into your castle that don't serve any purpose whatsoever. Like this one.

I was about to step into the room, but then froze. Several bodies lay strewn across the room. Most of them were human, but there was at least one reptilian. Instead of skin, it had overlapping ruby scales and a flat, ridged forehead. Its ears lay pressed against the sides of its head.

"What do you think happened here?"

"Maybe they were killed by something the dungeon threw at them? Or maybe they took each other out."

As the room was lit, I didn't need Spud to brighten the way. I turned off his smoldering glow and switched off my left glove, letting him fall into my hand, where I could feel his warmth through the leather.

"Still don't understand it," Spud said as I lifted him to my shoulder. "Teamwork makes the dream work. That's the motto of the Spud Squad. Though to be fair, I'm trying to think of something less cliché. I'm open to suggestions."

With Spud on my shoulder, I stepped into the room, my feet echoing on the stone floor as I approached the body of the reptilian.

Deceased Reptilian

It looks dead. Poke it with a stick!

Loot? Yes or No.

The buttons were grayed out. *Another senseless death. Over what? We could be teaming up, but instead we're killing each other. I suppose it makes for better TV.*

I turned away from the body. I really was getting sick of corpses. With a thought, I opened up my Map and found the room in which we stood. Through a door on the far side of the room was a set of branching corridors. Beyond them was the massive central chamber that formed the bridge between the castle's two wings.

"Crow, behind you!" Spud shouted in my ear.

I whirled around to find myself staring at a ruby-scaled reptilian, her lips pulled back in a snarl. She resembled the one that I'd seen on the ground. But that was impossible—that reptilian had been dead. The dungeon had told me as much. And yet, the body on the ground was missing, and a reptilian stood before me.

Silent Assassin (Geeta)

An intelligent hunter from the Emerald Isles, Geeta belongs to a fiercely independent race of bipedal lizards known as reptilians. Because of their pseudo-gills and overlapping scales, reptilians are capable of surviving a variety of conditions, though they tend to prefer the hot sun, dry sands, and warm beaches of their native lands. Enslaved aboard a pirate ship called the *Rancid Pearl*, Geeta and her companion Silvana were sentenced to Toroth-Gol for thievery when they were captured along with the rest of the crew.

Around Geeta's neck was a metal collar. Below it, a leather sash with decorative rivets ran from one of her shoulders to the other, covering her chest. A skirt made of similar material ran from her waist to her knees.

The reptilian's eyes swirled with the yellow and orange of a nebula. Instead of pupils, she had vertical black slits, like those of a goat. There was a strange look in those eyes, something malevolent.

Geeta jabbed a black knife toward my abdomen.

I got an arm up, batting away Geeta's forearm and making the stab go wide. Thank goodness for my defensive training with my father. I reached for Spud, but Geeta jabbed again, forcing me to abandon Spud in favor of another block.

"I saw you in the ballroom," Geeta said, her eyes blazing. "I saw you over Silvana's dead body. You will pay for what you have done. All of you will pay!"

As the reptilian swung a third time, I caught her around the wrist and yanked. I'd only been trying to throw her off balance, but her arm tore from its socket. Geeta stumbled back, leaving her appendage in my hand. I stared at the arm in surprise. For a moment, I thought it was a reflection of my strength, but then the creature laughed.

"Not used to fighting reptilians, are you," she hissed, a forked black tongue poking from between scaled lips. "This is not over. No matter where you go, I will find you. You have made an enemy, King Crow. You are mine."

Then she turned and ran. *By the Dregs, she's quick.*

"Wait!" I yelled. But she didn't stop. She headed through an archway to my right, disappearing around a corner. "You've got the wrong guy! I didn't do anything!"

Something smacked me in the side of the head. It was Spud. "What the heck, Crow?" he said. "Why didn't you use me? You're gonna give us a bad reputation. People are gonna think we're soft."

I shook my head, rubbing the spot that Spud had bumped. "She thought we killed her friend. The one from the ballroom. She thought we were responsible, but it was Cara Thorne and those pirates."

"Well, now we have a sworn enemy," Spud said. "That's kind of cool, I guess. At least you got that sick dagger. And her arm."

I remembered what was in my hand. "Gah!" I said, letting the arm drop. When it hit the ground, the fingers opened, sending a dagger clattering across the floor. I walked over to it, keeping an eye on the arm. I had a strange premonition that it might come to life. "Spud, watch the arch. Yell if you see that reptilian again."

I bent down and lifted the dagger. It was about a foot long, the blade and handle crafted from a single piece of dark brown metal. The cross guard, made from the same dark metal, was forged into two serrated fangs that pointed in the same direction as the blade.

Stiletto of Silence

In Toroth-Gol, no one can hear you scream. Same goes for your enemies, and that's especially true if you stab them with the Stiletto of Silence. Crafted in the vacuum of the Endless Void, this is a dependable weapon with a unique skill: once pierced with the blade, a victim will be unable to speak, yell, or otherwise make verbal noise for sixty seconds.

"I guess I can see this coming in handy?" I said, turning the blade over. "I'm not really one for the cloak-and-dagger kind of fighting."

"Big man needs big explosions. Big potato same way. Club, fire, blood, boom!"

"Are you making fun of me?"

"Yes. That's a gift from the dungeon. I doubt we'll come across those often, so be thankful."

I nodded, putting the dagger into my Inventory. With a last glance at the arch, I headed toward the doorway on the far side of the room.

Sworn enemy or not, I had a date with the Dark City.

14

Spud and I walked down a corridor after leaving Reception Room #3. It was like a lot of the other areas in the castle in that it was long and straight, with dusty stone floors and doors on either side that led to far-flung locales: Ancient Coast, Uncharted Caldera, and Mushroom Kingdom. This was one of the human-sized corridors, which differed from the giant-sized corridors in that the ceilings were ten feet overhead and not, say, a hundred and twenty.

"I'm just thinking out loud here, but do you think Geeta is naturally fast?" Spud asked. "Or do you think she got a speed boost from her Silent Assassin class? Because she wasn't only fast, but like, *way* faster than you. I'm talking, 'Watch out! I'm in the Bank District and I need to be in the Tower Section, but the funiculars are down, the monorail is broken, and the ferry isn't coming for another twenty minutes so I should run' fast."

"What?"

"My point is, you're a strength and endurance guy. She was all about speed and dexterity. She carried a stiletto, which is basically every assassin's weapon of choice, and she clearly had a special skill that allowed her to blend in with dead bodies. Remember? She was dead. We saw her. And then, just like that, she was alive and trying to gut you like a fish." He bounced excitedly on my shoulder. "Man, you picked a heck of a person to have as a sworn enemy. Natural armor, the ability to breathe underwater, and can regrow her limbs. Imagine getting your arm chopped off and being like, 'That's not a problem.' Or getting caught in a situation without a weapon. You could, like, pull off your arm and beat people with it. What's *your* advantage?"

"I'm exceedingly clever. And good-looking."

"A lot of things are more clever. And better looking."

"Yeah, well, a lot of things probably breathe underwater better than the reptilian. If you like the reptilian so much, why don't you go travel with her?"

Spud turned and stared mournfully down the corridor. "I can't," he said. "You chased her away."

We followed a sign for the Dark City around a corner. At the far end of the hall was an archway illuminated by the light that came from the room beyond. There was something else as well: a clanking, clicking, grinding noise, kind of like someone was dragging a lightball bat across a concrete floor.

"Do you hear that?" I asked. Every muscle in my body felt tense. I couldn't explain why I was so on edge, but a childhood in the Dregs had taught me to trust my instincts.

"I used to fool around with a sapient deep fryer who made noises like that," Spud said. "Man, that's really bringing me back. Those were wild nights."

I approached. Even though it wasn't particularly hot, a bead of sweat dripped down my cheek. I wiped it away, then brought Spud into my hand.

"I was having fun on your shoulder," he said as I activated my glove and set him to hover above my palm. "Can't I stay there?"

I shook my head. "I'm not sure what's in there, but I don't think we'll like it," I whispered. "I want to be ready for anything."

Spud sighed. "Fair enough," he said. "If I die, scatter my skin from the roof of the castle."

With Spud hovering over my palm, I crossed into the room and immediately saw the source of the grinding: the room was filled with gears. Hundreds of them. Maybe even thousands. They covered all four walls, the ceiling, and even the floors. There were fast-spinning little gears the size of Spud, along with massive, slow-moving ones as large as the fireplace in Sammy's Kitchen. They turned in unison, some faster, some slower, but all of them moving and making noise as they moved.

On one wall, light shone through frosted glass that sat behind the gears. A series of catwalks that ran from wall to wall allowed one to cross the room without stepping on the gears that lined the floor. Ladders to my left and right led to another three levels of catwalks, which stretched to the ceiling. In the center of the room, a suspended platform held a small mountain of inert gears, which I guessed were spares for when the others broke down.

"The sound of metal on metal," Spud said dreamily. I had a feeling he was thinking about his lost paramour. "I knew I recognized that sound. Layla, how I miss you!"

Then the bodies came into view. At first, I didn't recognize them, as they'd been brutally savaged. As my eyes crossed over the first, I got the now-familiar message: *It looks dead. Poke it with a stick!* It came up half a dozen times, sometimes when I didn't even think I was looking at a body part.

There were more dead here than I'd seen anywhere else so far, and the remains dotted the catwalks. One body hung from the catwalk above us, rigor mortis keeping its cold hand locked around the railing. Another body was little more than gobbets of flesh sitting atop two massive gears on the floor. I shuddered to imagine the slow, painful grinding of bones that must've occurred.

The Castle of 1,000 Doors (Engine Room)

The gears in this room power the teleportation features of the castle. At one time, it was serviced by over three hundred human technicians who kept the gears lubricated and running. Today, the room runs on its own volition, which means it could break down

at any moment. If that happens, you'd be trapped here with the Clockwork Guardian.

"Clockwork Guardian?" I said.

Those were the wrong words. A second later, there was a noise that didn't sound like the turning of gears as much as it sounded like a large, malevolent creature moaning and grunting. Sure enough, the mountain of spare gears in the center of the room shifted, sending gears tumbling off the sides of the platform. There was a horrific screeching as they interrupted the motion of whatever gears lay below.

The noise was nothing compared to the roar of the creature that emerged from beneath the mountain.

At first I couldn't get a sense of it, as it wasn't like anything I'd seen before. There was pink flesh and wispy white hair. Then the creature got to one knee and I recognized two arms. A leg. The mountain of gears shifted again and a second leg emerged from the pile.

"Sh—should you shoot that?" Spud asked, his voice cracking. "Wait a minute. I'm your ammunition. On second thought, *definitely* don't shoot."

The creature stood. It was humanoid, but far larger than even the biggest human—perhaps thirty feet tall, the top of its head reaching a third of the way to the ceiling. Its face was hideous and seemed to be made mostly from forehead, with a single large eye in the center of its face. Beneath the eye, I recognized a smashed nose that hung over a mouthful of jagged teeth. The creature wore a pair of canvas shorts. In one hand, it carried a chunk of wood that I assumed was some type of club. Incongruously, it had a huge brass hoop through one nipple.

"Ack," I whispered as the creature roared, spittle flying from behind its cracked teeth. Even from where I stood, I could smell its putrid breath.

Clockwork Guardian (Cravag)

What do you do with the cruel, lumpy son who can't do anything

right? You certainly don't put him at the front desk, where he'll scare customers by drowning butterflies in formaldehyde and pulling the legs off spiders. No, you place him behind the scenes and make him the master of his own small domain. That's exactly what happened here.

The second son of Giant King Elrond and Contessa Georgia, Cravag shamed the royal family when he was caught using a magnifying glass to light the kitchen staff on fire (RIP, Chef Sammy). His parents placed him in the Royal Forests and gave him the title of Forest Keeper.

Elrond and Contessa Georgia died of the Insanity, so Cravag placed himself here, in the Engine Room, where he gave himself the title of Clockwork Guardian and stepped into the very important task of disciplining the human technicians who kept the gears running. He did his job a little too well.

"Cravag?" I said. "That thing has a name?"

Spud wasn't as incredulous about Toroth-Gol's quirky imagination. "Run, Crow!" he said. "Cravag is huge. That thing even looks at us wrong, and we're dead. Caput! That's it for Spud and Crow. We're mashed potatoes!"

Cravag did more than look at us. With another roar, the giant reached toward us with his free hand, one massive palm swiping down with the force of a freight train. Cravag was trying to squash us.

Leaders don't often talk about this, but we get scared, too. Everyone gets scared. I've rubbed shoulders with the most famous athletes in the world, big and small, men and women, and I know that every single one of them still gets butterflies before important games. Heck, I was one of the most decorated athletes in the world, and I still got butterflies, even ten years into my career.

As our coach had told us time and time again, what separated top performers from laggards was the ability to manage fear. While laggards let fear cloud their judgment, top performers compartmentalized. Usually, I was better at compartmentalizing than anyone.

But in that moment, fear got the best of me. I panicked.

By the Dregs! That thing is huge and it wants to kill me. Get away, get away, get away!

If I'd been thinking clearly, I would've run back the way we'd come. Safe in the human-sized corridors, we could've found a way into the second wing that didn't involve entanglement with a deranged giant. But I wasn't thinking clearly, so I took off down the catwalk, my feet ringing against the black metal.

"No, Crow!" Spud shouted. "The other way! You're headed in the wrong direction!"

Behind me, Cravag roared. Perhaps it was this bellow that made me remember my training, or maybe it was Spud's yelling, but either way, my athlete's instincts kicked in.

Better late than never. I'm not going down without a fight. You can beat this monster. He's just a giant swinging a massive hand at you. Just a giant hand coming at you. Pretend it's an enforcer's bat. Pretend you're playing a game of lightball!

The giant's palm slapped the catwalk behind me.

15

As the entire catwalk shook, I almost slipped, but managed to keep my feet.

"*Agh!*" Spud screamed as he blazed with flame. "Oh, baby! Into the tunnels. Go!"

After his failed smash, Cravag pulled back his hand. He looked like he was about to try again. However, maybe he wasn't as dumb as he appeared, because he stopped with his head cocked.

Maybe he realizes we're sapient. Perhaps he understands that we're living, breathing creatures just like him. He knows we deserve to live!

When the giant's fleshy lips spread into a cruel smile, I knew that wasn't the case. Even as I ran back toward the doorway through which we'd entered, Cravag lifted his other hand, dropping his giant club in front of it. The huge piece of wood hit the catwalk with the same force as his palm strike, shaking the metal and sending shockwaves reverberating around the room. From somewhere below came the shrieking sound of metal tearing away from metal. The catwalk dropped another few inches before catching, which sent me stumbling. The shift caused a torso that had been hanging off the edge of the catwalk to fall in between two gears, where it was ground to bloody leather without so much as a sound.

"*Arrrghhhhh!* That's not gonna work," Spud said as I regained my balance. "Head for the far archway. Your—oh, baby—two o'clock."

I glanced at the entrance, which had been completely blocked by the club. Then I looked at the far archway. In theory, running for the archway was a good idea, as it was the only other way I could get out of the room. Additionally, if the tunnels on the other side of the archway were as small and cramped as the wing we'd just left, we could escape from Cravag and he wouldn't be able to follow.

However, no sooner had Spud shouted than the giant pivoted, seemingly noticing the far archway for the first time.

"Stop calling out our plans, Spud!" I said. But it was too late. Grunting, Cravag leaned over and tore a huge gear from the clockwork on the far wall. He raised it above his head and slammed it into the catwalk, sending yet another shock through the metal.

Please, catwalk, don't collapse, I thought, but since when did I have any luck? The force of Cravag's slam drove the far catwalk into the gears below, which chewed through the metal with a sound like a chorus of metal angels. Even if I'd still been thinking about trying to find a way through the far archway, Cravag made it a moot point by lifting the massive gear and embedding it into the wall in front of the exit.

He blocked the only two exits. To Cravag, this was now a game of cat-and-mouse. He was toying with us.

Classic deranged giant behavior.

As the far catwalk was chewed to iron chips between the gears, the segment of catwalk on which we stood fell another several inches. In another few moments, I knew the metal beneath our feet would join its cross-room counterpart in the gears below, delivering us to a slow, painful demise. I expected Spud to make a joke or some sort of pun, but for once, he remained silent. I glanced down at him and he stared back at me, expectant. With a shock, I realized he was waiting for my orders.

"If we stay here, we're gear meat or giant food," I whispered, taking care not to project my voice. "But Cravag has blocked both entrances. There's only one way out of this, and that's up."

"You—*aghhhhh*—climb those ladders and we're both dead," Spud said. "That oversized baby will swat you down in a second."

"I don't see another choice," I said. "And I think I can make it. But only if you distract him."

"Distract? *Argggghhh!* What do you mean? Crow, I'm *very* against this plan."

Spud's flames made him scream. Was that something I could use?

An idea came to me. "Calm down," I said to him. "The giant understands us, but I don't think he's smart. On the count of three, I want you to tell me to head through that other entrance behind Cravag. Scream it as loudly as you can. I know you're good at screaming. Make sure Cravag can hear."

"*Argggghhh!* But there isn't a—oh. It's a distraction. Nice, Crow. For a second, I thought you were going to shoot me at him or something. I —oh baby—thought that would be the distraction. But this is a—*ugh*— much better plan."

"I'll go for the ladder." I tensed the muscles in my legs as preparation for what came next. "Turn off your heat and I'll put you on my shoulder. I'll need both hands to climb. Ready? One. Two. Three!"

I called out the last number and Spud's flames winked out. Then he yelled, "Crow, head for that other entrance! The one behind the stinking giant!" Cravag, who'd been leering at us with a triumphant look, narrowed his eyes and glanced over his shoulder. That was my cue. I dropped Spud's warm body into my palm, set him on my shoulder, and jumped for the ladder. The metal rungs were surprisingly cold against my gloves.

"Climb like the wind," Spud said, and I shot up the ladder. I didn't know if it was my strength or adrenaline that propelled me, but something made the journey easier than it had any right to be. I'd made it halfway up before Cravag realized what had happened.

"Oh no," Spud said as the giant roared. "He's onto us. Crow, you've got to do something. He's about to smack us down!"

My back was to the giant, but I hooked my legs over one of the rungs and let myself fall backward. Blood rushed into my head. Now that I was upside down, I could see Cravag reaching toward us.

"Keep him distracted," I said.

"Crow? What? You're going to shoot me, aren't you? Crow, this is a bad idea! You're going to murder me!"

"You'll be fine." I took aim. It was difficult, but I'd had a decent bit of practice. Years and years of practice. Not only with my team, but with my father. Valentine had been insistent that I know how to shoot under any conditions, which had meant a variety of strange, grueling, and often humiliating exercises. At the time, I hadn't understood their value, one of which saw me trying to hit targets during the hottest day of summer while hanging from ropes by my ankles and having his staff pepper me with rotten produce. Now, though, I was grateful for the experience.

"Do you know what happens when I die?" Spud said. "Do you know where I go before I come back? It's Hell, Crow! Potato Hell! Not lowercase h. Uppercase H! It's awful. I'm surrounded by evil potatoes who scream at me in some unintelligible language and poke at me with pitchforks. They—*ahhhhhhh!*"

I activated Spud's flames and launched him at Cravag. One day years ago, before lightball practice, our coach had pulled out a speed gun and measured a few of our shots. Most people on the team could shoot a lightball at eighty, maybe ninety miles per hour. I regularly hit a hundred and twenty miles per hour. On that day in the Engine Room, I would've put the shot at pretty darn close to a hundred and fifty miles per hour.

A screaming Spud hit Cravag in his outstretched palm. While shooting Cravag with a regular, electromagnetically charged potato might've been like throwing pebbles at a bear, I could tell Cravag felt the searing heat of Spud's flames. The giant recoiled as if stung and stepped backward, a motion that carried him off the side of the platform.

After that, two things happened. First, Cravag smashed his hands together, catching Spud between them. It happened before I could yank him back. I was hopeful that Spud was small enough to avoid getting crushed, but no: the potato's screams were cut short the second the massive palms came together. When the giant opened his hands, Spud's flattened, flaming skin tumbled to the central platform.

"Spud!" My heart sank. *What did you do? Poor, innocent Spud.* The plan had been my idea and now my friend had been smashed. I'd get him back, but that didn't take away from the fact that I'd knowingly sent him into danger. A part of me attempted to rationalize the decision: *it was the only way to distract Cravag.* But another part of myself— a louder part—wouldn't accept that. *He trusted you, and you got him killed. You can't brush that away so easily.*

There'd be a reckoning and I'd deserve every second of it. But for now, I needed to focus on survival. Spud might've been crushed, but his death had served a purpose. When he'd smacked into Cravag's palm, the giant had stumbled backward. He'd stepped off the platform and his back foot had settled between two gears. I thought they might drag Cravag into their depths, but that would've been too easy. Luckily for me, though, they trapped him. The gears screeched, trying to turn, but Cravag's ankle was too strong. Instead of breaking the bone, the teeth just caught the giant's ankle and held him fast.

I didn't wait to see what would happen. Instead, I pulled myself upright and climbed the rest of the way up the ladder. I reached the top just in time to duck under a spinning gear that flew over my head and smashed into the wall behind me.

You'll keep Spud alive for the rest of your time together, I vowed to myself as I stood upright. At the same time, I knew that to fulfill my promise, I had to beat Cravag. But how to kill a thirty-foot-tall giant? Fortunately, Cravag was no longer mobile. He tried to lift his leg, but the gears held him tight. As if in response, he roared in pain and reached for another gear to throw my way.

Stay calm. Analyze the scene. Work with what you've got. What can you do here?

Everything that happened next occurred in slow motion. I'd like to say that I'd had some sort of grand plan from the beginning, perhaps some brilliant vision that I executed with crisp, tactical precision like I was back on the field. In truth, I was simply reacting to my environment—except now, I was doing it with a clear head.

There was only one move left. Ducking a second gear that Cravag hurled at my head, I ran along the catwalk until I was positioned above him. Leaning over the edge of the railing, I called the barrel of Sammy's Spider Killing Solvent from my Inventory. The four-hundred-pound barrel appeared in my arms, smashed against my chest and supported by the catwalk's railing, and the catwalk moaned under its weight. I almost dropped it.

Don't you dare. Grunting with effort, I set my legs and pushed with all my might. The wood of the barrel scraped against my forearms and I thought I might fail, but then gravity caught the barrel and it fell over the side of the catwalk.

Straight toward Cravag.

I peered over the railing, a smile on my lips as I prepared to revel in the sight of Cravag's crushed noggin. Of course, that's not what I saw. Instead, the giant had snatched the barrel out of the air like it was little more than a slow-moving fly.

What other weapons do I have? That had really been my best option.

I thanked every god I could name as Cravag popped the barrel into his mouth.

Spud might've been gone, but the little pile that had once been Spud still burned on the central platform. *Please let Spud's electromagnetism still work.* If it didn't, I was toast. But someone must've been watching over me that day, because when I activated my glove, the blazing husk shot toward me.

"Yes!" I yelled. When the flaming skin was in front of me, I used my other glove to shoot it toward Cravag. Spud couldn't scream, but I screamed for both of us.

"You won't beat me, Toroth-Gol. I'm getting out of here alive!"

My shot was perfect. Like, the kind of shot that would've earned me a spot on *SportNetwork Top Ten*. I would've gotten the game ball and a shoutout from my coach. Not only had I put the flames through Cravag's lips, but I'd also threaded the forest of jagged teeth. His single eye widened as the burning potato skin went straight down his throat.

"That's for Spud!" I shouted. If the potato had been there, he might've shouted a pun. "Beware, Cravag, for I yam Death!" or "You've been roasted." But he wasn't, so it was just me, screaming impotently at the massive, half-trapped giant.

"I hate you, Cravag! You're ugly and I hate you! That's for Spud!"

The giant blinked. I stared at him, expecting him to explode at any second. But he didn't. A second ticked by. Then another.

"Uh, you're supposed to burn now," I said. After another few seconds, when nothing happened, Cravag smiled. "No!" I said, backing away from the railing as he reached toward me.

When his hand was about halfway to me, Cravag stopped and screamed. The noise was so loud that the frosted glass in the windows shattered. The catwalk reverberated like it'd been struck with a mallet. I fell to my knees and clapped my hands over my ears.

"Yeaaggghhhh!"

The scream was so loud that it made my eyes water.

Stop. Please stop!

But the noise didn't stop. If anything, it only got louder. The sound hit me as a physical force that made it difficult to breathe.

There was the screech of metal as one of the catwalk's supports broke. Whether it was from the scream or something else, I couldn't tell.

Grab onto something. If the catwalk broke and I wasn't holding on, I'd be spilled into the gears. *The railing. Grab the railing!* But no matter how hard I tried, I couldn't will myself to take my hands from my ears.

When I was sure the railing would break, the screaming stopped. I took my hands away from my ears. Crawling forward, I peered over the edge of the catwalk. Below me, Cravag clutched at his neck, tearing away handfuls of skin from his own throat. From between his lips, and then from the holes in his neck, emerged swirling green flames. His mouth was open like he wanted to scream, but the flames had burned away his vocal cords. I didn't feel sorry for him. A second later, he toppled to one side and crashed bonelessly into the sea of gears. Without his strength to resist them, the gears started to pull his corpse into their depths.

"Good riddance," I said to the empty room. I'd burned the giant alive from the inside out.

16

Over the next few minutes, the gears did their grisly work, grinding Cravag's twitching body to pulp. After the screeching of twisted metal and the dying giant's roars of pain, the comparatively quiet turning of the gears put me into an oddly meditative state. Within seconds, the only sign that a murderous giant had ever inhabited the platform was the blood-slick gears and the puddles of green fire burning atop the metal.

When I was sure I wasn't in any imminent danger, I pulled a jar of pickle juice from my Inventory and took a long sip, gazing out over a field of turning gears and twisted metal. The tangy liquid made my eyes water. *Or maybe that's the stench of dead giant.* Before I recapped the jar, I poured a few drops of pickle juice over the edge of the catwalk.

"RIP, Spud," I said. "This is your victory. See you soon, my friend."

Per the description of my Food Fighter class, I had to believe that the potato would reappear in my pouch. As for where he went in the interim, I didn't know if he'd been telling the truth or not.

Is there actually a potato-themed version of hell? If there is, I hope it's not too painful. Either way, I'd need to make amends when he returned.

But I could worry about that later. As I returned the pickle jar to my Inventory, I realized I had another problem: my weapon set had only come with a single projectile. With Spud gone, I didn't have anything left to shoot.

My gloves were shiny from wear and sweat. On the lightball field, that layer of grime was a point of pride. When a new crop of players arrived each year, you could always tell the flakes from the competitors by the amount of scum on their gloves. The more well-worn the gloves, the better the player.

Right now, however, they weren't useful to me. I pulled open the straps, unzipped the sides, and pulled them off. It felt good to stretch my fingers. Then I hung the gloves from a loop in my belt and considered my next move.

I could head back into the cellar and grab another barrel of Sammy's Spider-Killing Solvent. That had been the difference between life and death against Cravag. On the other hand, Spud's death left me without my best weapon, which was a good argument for pushing forward.

I was stepping toward the door when text flashed in my vision.

You killed Clockwork Guardian (Cravag)

Congratulations, murderer. You just killed the last giant in existence. Hope you didn't need those idiots for anything. That's right —I said idiots. I didn't like them either, okay? They smelled like dead raccoon and I couldn't stand it when they used each other's hair to floss the gristle from their teeth. Is that what you wanted to hear? That they weren't my favorite? Loot the thing and get out of here.

Loot? Yes or No.

Sheesh. It sounded like whoever was writing those descriptions needed a day in the Pleasure Gardens. But at least it reminded me that I needed to loot Cravag's body. Mentally, I selected "Yes," bringing a new block of text into my vision.

Loot acquired. From Clockwork Guardian (Cravag), you've gained special weapon type "Clockwork Guardian's Club." Good luck lifting it! Item sent to Inventory.

I entered my Inventory and there it was: a miniature image of Cravag's club. However, the box in which it sat was grayed out, and I couldn't click into it.

Hmm. I wonder what that's about.

I was disappointed I couldn't wield the club, but the next message made me feel better.

Loot acquired. From Clockwork Guardian (Cravag), you've gained special material type "Clockwork Core." Combine with additional special materials and a schematic to create a special item. Special materials missing. Schematic missing. Item sent to Inventory.

What's a special item? It seems that if I gather enough materials and have the right schematics, I can make more powerful gear. But how?

I'd never been a particularly strong engineer, but if combining materials was as easy as hitting a button, I'd be in good shape.

My questions were answered by the block of text that appeared in my vision, which was also loot-related.

Loot acquired. From Clockwork Guardian (Cravag), you've gained schematic "Clockwork Automaton Companion." Combine with special materials to create a clockwork automaton companion. Special materials missing. Item sent to Inventory.

I opened my Inventory and studied the schematic. The left side of my screen showed a diminutive humanoid made from metal. Armored plating covered its jointed arms and legs, and a series of overlapping segments made up its bulbous head. To be honest, it looked kind of like a cross between Spud and a lightball. With arms and legs. I didn't get a description of the creature, but the right side of the screen showed me the additional materials required to make it. In addition to the Clockwork Core, I needed six pieces of sheet metal, two sheets of glass, a hundred feet of copper wire, and something called an Automaton Housing. I also needed to find something called an Engineer's Bench.

Beneath the list of required items, a grayed-out button said, "Create?" I assumed that once I gathered the right materials and found the bench, the button would become clickable.

You've unlocked a Unique Achievement: Last of the Giants.

The bigger they are, the harder they fall. Today, the universe waved goodbye to a race of horrifically inbred monstrosities called giants. It's because of you. You killed the last giant. Good thing his mother isn't around to blame you, because she wasn't very nice, either.

Reward: Giant's Roar. This special skill augments your strength by 1,000 percent for thirty seconds. However, after those thirty seconds, you'll be weak as a baby for five hours. You'll also be *super* nauseous and your bones will ache something fierce.

I didn't know the full range of special skills that were available, but as far as this one went, it seemed fine. The strength boost was huge, though I definitely didn't like the thought of being weak as a baby in Toroth-Gol.

And for five *hours. I'd have to be in pretty dire straits to think about using that.*

My thoughts were interrupted by a new message that flashed across my vision.

Warning: Due to a system malfunction in the Castle of 1,000 Doors (Engine Room), many of the doors have been disabled. Error. Malfunction. 128 of 1,000 doors disabled. Error. Malfunction. 129 of 1,000 doors disabled. Error. Malfunction. 130 of 1,000 doors disabled.

"By the Dregs! That's not good." I needed to get to the next room.

Of course, that room was now blocked by a massive gear.

I slid down the ladder and ran to the blocked archway. The gear that Cravag had slammed into the wall had been one of the biggest in the room. It was made from solid metal and there was no way around it. Perhaps Spud could've slipped through the tiny space between one of the teeth and the bottom corner of the door where the metal didn't quite cover the opening, but that was it.

Still, I could wedge my hand through the opening, so I pushed my arm through the hole and wrapped my fingers along the back side of the gear. It was embedded about a foot into the stone. Bracing myself, I pulled. Nothing. I pulled again, this time giving it my all, yet the gear still didn't budge.

Is it worth backtracking through the castle, finding a way onto a different floor, and then trying to chart a path to the other wing? I checked my Map, trying to find an alternative route.

My thoughts were interrupted by new text that flashed across my vision.

Warning: Due to a system malfunction in the Castle of 1,000 Doors (Engine Room), many of the doors have been disabled. Error. Malfunction. 147 of 1,000 doors disabled. Error. Malfunction. 148 of 1,000 doors disabled.

No time to backtrack. I closed the Map. *But I can't move the gear. What are my options?*

In a crisis situation, the body's fight-or-flight instincts engage and a part of the brain called the amygdala shuts down the prefrontal cortex. The prefrontal cortex is what's responsible for critical think-ing. If you've ever seen someone freeze in a difficult situation, or make a crazy decision, that's why.

However, I'd trained to stay calm under pressure. Consciously, I made an effort to slow my breathing. A few seconds later, a dispas-sionate filter crept over my thoughts. This was the rare state of being that I entered when the game was on the line, or when an enforcer charged toward the back of an unsuspecting teammate. As rational thought returned, I knew what needed to happen.

Activate Giant's Roar. Strength flooded my body. Heck, with Giant's Roar activated, I probably could've punched a hole straight through Cravag. But Cravag was dead, and I was on the clock. The numbers in my vision made that abundantly clear: as soon as I'd activated the special skill, a timer had appeared in the air, counting backward from thirty.

I pulled up my Inventory and found the Clockwork Guardian's Club. As I'd expected, the grayed-out "Equip?" button was now blue. When I mentally clicked it, the club appeared in my hand. Although it was still massive, it'd been scaled down for someone my size, perhaps five feet long from end to end. The handle fit comfortably in my hand, but the club tapered out, widening until the tip was as large around as my thigh. It hummed with power. With the buzzing weapon in my hand, I felt like I could conquer armies.

Gripping the club in both hands, I lifted it over my right shoulder and swung it toward the gear with all my might. Wood struck metal with a clanging sound like the world's largest bell. I swung again. And again. Each strike shook more dust from the places where the gear met the wall. After seven or eight swings, I noticed a crack in the metal. That was enough to spur me on. I struck again and again, each strike enlarging the crack, until finally the gear shattered.

"Yes!" I said. I put the club back into my Inventory and ran through the archway. After the giant-sized room, it felt strange to once again stand in a human-sized corridor.

How had Cravag even gotten into the Engine Room? Wouldn't he have been too big to fit through the corridors? But the thoughts were a distraction. Belatedly, I noticed that I only had seven seconds left on my timer. Seven seconds until I was weak as a baby for *five hours.*

Adrenaline flooded my veins and I pelted down the corridor as fast as my legs could carry me. Five seconds. Four. I entered a square room, empty save for a door on the far side.

Dark City.

That's it! Since I'd been following the signs through the dungeon, I wasn't surprised I'd found the right door. As the final seconds of my Giant's Roar ability ticked away, I lurched forward. *I'm going to make it!*

Five feet in front of the door, the timer ran out and I collapsed.

I felt like a mule had kicked me in every major part of my body at the same time. My bones ached, and nausea swelled in my gut.

Get up, Crow. A message appeared: 280 of the 1,000 doors were now inactive. *You've faced worse. You're five feet away from your goal and if you don't keep moving, the doors will stop working and you'll be trapped here during the Purge.*

I tried to crawl forward, but my body didn't respond. I couldn't move.

You're giving up? I didn't have a choice.

I was tired. So, so tired.

"Sorry, Spud," I mumbled. "Sorry, Father."

Warm hands gripped my jumpsuit under the armpits. *Is someone pulling me? Or is that my imagination?*

Everything went dark.

17

"**G**ah!"

I sat up. I was still breathing. In the moments before I'd collapsed in front of the door, I'd made peace with my demise. I'd welcomed it. The sudden weakness I'd felt after using Giant's Roar had made death an attractive option—as it was now. My body ached. I felt like I'd been beaten by a dozen enforcers, resurrected, and then crushed by falling boulders. My mouth tasted like someone had pulled out my tongue and replaced it with a cockroach.

Groaning, I hunched over my knees and waited for the world to stop spinning. Even with my eyes closed, I could see that the timer in the upper right-hand corner of my vision had reset. Now, it showed two weeks.

Two weeks until I get eaten by a horde of cicadas. At least it won't be a wall of living flame.

I took a deep breath, trying to work oxygen into my aching lungs. The air was damp and cool, though it smelled of charred wood. A crackling came from beside me, and I opened my eyes. I sat next to a fire. It was small and orderly, surrounded by stones, the logs built into a pyramid.

"Welcome back." I turned my battered neck to see a reptilian sitting on a log. She had ruby scales and the yellow in her eyes swirled around a vertical pupil like hot gas. Both her voice and the look she gave me were completely devoid of emotion. She bore a striking resemblance to Geeta.

Oh no. That's definitely Geeta.

At the sight of my sworn enemy, I scrambled away. My body screamed in protest, but the instinct to survive outweighed comfortable immobility. I reached into my pouch for Spud, only remembering what had happened a few hours ago when my fingers found empty air. Besides, even *if* he'd been there, I wasn't wearing my gloves. They lay on the ground beside the fire.

Geeta hadn't moved. She sat on the log, staring at me with those strange yellow eyes. "I dragged you through the door while the castle was collapsing. To be honest, I thought about leaving you behind. But I heard what you said to the *drughyr* after I fled. You are not responsible for Silvana's death. I know this, now." When I didn't respond, Geeta said, "If I had wanted to kill you, I could have done it many times by now."

I'd imagine I looked pretty dumb as I sat there, blinking and staring at her. It's not often that you fight a giant lizard, pull off her arm, steal her blade, and then have her save you from certain death.

Then again, it's a pretty good week for firsts.

"Take this."

From the ground beside her, Geeta lifted a leather waterskin, shaking it so I could hear the contents sloshing around inside.

Endless Waterskin

After three to four minutes without oxygen, the average human body undergoes permanent, irreversible brain damage. After four to six minutes, a person dies. It would take around three days to die without water, and a month or two without food. So get your priorities straight: oxygen, water, food. Don't go playing in any

vacuums, and keep yourself hydrated. The Endless Waterskin is here to help. Though it looks like it can only hold a few mouthfuls, this enchanted waterskin never runs dry.

Geeta threw me the skin and I caught it, though my aching arms screamed with the sudden movement.

That's the last time I'm using Giant's Roar, I thought as I pulled at the plastic nozzle and slurped at the contents. The water inside slid down my throat and every molecule of my body sang with joy.

"Slowly." As soon as the words left her mouth, I gagged, my water-starved body trying to reject the nourishment. I managed to keep the liquid down. "What happened to you?" Geeta continued. "You went limp right before you reached the door."

I took a few more small sips until I was sure my stomach could handle the intake. "Thank you," I said. At least, that's what I tried to say. With my cracked lips and mouth full of water, it sounded more like, "ankoo."

Geeta reached to a holster held to her thigh with leather straps and lifted the Stiletto of Silence, its brown-black blade glinting in the fire-light. I tensed, but a moment later she reached down again, and this time lifted a whetstone. She drew the blade across the stone, which made a soothing sound. *Snick*. She must've taken back the blade while I was out.

"There was a gear blocking the hallway I needed to take," I said after I'd swallowed another few mouthfuls from the waterskin. Since she'd saved me, I felt like I owed her an answer to her question. "I have a special skill that let me smash it. It leaves me pretty weak for a few hours after I use it."

Geeta went back over the stone with the blade. *Snick*. When she didn't say anything else, I looked around. Above me hung two moons, one red and one blue. In the far distance, bridges connected the land we were on to a plateau—at the far end of the plateau was what looked like a castle, where every window was glowing with blue light.

The Castle of 1,000 Doors (Dark City)

Of the 1,000 doors, you chose the door to the Dark City. It wasn't the easiest door to reach, but hopefully you'll find its treasures rewarding.

Originally constructed as a safe haven for dwarves escaping the Insanity, the place has certainly seen better days. What threatens the dwarves in the Dark City? That's one of many secrets you'll have to uncover.

As I finished reading, Geeta said, "Where is your friend? The *drughyr?*"

I assumed she was talking about Spud, but I wasn't sure. "You keep using that word. *Drughyr.* What does it mean?"

"That is the word my people use to describe a spirit. It is correct, yes? You are some type of enchanter? You used great magic to trap a spirit in that vegetable?"

At that, I could only laugh. I regretted it as pain shot through my ribs. For one, I couldn't imagine using magic. Even if I could, I wouldn't use it to harness a spirit to a potato.

"I wouldn't call Spud any type of spirit," I said. "He's my weapon, like you have that blade. I got these gloves that let me shoot him at my enemies. Apparently, if he dies he reappears in my pouch after twenty-four hours."

Geeta's brow furrowed. "Your weapon is an immortal talking potato?"

"An immortal, sapient, electromagnetically charged potato. With elemental powers."

I reached toward my belt, exhaling a quiet sigh of relief when my hands touched the pouch. But not Spud. He wouldn't be back for a while. I remembered the events of my fight with Cravag and was shocked to realize that I missed the fast-talking potato. For most of the last day so far, he'd been a constant companion, and there was comfort in the familiar.

Geeta's blade hovered over the whetstone. "It is good to know you have not lost your friend." I could tell she was thinking about her own companion.

"That other reptilian was your friend?"

Geeta went back to sharpening her blade. "Our kind comes from the Emerald Isles." *Snick.* "Most of the time, humans left us alone, because the Isles are dangerous to reach and there is not much down there that humans want. But every once in a while, we got raided by slavers. Silvana was my partner. We were hunting when we were ambushed. We ran, but the slavers were waiting for us. Trapped us in nets and brought us aboard their ship. They brought us north to Atlantis, where they sold us to a pirate named Cara Thorne."

I nodded. I'd heard tales of the strange south, where slavery ran rampant.

And I'd met the dangerous Cara Thorne.

"Reptilians are popular among pirates," Geeta continued. "We are docile. We are also resilient. We do not get seasick, and we do not get diseases like scurvy. We can also breathe underwater. We were with Cara for a month before she got herself captured by the Empire. They did not care if we were enslaved or not. They sentenced us to Toroth-Gol with the rest of the crew. Even once we were down here, Cara treated us like we were still enslaved. I escaped, but they caught Silvana. I was coming back to help her when..." She trailed off. "Then I looked into the room and saw you."

I imagined the situation from Geeta's point of view. She'd been stolen from her homeland, forced into slavery, and sentenced to die with her captors. Then she'd escaped, only to have her lover killed by the very people who'd enslaved them.

"I'm sorry," I said.

We sat in awkward silence for a few seconds before Geeta shook her head. "I will find Marland Thorne," she said without a hint of doubt. "I will also find Skeev and Cara Thorne. Their whole cursed line will die by my blade. Then I will hunt down the Heart of the World and escape this place. I will set the *Rancid Pearl* aflame. I will destroy slavery in the south. I will go back to the Emerald Isles and drink *gorda* on the beach. I swear this, on the ghost of my dead Silvana."

I didn't say anything. *Snick.* Geeta's blade slid across the whetstone. After another few seconds, she remembered that I sat across from her. She glanced over at me.

"How did you choose this door?" she asked. "Dark City? You seemed very intent on getting through when I found you. There were easier doors to choose. But you wanted this one, no?"

I nodded. I still didn't know if I could trust her, but she'd already saved me once. So I told her what Jocko had said to me on the rail car.

"That is it?" she said after I'd finished. "No other reason?"

I shook my head, the motion making my skull throb. "No."

Geeta set her whetstone on the ground and slid the stiletto back into the holster on her thigh. She shrugged. "Bold, to follow advice like that," she said. "But when one choice is as good as any other, you might as well go with what you have got. So we head to the fortress and try to find this Jocko. I am guessing that is the fortress over there."

She pointed across the chasm to the massive building illuminated with blue light. I was about to reply, when I noticed something happening on one of the bridges that connected the land mass we were on to the distant plateau. "Look," I said, pointing toward one of the bridges. "What's that?"

A light appeared on the bridge. Then another. And another. The lights started in the gatehouse on the side of the bridge closest to the city but spread across its entire length. The bridge was also covered in soldiers. Even at this distance, I could see spears poking over their shoulders. There was something else in the air around the soldiers, something that looked like birds.

A second later, Geeta confirmed my suspicions. "Those look like trained birds. Those soldiers are all facing the same way, and they are looking at the dark. They look like they are watching for something."

Her words brought goosebumps to my arms. I felt exposed. I didn't miss the claustrophobic confines of the Castle of 1,000 Doors, but a wall at my back would've been nice. Despite the illusion of open skies, we were still in Toroth-Gol. We were still trapped in a dungeon that was trying to kill us.

Geeta glanced at me, seeming to understand my unspoken worries. "Sleep now. I will watch. When you wake, I will scout. Then your friend will be back, and we can make our move."

We? I thought, though I was too exhausted to think about it.

I fell asleep instantly.

18

When I awoke, my first thought was that Geeta hadn't moved. The reptilian sat exactly where she'd been on the log nearby, her strange yellow eyes reflecting the orange fire. Then I smelled roasting meat. I glanced at the fire and saw the spit built above it, the stick holding the unmistakable form of a skinned rabbit. From the countdown timer in the upper right-hand corner of my vision, I realized that four hours had gone by since I'd fallen back asleep.

"You can eat this once it is done," she said, nodding to the rabbit. I sat up and was surprised to find that I had an appetite. In fact, I felt almost one hundred percent better.

"You don't want any?" I asked.

"I have already eaten," Geeta said. She stood and slipped the Stiletto of Silence into its holster. I didn't even hear so much as a whisper as the blade slid home. "Now that you are awake, I want to get in as much scouting as possible so that we are ready to move when the *drughyr* gets back."

I glanced at the rabbit. *Pop.* The fat hissed and crackled as it dripped into the fire. "Can I help?"

Geeta shook her head. "You should continue to rest. I will assess the situation and let you know what I find. If two hours pass and you have not heard from me, then you can help by coming to find me."

I nodded. While I was still recovering, and while Spud remained in Potato Hell, I was happy to stay out of danger. My hands were good in a pinch, but it was Spud that made me a threat. In this situation, the sensible thing was to play to our advantages. I'd watch the camp while Geeta scouted the terrain between our camp and the bridge.

"Good luck," I said.

On silent feet, Geeta slipped toward the edge of camp. There was a sinuous grace in her movements, a dexterity that I'd often admired in some of my favorite lightball players. In certain positions, like enforcer and center, you wanted someone big, like me. But for attack or even keeper, it paid to have someone with finer motor control. Sometimes, when the batons swung heavy—or the crowds of screaming fans surged thick—I wished for nothing more than the ability to disappear.

Geeta disappeared into the woods. Once she was gone, I stretched.

Amazing what some water and a few hours of sleep can do. I squinted at the distant bridge, where I was still able to make out the shapes of the soldiers by the light that lined the path. From what I could tell, they still faced the dark. Watching. Waiting. I couldn't tell exactly how many soldiers lined the bridge, but I knew it was more than I wanted to fight. Either they were friendly, in which case we could talk our way into the city, or we'd have to find another route.

Geeta hadn't left me her Endless Waterskin, so while I waited for the rabbit to finish cooking, I pulled out a jar of pickle juice and twisted off the cap.

DELAYED MESSAGE

You've unlocked a Unique Achievement: Blessed.

Against all odds, you've managed to kill a *really* powerful enemy, which earned you this unique achievement. Wipe that sweat off your brow and get back out there. It's time to get naughty.

Reward: Ring of Naughtiness. Who said you can't find love while fighting for your life? And if not love, maybe some lust? Equip this ring to make any humanoid within a ten-foot radius feel positively disposed toward you for ten minutes. After each use, the Ring of Naughtiness needs to be recharged for five hours under the naughty light of a full moon before it can be used again.

Huh. That's weird.

I went back into my Inventory and found the ring. The band was a yellow-gold color, and the ring was inlaid with three rubies cut into the shape of hearts. It was fairly gaudy, which was one of the several reasons I didn't put it on right away. Frankly, I didn't like the idea of using magic to induce lust. That made me think of Cara Thorne. In my mind's eye, I saw her sharp cheekbones and salt-streaked hair.

I shook my head. *That's her charm magic. Don't let her get the best of you. You're stronger than that!*

I closed out my Inventory. I'd use the Ring of Naughtiness if I was in a pinch.

For now, I didn't need it.

When no more messages showed up, I turned my attention to my bodily needs. Over the next hour, I had myself a feast: pickle juice and roasted rabbit. The briny juice was nothing to write home about, but the rabbit was the first hot meal I'd had since entering the dungeon, so I enjoyed every tasty morsel. I'd just finished sucking the last bit of meat from a leg bone when I looked across the fire and saw Geeta sitting across from me.

"Gah!" I said, dropping the bone into the dirt as I stumbled backward. When I recovered, I said, "Geez, don't do that. You scared me!"

Geeta stared at me, her yellow eyes reflecting the firelight. "The creatures on the bridge are dwarves. Most of them carry spears that make a humming noise. They are filled with the same energy that powers your lights. I do not know what you call this in your language."

"Electricity?"

"Perhaps. The dwarves also have flocks of birds that live in cages on the bridge. They are called bladed sparrowhawks. They are not real birds, but creatures made from metal. There are many of them. Too many to count. They have knives for toes. By themselves, they do not appear particularly powerful, but in a group they represent a threat."

"The birds are on the same side as the dwarves?" Geeta nodded. "Good to know. Are the dwarves friends or foes?"

Geeta shook her head. "I did not talk to them. Considering what they are fighting, I imagine they will be our allies. Their enemies are insects called lampreys. The ones I saw were a foot, perhaps two feet long. They are pale as bleached bone. On one end, they have a gaping mouth with rows and rows of teeth. It seems like they can burrow into the ground in the time it takes to blink."

That doesn't sound good. Especially while I'm still missing my primary weapon.

"Anything else you can tell me about the lampreys?"

"The lampreys do not have eyes, but they are drawn to the buzz of electricity. It infuriates them. Drives them to madness. They want to destroy it. They can also hunt by sound. I saw a group of them attack a dwarf. I have never heard such screams. This is what the dwarves seek to keep from invading their city."

I was getting used to Geeta's clipped pattern of speech. *Is that a Geeta thing or a reptilian thing?* It was strange that there was an entire second race of humanoid creatures that inhabited the southern part of the planet, and that I didn't really know anything about them.

"We will have to cross the bridge at some point, which means crossing through lamprey territory," Geeta continued, interrupting my thoughts. "We will do this when the *drughyr* returns. Until then, I found something else. I would like your opinion on the matter."

"Oh?"

"It is this way." Geeta pointed to the woods. "Perhaps it would be best if I showed you."

I swallowed. I didn't know Geeta that well and I didn't think it was the best idea to follow her into the darkness of the woods. However, I consoled myself with the knowledge that if she'd wanted to kill me, she could've done it a hundred times already. Just in case, I palmed the Ring of Naughtiness. I didn't know if it'd work on Geeta, and I hoped I wouldn't have to try, but unless I wanted to use Giant's Roar and the club again—which I definitely did *not*—the ring was my best weapon until Spud returned.

I stood and cautiously followed Geeta, who encouraged me to stay silent by pressing a scaled finger to her lips. In the darkness of the woods, it was almost impossible to avoid every patch of dry leaves or cracking branch. Still, I'd like to think I did a fine job, as no maw-mouthed lampreys exploded out of the ground to burrow holes through my groin.

After a few minutes of walking, Geeta stopped. I found myself staring at a dilapidated structure that looked like it'd once been a house. The walls were made of mortared cobblestones, and the shingled roof was mostly covered in roots and weeds except for one place where an entire tree sprouted out from between two broken beams. If the structure had ever had a door, it'd long since rotted away.

"Here we are," Geeta whispered, motioning toward the structure. "What I want to show you is in there." She pointed to the yawning darkness of the door frame.

"I see," I said, preparing to slip the Ring of Naughtiness onto my finger. "Tell me what we're looking at."

Geeta stepped toward the structure. "Do you see this?" She moved a finger in a lateral line from one side of the door frame to the other. "This string?"

"I'm not—" But then I did see it: a glinting yellow string running between the door frame exactly where Geeta had been pointing, about a third of the way down from head height. I took a step closer and examined the line. "Huh. What is that?"

I went to pluck the string, but Geeta grabbed my wrist. She moved so quickly that her hand appeared as a blur. She stopped me before I could touch the string.

"Do not touch that. That is a trap. If it is triggered, it will blow the entire structure."

I stared at the yellow string. *Close call. If I'd been alone, I would've triggered that for sure.*

Geeta released my wrist and ducked under the string, moving with the grace of an acrobat. "Follow me," she said as she disappeared into the darkness of the house.

19

As it turned out, Geeta had found the Dark City's Fountain of Wishes. It'd been hidden in the wreckage of the house, overgrown with roots and weeds and protected by a booby trap but still active. That only left one problem.

"Where do we get our gold coins?" I asked. I cast around for the tray, though I didn't see anything. I stuck my hand into the fountain until the water reached my elbow and felt around the tiled base. It was smooth and cool, but there were no coins inside.

"I have one in my Inventory," Geeta said from behind me.

I glanced over my shoulder. In the darkness, Geeta's eyes glowed yellow. "Did you save your coin from the first room?" I asked.

Geeta shook her head. "No. I got a coin from someone else."

I remembered the bodies around the Fountain of Wishes in the promenade. *Did Geeta kill another hunter and steal his coin?* That didn't seem right, but then again, I didn't know Geeta that well. Come to think of it, I didn't really know her at all.

"Did you... did you murder someone for it?" I asked.

Geeta snorted. "No. There was a fourth pirate with Cara Thorne's crew, a man named Hildar. He kept the enslaved in line. I hated him. When we got our coins in the promenade, he picked a fight with me and Silvana, insisting that we were still enslaved and should give our coins to him. The other prisoners stood up for us. A fight broke out and another prisoner killed Hildar. It was self-defense. When the other prisoner took the coin off Hildar's body, he gave it to me. Said it was an apology from humanity for the time we spent enslaved."

She held up the coin which had appeared in her hand, the metal glinting in a slash of blue moonlight that came through the dilapidated ceiling. Dexterously, she rolled it over her knuckles. The heavy coin clicked as it danced across her scales.

"Do you know what it'll give you if you toss it into the fountain?" I asked.

Geeta shook her head. "Back at the promenade, I got a special skill called Play Dead, which was the one I used to trick you when we first crossed paths. The skill lets me pretend to be a dead body for two minutes every hour." The coin stopped its journey across her knuckles, caught between her index finger and thumb. "I tell you this because I want to fight beside you. I think we will get further in this dungeon if we are a team. Do you agree?"

I stared into her swirling yellow eyes and thought about the potential. *She was the one who recognized the booby trap I would've triggered. She can play dead and regrow her limbs. And she's quick. Her skills are good complements to my style.*

"I do think we'd work well together," I said. "But if we're going to be a team, one of us needs to be the leader. I have experience leading teams and so I think it should be me."

"Agreed," Geeta said. I blinked. Usually, people wanted positions of power for themselves. But Geeta had acquiesced without even a moment of hesitation. "I want to survive," she added. "You have experience with leadership. Besides, I am better at staying behind the scenes. Leaders need to be out front. So you will lead."

"We're a team? Just like that?"

"We are a team. This means you should have some input in the upgrade that I choose. I will tell you my options." With a flick of her hand, Geeta tossed her coin into the fountain. *Plink.* The metal disc hit the water and sank beneath the surface.

That's a lot of responsibility to give me, I thought as we waited for Geeta's options to appear. *But hadn't I been saying the hunters should find a way to work together?*

"What did you get?" I asked after a few seconds.

Geeta nodded. "I have three choices here: Weapon Upgrades, Armor Upgrades, and something called Misc. Upgrades. I have three choices in Weapon Upgrades, but only two in Armor Upgrades and Misc. Upgrades."

"Walk me through each one."

There was a second of silence as Geeta clicked into her first menu. "The Weapon Upgrades apply to my Stiletto of Silence. The first one is called Cast of Silence. It says, 'Hush, little babies, don't make a sound, not with Cast of Silence around. Cast of Silence eliminates any sound within a twenty-foot radius of you for thirty seconds.'"

I nodded. "I could see that being very useful if you want to silence a group that's sneaking somewhere with you. As long as they stay close, no one will hear them."

"Yes. The next upgrade is called Cone of Silence. It says, 'What do you get when you build a three-dimensional shape that tapers smoothly from a flat base to a vertex? A cone! Project a static cone with a thirty-foot diameter for up to a hundred feet. Anything that falls within the cone is silenced. Cone lasts for two minutes.'"

I considered. *Cone of Silence can be cast farther, and the area of effect and time limits are better, but the cone is static. The Cast of Silence only affects a small area, but it moves with Geeta, which makes it a much more versatile skill.*

"So far, I'm a fan of the first one, personally," I said. "What's the last choice?"

"It is called Mark of Silence. It says, 'You do not know it yet, but you are already dead. Well, not you. Your enemies. That is because they have been hit with the Mark of Silence. Cast this mark on a single target. As long as you maintain a direct line of sight, that target is silenced. Mark of Silence also silences anything within a five-foot radius of the silenced target.'"

I whistled. "That's a pretty good one. The best yet, I think."

Geeta nodded in agreement. "Yes, well, now we can get into the Armor Upgrades. The first one is called Chameleon. It says, 'Where did they go? I cannot see them. I think they went—*argh!* That is what your enemies will be saying when you have got this passive Armor Upgrade. As long as you are completely still, Chameleon makes you invisible.'"

I shivered as I considered the possibilities. *If Geeta had possessed the Chameleon power when we'd first met in the Castle of 1,000 Doors, I'd be dead.*

"That complements your Play Dead ability," I said. "It would really make you into a cloak-and-dagger type. Although you can't move while it's active, since that would disrupt the effect, so I'm wondering if that ruins some of the potential. But it's still a powerful upgrade."

Geeta nodded. "My other choice here is called Bad Blood. It says, 'You ever bite into a piece of rancid meat soaked in battery acid and wrapped inside a pair of damp, maggot-filled underwear? With this passive Armor Upgrade, you become as unappetizing as that previously mentioned morsel to any hungry beast that might want to crunch on your bones.'"

"Gross, but interesting," I said. "I can see the applications. And what are your final two options?"

Geeta pulled them up. "Both of them affect my eyes. The first is called Ophthalmic Augmentation: Hypnotic Stare. I can use my eyes to put an enemy to sleep, though I need to make eye contact with my enemy for at least five seconds, and the effect only works half the time."

My eyes widened. The ability to put someone to sleep with your eyes was powerful. However, I didn't like that it only worked half the time.

"And the last one?

Geeta pulled up the final description. "This one is called Ophthalmic Augmentation: Second Look. It is a passive ability that negates concealments."

"Interesting. If we hadn't seen this, I might've told you to go with Chameleon. But now I'm wondering about its utility. Because if you can get the ability to negate concealment, I'm wondering if that's a common thing for other people."

Geeta nodded. "I was thinking the same thing. And, as you mentioned, Chameleon requires me to stand completely still. It is not very versatile."

I tapped my chin. *What would be the best choice for the team?*

"I like Mark of Silence," I said.

"It makes the most sense," Geeta said. "It would be good for taking out enemies without alerting others. How do you call this?"

"Maintaining the element of surprise."

Geeta flashed a grin that showed a mouthful of sharp teeth. "Yes. With this power, I can silence our enemies while you can shoot them with your *drughyr*. The enemy would not know what was upon them until it was too late."

That's a compelling vision. Though if we start going by "Surprise Squad," Spud is going to kill us.

Before Geeta could make her final choice, I held up a hand. "Are you sure about this? It's your upgrade. I'm all for teamwork, but you're the one who earned this coin."

Geeta nodded. "Mark of Silence. I am choosing it."

A second later, it was done. The obvious next move was to go back to the campsite and explore Geeta's new abilities. However, before we did, I had an idea: the fountain was a fountain and my jumpsuit was encrusted with gore. In some places, it'd gotten so stiff that it probably could've turned a blade. And it was *ripe*. I'd gotten used to the smell, but from the way Geeta turned aside when I got close, I had a feeling I'd be doing our fledgling team a favor by taking a bath.

I unclipped my belt and removed it from around my waist. There was so much sweat and blood caked into the leather that it came away with an audible *crack*. I set it on the stone edge of the fountain and started opening the buttons of my jumpsuit. I thought Geeta would turn away, but she stared at me expectantly.

Maybe you need to give her a hint.

"I'm going to take off my jumpsuit," I said. "Dunk it in the water and give it a good wash."

Geeta nodded. "Good idea." When I didn't continue undoing my buttons, she said, "Is it too cold? Why are you waiting? You do not need my permission to get into the fountain."

How do I explain this?

"Oh!" Geeta said. "You need assistance with the buttons. Are they on the backside of your suit? Turn and I will help you."

"It's not…"

Before I could finish, Geeta grabbed my shoulders and turned me around. "But that does not appear to be the case," she said as she looked down the back of my jumpsuit. She spun me to face her. "I do not understand. What is the problem?"

"You're a woman," I said. "I'm a man."

"Yes? That is a fact."

"So…"

Geeta's eyes went wide. "I have read about this. Humans and modesty. I am sorry, Crow. I did not realize at first because we do not have such a thing in our culture. The body is not an object of sexualization." She shrugged. "I will not turn around. Even if it means everyone in the Empire will watch. Best we help get you over this now, as I cannot imagine how modesty will protect us in Toroth-Gol. What if I turn my back and something attacks you? I think we would both feel worse if you died than if millions of people saw your human sex organs. Right?"

I sighed. *I'm not sure I agree. They'll probably blur the feed. If not, at least you'll give them something to talk about.*

I undid my buttons and let my jumpsuit fall to my feet. Then I stepped out of the crusty fabric, naked for the first time since entering Toroth-Gol. There was a slight chill in the air and I rubbed my hands together to keep warm.

"There," Geeta said. "Was that so hard?"

I bent and lifted my jumpsuit before tossing it into the fountain. The movement gave Geeta a view of my back. When she saw it, she sucked in air through her teeth.

"You had another reason for not wanting me to see you without clothes," she said quietly. She was referring to the criss-crossing scars that made my back look like a bad painting in the Gomindor Museum of Art. The scars no longer hurt, but they looked as ugly as they had when I'd gotten them.

If the Empire didn't block out that last bit, they're definitely cutting this. Those in power didn't like anyone to know how bad society could get.

"Who gave you those scars?" Geeta said from behind me.

"When I was younger, I was enslaved, too," I said. "I worked in a warehouse and the overseers kept us in line with a whip. If you did something they didn't like, it was five lashes, ten lashes, stuff like that."

I glanced over my shoulder and saw Geeta follow one of the scars with her eyes. "And you did many things they did not like."

"I was a kid." I turned back to the fountain. "No kid wants to be told what to do. When you're enslaved, you get told what to do a lot."

"I know," Geeta said. As I stepped toward the fountain, a scaled hand settled on my shoulder. I turned to see Geeta looking into my eyes.

"We will fight together," she said. "We will win together. This I promise you, on the ghost of Silvana."

I bowed my head and closed my eyes. I didn't like to dwell on my time as an orphan in the Dregs. They weren't good memories, and I hadn't thought about them in a while. Before my father had saved me, I'd gone through horrors that no one should ever have to experience.

Maybe it was a good thing she saw my back. If anyone can understand the terror I felt in those days, it's Geeta. I wouldn't wish those experiences upon anyone, but she has had them, too. Perhaps our shared history will bring us closer together.

"Thank you," I said. I opened my eyes and placed a hand on her shoulder. The scales beneath my palm were solid but surprisingly smooth. "We will survive together," I continued. "As you promised on the ghost of Silvana, I make you this vow on my own life."

It was dramatic, though it felt right. From my time playing light-ball, I knew that the best teams weren't formed by a desire to win, but the motive behind the desire.

Necessity was the strongest motivator of them all.

With a nod, Geeta accepted my words. I went to my knees in the shallow fountain and rubbed at my skin, letting the water take off what felt like a year's worth of blood, sweat, and dirt. The cool water felt so good that I let myself slip beneath the surface. When I came back up, the water dripped off my scalp and into my eyes, filling up my mouth and rinsing away the sour taste of vinegar and bile.

For the first time since entering Toroth-Gol, I felt hopeful. I *would* survive. And gods help anyone that stood in my way.

20

When we got back to the camp, Geeta breathed life back into the fire and I laid out my jumpsuit to dry. Then we experimented with Geeta's new power.

During our first test with the Mark of Silence, Geeta stood on the opposite side of the campsite from me, facing me down like we were in an old-fashioned duel. We were perhaps twenty yards apart. The description had mentioned that she needed direct line of sight, so for this experiment, there was nothing between us.

"Okay," I said. "Go for it. I think you should—"

That was as far as I got before Geeta raised a scaled hand in my direction. It was an unnecessary flourish, but I suddenly couldn't speak. And it wasn't for lack of trying. I tried to talk, yet nothing came out.

It was the strangest sensation. My mouth moved and my tongue formed the words, but something sucked away the sound before it left my lips. I tried yelling. This time, I could hear myself, but the sound was barely audible.

"Help! Help! There's an assassin in the building!" I screamed at the top of my lungs, which only came out as a whisper.

I nodded at Geeta and she let the Mark of Silence fall. I laughed, relishing the ability to make noise again. Before experiencing Geeta's power, I hadn't realized how much I'd relied on sound to make sense of the world.

"You'll want to keep this handy when you meet Spud," I called to her. "He can be a bit talkative."

We continued practicing, testing the limits of her newly learned power. My loudest noises still got through. For instance, when I yelled, I could still hear myself. Barely, but it was audible. This was also when we discovered that Geeta didn't need to be holding the Stiletto of Silence to use the spell, though it needed to be nearby. After a few tests, we found that as long as she was within about ten feet of the blade, she was able to use the upgrade. To activate the power, she simply needed to look at a target and think, *Mark of Silence.*

After several additional experiments, we found that the silencing effect worked as long as Geeta could see me. And "me" included anything that could reasonably be considered a part of my person. For instance, when Geeta could just see the corner of my jumpsuit sticking out from behind a tree, the spell held. However, when I took the jumpsuit off, tied one leg to a branch, and crouched behind a tree while holding the other leg, the spell didn't work.

The magic is surprisingly complex, I thought as I slipped back into my jumpsuit. But why wouldn't it be? The scars on my back proved that the Empire wasn't the kind, benevolent force they pretended to be, but I suppose some of their propaganda *had* worked, because I *did* have an unconscious bias against magic, and in the same way it was denigrated in official Empire media.

Magic is savage. But that wasn't true at all, was it? I'd believed the messaging, though Geeta's power proved otherwise. Magic could be subtle and sophisticated.

It could be dangerous.

Magic could destroy the Empire. The realization came out of nowhere, and it was a testament to the efficacy of the Empire's propaganda that I immediately chastised myself for letting it cross my mind. *But it could, couldn't it?* The answer was obvious: *yes. That's why the Empire hates it.*

It was a powerful thought, though I'd need to consider the implications at another time. For now, I needed to focus on my survival.

After a few hours of experimentation, I taught Geeta a few commands I'd learned on the lightball field. *Attack. Pull back. Enemy ahead.* As we practiced, she proved to be quite the strategist. Together, we developed several new moves, including one called "peek-a-boo" that would let us maintain the element of surprise while entering a room that contained an unknown number of enemies.

There's more to Geeta than she's letting on. But that was fine. Hopefully, there'd be time to deepen our bond and learn the extent of her story.

Once I felt that she'd grasped the commands, I took watch and let her rest. Before she fell asleep, I asked about the strange collar around her neck.

"Is that a holdover from when you were enslaved?" I asked.

Geeta sleepily shook her head. Already, her eyes were closed. "No. Reptilians are cold-blooded. In the Emerald Isles, the sun maintains my body temperature. On the *Rancid Pearl*, and here in Toroth-Gol, I need an external form of heat. The collar is a portable heater."

"Ah. That makes sense."

As Geeta drifted to sleep, I considered what she'd told me. Without the sun, and without the collar, Geeta would slow down until she was unable to move. It was good to know. As Valentine had always told me, the first step in building any team was to get a sense for the strengths and weaknesses of your allies. Geeta's strengths were obvious: she was a fast-moving, silent assassin. However, her attacks wouldn't help much against well-armored opponents. And she'd freeze if she lost her collar.

When Geeta awoke, she went on guard duty while I rested. After I rejoined the living, we made a plan. The trick was getting across the bridge, which was heavily guarded by the dwarves and bladed sparrowhawks. We still didn't know if they were friendly or not. *In a worst-case scenario, I wonder if I could use my gloves to throw around the bladed sparrowhawks.* However, at the end of the day, I was only one person with two hands. I could hold my own against a few opponents, but if Geeta's scouting report was correct, there were way too many to face by ourselves. If we got into a fight with the dwarves on the bridge, we wouldn't win.

So we needed a peace-offering. It was Geeta who came up with an idea. I didn't like it, but honestly, I couldn't think of a better plan. Against my better judgment, I resigned myself to my role.

While we waited out the last few hours on Spud's timer, Geeta did some more scouting and I resumed the training regimen that my father had prescribed for me on off-days from lightball practice. His theory was that even when I wasn't explicitly practicing, it was important for me to stretch both my mind and muscles. Over the years, I'd done at least a hundred different versions of the off-day workouts, and I'd memorized several dozen of them. A few required equipment that I didn't have at the campsite, but most were designed to be completed anywhere at any time without specialized gear.

By the time Geeta returned, I'd worked up a pretty decent sweat. I took a seat by the fire while she showed me her haul: a shirt full of small, dark purple fruits that the text in my vision identified as "blackberries." I hesitated before eating them but Geeta assured me she knew the fruits from the Emerald Isles, where they grew within massive copses of thorny brambles. Frankly, I had been getting tired of pickled cucumbers and onions, so I popped a handful in my mouth and immediately asked her to go back for more.

It was while Geeta was gone the second time that Spud returned. I knew the second he appeared in my pouch because I heard him yelling. Although the sound was muffled by the leather, the words were impossible to ignore.

"I hate you! You stinking boil on the butt of a donkey with pox! I hope you drown in an ocean of your mother's blood! I hope you eat bad taco meat and get diarrhea for a thousand years!"

I reached into the pouch and immediately felt a sharp pinch.

"Ah!" I said, yanking out my hand. "By the Dregs, Spud, it's me. It's Crow. You're back, buddy. Don't bite me!"

"I know who it is! You murdered me! You sacrificed me! I hate you!"

I didn't know what to do, so I waited for a while and eventually the yelling stopped. When it did, I reached into the pouch again and *carefully* drew Spud out. This time, he didn't bite. He didn't even make any noise. Instead, he stared at me, his bright eyes narrowed, angry heat pouring off his skin.

"Um, hey Spud," I said. I'd known this was going to be awkward, but it was even worse than I'd expected. "I, uh, I'm sorry. If it makes you feel any better, you were terrific. You saved my life. I thought we were goners, but you gave me time to hit that giant with the barrel and then I used your... ah, I lit the solvent on fire with your flames. We burned him from the inside out. Then he fell into the gears and they blended him up. We're in a new part of the dungeon now, and we've got a companion. Another hunter. She's scouting right now, but I'll introduce you as soon as she's back. It's a good position, buddy, and I couldn't have done it without you. Really. You saved the day. I couldn't have done it without you."

Spud was still. Too still. The stillness was definitely worse than the yelling.

"You sacrificed me," Spud said quietly. "You murdered me. Even after knowing what would happen. Even after I told you where I'd go."

"Ah, yes," I said.

"You condemned me to Potato Hell."

I couldn't argue, because everything Spud had said was true. We stared at each other, anger pouring off of him in waves, and then his upper lip quivered. His eyes grew wide and soon he was blubbering into my hand.

"Oh, Crow, it was awful," he said, tears and snot spilling into my palm. "You don't know what it was like down there. You could never imagine the horrors. The fire! The pitchforks. And the things they said! They told me... they told me..."

He couldn't finish the sentence. I had no clue what to say. I'd never been very good at comforting someone. Probably had something to do with a childhood in the Dregs. No support system and all that.

But I knew I needed to try. I owed him that.

"You're okay, buddy," I said, cradling the potato to my chest. Was I doing it right? I switched him to my left hand and wiped the wetness on my jumpsuit. "Hush now. I'm here. You're here. You're back. And you look great, by the way. Your skin is practically glowing."

Spud blew his nose into my hand, a loud *honk* that sent sticky mucus streaming into my palm. "I might look good on the outside," he said. "But what about my insides, Crow? What about my emotions? I'll be on the therapist's couch for a year. It's terrible, Crow. I'm broken. I'm so broken."

"You're not broken," I said. "And if you are, then I'm broken, too. We can be broken together."

It was a dumb thing to say, but it had the intended effect. Unfortunately, Geeta chose that exact moment to return. She arrived as silently as she'd left, reappearing across the fire from me without a sound.

"Uh, Geeta," I said, nodding to her. "This is the friend I was telling you about. The one who saved me? Spud. Spud, this is the other hunter I mentioned. Can you say hi to Geeta?"

Spud looked up from where he was curled in my hand. At first, he looked angry again, but when he saw Geeta, his eyes went wide.

"She's not another potato?" he said.

"What?" I said. "No. Why would she be a potato?"

It was like someone had flipped a switch. Spud's tears dried and the quaver disappeared from his voice. He rolled back a bit and shook the mucus from his skin, which ended up coating my hand.

"I thought you were trying to replace me!" he said. "My goodness. This changes *everything*. How do you do, Geeta? I'm Spud. Say, you look a lot like the lizard that was trying to kill us. She does, doesn't she, Crow? What was her name? It started with a 'G,' too. Maybe Grita or Gina or something like that. Anyway, it's a pleasure to meet you."

"Greetings, honored *drughyr*," Geeta said. She bowed her head to Spud. "Your friend tells me you are quite an accomplished fighter."

"*And* she's a charmer," Spud said. "I like her already. We're going to get along fine. Geeta, I don't think it'd be a stretch to say that I've taught Crow everything he knows. Why, in our first battle together..."

As we listened to Spud's exploits, the dual moons disappeared beneath the horizon. The sky remained dark, but that only provided contrast for the twinkling stars. One by one, the lights on the bridge went out. I knew I'd never feel safe in the dungeon, but I felt okay. Like maybe, with Spud and Geeta at my side, I might be able to find my father. Like I might survive.

To my knowledge, no one had ever escaped Toroth-Gol, but why not me? My whole life, I'd beaten the odds. While there was still much I didn't know about Geeta, it seemed like she was used to beating the odds as well.

After an hour of stories about Potato Hell, Spud said, "We gonna gather moss on our feet or are we going to keep moving? I say we make a push for that fortress. Maybe it holds an armory with unstoppable weaponry, like a sword that can slice through reality. Or no! Maybe it contains a cloning machine. That would be okay, because a clone wouldn't replace me. It would *be* me. I mean, think of how powerful I am by myself. Imagine a hundred *more* of me. Imagine!"

"That would be quite a fighting force," Geeta said. I couldn't tell if she was humoring him or if her people really had some sort of cultural norm around giving respect to talking vegetables. What had she called him? A *drughyr*?

"I'm ready to go," Spud said. "Just try not to kill me again, okay Crow? I hate Potato Hell."

I nodded. "You got it," I said. "Geeta, care to explain our plan?"

For the first time since we'd met, Geeta smiled. "Honored *drughyr*, I sense that you will like this one," she said in her strange, halting pattern of speech. "It involves using Crow as bait."

The plan was simple. The dwarves were clearly at war with the lampreys. So, we'd kill some lampreys and bring their dead bodies to the dwarves as a peace offering.

I stepped onto the soil and flashed my gloves. "Flashing" was a lightball term that described a standard pre-game warm-up. To ensure that everyone's gloves were working correctly, we switched from "push" to "pull" while the technician checked our readings. It was the equivalent of a singer leaning into the mic and saying, "test test, test one, two, three."

"Here we go," I said. "As soon as we've got one, we retreat. If we find ourselves overwhelmed, we retreat. And in the event we accidentally attract anything stronger than a lamprey—"

"Yeah, yeah, we retreat," Spud said. "We all know the plan. Can we start on the killing already? That's the fun part."

After the hard stone beneath our campsite, the mossy ground felt strangely buoyant. A few more steps and I stood in the center of the clearing. Light from across the chasm filtered through the surrounding trees.

"Come on, you juicy buggers," I whispered as my battery pack began to whine. "Come to daddy."

I set Spud to hovering above my left glove. Then I crouched and waited. My right hand hovered behind Spud, ready to shoot him at the first thing that moved. The air was cool but tense. There was no sound save for the hum of my battery pack and the thump of my own heart. I felt like I did as I took the line at the beginning of every lightball game, readying myself for the face-off. I was tense. Nervous. It didn't matter how much I'd practiced or how many professional games I played. Every time I took the line, the butterflies started flapping around my stomach.

At first, I didn't see what attacked me. It came out of the ground behind me and not even the quickest reflexes in the world could've stopped it. In less time than it took me to pop a lightball into a net from a foot away, the blood-sucking monster latched its mouthful of needle teeth into the flesh of my glute.

"Agh!" I said. From above my glove, Spud screamed, too. I'm not sure why, as he wasn't on fire, and nothing was attacking him. I looked over my shoulder to see a foot-long, cucumber-like shape sticking out from behind my right butt cheek.

Lamprey

The lamprey is a sightless carnivore most often found in the forests surrounding the Dark City. Upon reaching maturity, the lamprey spins a nearly impenetrable chrysalis and enters a state of pupation. After two to three years, the lamprey emerges as a winged imago, which eats any nearby chrysalises to build the strength it needs for mating. Because of its cannibalistic nature at all stages of its lifecycle, only one in every hundred thousand lamprey successfully make the transition to winged imago. Like other members of its family, the lamprey hates electricity.

The pain was excruciating. In my mind's eye, I got an image of the creature's maw, with layers of bloody gum between circular rows of needle teeth. All of that was currently digging into my soft flesh. It was enough to make even the heartiest soul have nightmares.

"Retreat, Crow," Geeta said from somewhere beyond the trees. "Remember the plan. Fall back!"

"Listen to Geeta," Spud said from my palm. "Fall back, Crow! We had a plan for a reason."

Dimly, I remembered what we'd discussed. *It's tough to stay focused when you've got a monster biting your butt.* With my right hand, I grabbed the lamprey around its middle and tried to keep it from burrowing even farther into my skin. At my touch, the creature hissed; to my surprise, it also released its grip. As I was feeling a split-second of relief, it arched its pale, segmented body and latched onto my wrist.

"Agh!" I said again. At the sight of the creature's head, I almost threw up. The *entire* thing was a mouth, just a circle of darkness ringed with white spines like some inside-out sea urchin. The spines were covered in blood. Before the creature locked onto my skin again, I glimpsed all the way down its maw to the other end, where I caught sight of a mass of orange goo with the consistency of toothpaste. Its brains? Its guts? Leftovers from a previous meal? I didn't have the presence of mind to care.

"This way, Crow," Geeta shouted. "Over here!"

I stumbled toward her voice. Spud was still screaming. Something like "Ohgodohmygod, Crow, Crow, ohImightbesick."

I couldn't keep him hovering, since I needed both hands to deal with the lamprey. But I didn't want to leave Spud to his own devices; we'd just gotten him back, and I didn't want to get him killed again. I unlocked my left glove, which dropped Spud into my palm, and hurled him toward Geeta.

"Catch me, Geeta!" he yelled. "Oh, you beautiful woman. Thank you, my sweet, scaly friend. You're a legend."

I couldn't spare him another thought. It felt like the lamprey on my wrist was rotating its ring of teeth. Only my iron hold on its round body kept it from getting to the bone.

With my left hand free, I squeezed the lamprey's body closer to its head. But the harder I gripped, the harder the lamprey bit, and I couldn't make it let go.

I was yelling. I didn't know where Geeta and Spud had gone. Another lamprey jumped out of the ground in front of me, this one several feet long and possessing a mouth as wide around as my bicep. As it surged toward my face, my reflexes took over and I batted it out of the air. It made a keening sound as it struck the ground, wriggling like a fish. Instantly, two more lampreys popped their sightless heads from the ground and latched onto the first, screeching with pleasure as they bore through its hide.

I retched. *What a terrible plan.* I made it to the edge of the clearing and collapsed onto the stone, hardly noticing that I skinned my knees through my jumpsuit. I still clutched the lamprey trying to burrow through my wrist. Something warm and wet ran down my forearm. I assumed it was blood.

Or is it urine? Maybe I peed myself. That would be a first.

Even if I had, I didn't care. I couldn't think straight. I rolled on the ground, beating my wrist against the stone. I was oblivious to everything except removing the lamprey. Squeezing didn't work. Neither did pulling. I punched at the creature's segmented body, trying to catch it between my fist and the ground, but my angle was off, so that didn't work.

Think through this, Crow. What can you do?

I grabbed a jar of pickles from my Inventory and used it to try and smash the lamprey. I missed, and the jar shattered against the hard ground. Now, I wasn't only grappling on stone, but stone covered in glass shards, onions, and vinegar.

"Get it off me!" I shouted as Spud rolled in panicked circles.

"The ham, Crow," he cried. "Try the ham. Maybe it'll like pig meat better than yours!"

I was game for anything. Even as the lamprey continued its relentless assault, I managed to get the ham out of my Inventory. Once it fell to the stone, I beat my wrist against it.

"Eat the ham!" Spud shouted. "Come on, you ugly thing. Eat the ham!"

The lamprey didn't take the bait. Belatedly, I realized that I didn't even have Sammy's Spider-Killing Solvent, which I probably could've used to douse the lamprey. I'd used my only barrel to kill Cravag.

I was about to activate Giant's Roar when Geeta appeared beside me. With a flick of her wrist, the Stiletto of Silence sliced the lamprey down its segmented middle. Finally, the creature went limp. Still, it didn't let go of my arm, though at least it'd stopped trying to burrow through my bone.

I lay on my back in the mess of pickled onions, glass, and blood. So much blood. I'd been cut by the glass in a dozen places, not to mention the wounds I'd taken from the lamprey. Above me, the stars of the Dark City twinkled brightly.

"Hold still," Geeta said. "I am going to try and cut this off of you."

I almost laughed. *Where would I go?* Gently, she probed around my wrist. I closed my eyes and let her work.

"Done," she said after a few seconds. I opened my eyes and she stood above me holding a butterflied lamprey on the end of her stiletto. Rather, she held several pieces of one. From the beginning, the foot-long lamprey hadn't looked like much of a threat, and now that it hung in tatters from her blade, it was difficult to even tell that it'd once been a parasitic predator.

"How did such a small thing hurt so much?" I asked.

Geeta shrugged. "It is not the size of something that makes it dangerous," she said. "Consider the honored *drughyr*. He is tiny, but he makes a forceful weapon."

"That's right," Spud said from beside my head. "Consider *me*."

"And in this case, the creature caught you unaware," Geeta continued. "Given the circumstances, I would consider you lucky."

I closed my eyes again. Maybe Geeta was right. Either way, we needed those lamprey bodies and it was going to be a while before I was in a position to make another go at catching them.

Which meant a while until we reached our destination.

"Do not despair, Crow," Geeta said. "I was busy while you were screaming." I opened my eyes and saw that she held three dead lampreys by their tails. Unlike the dark strip of leather that had once been the lamprey latched to my body, all three of these were at least four feet long, their pale, segmented bodies unmarred save for the wounds that marked the tops of their heads and oozed out green ichor.

"See?" she said. She shook the dead lampreys. "Not about the size, but how it is used."

If I'd had any strength left, I would've kissed her scaled reptilian feet.

22

In Geeta's Inventory, the lampreys showed up as a common raw material. I couldn't see the description, and I was squeamish about putting the dead lampreys in my own Inventory, but Geeta told me they'd each become a single unit of something called "Lamprey Hide." Apparently, she had a schematic that would let her combine twenty of the hides with a needle and catgut to make a set of Forest Beast Chest Armor, and another ten could be combined with the same materials to make a similar set of armor to cover her legs.

"Nothing like wearing the skins of your enemies for protection," Spud said. "Crow, we should make *you* a set of that."

I ignored him. "I need to get to the Fountain of Wishes," I said. "Back in the promenade, the water from the fountain healed me, and I'm willing to bet that this one will do the same thing."

As soon as he heard 'Fountain of Wishes,' Spud's eyes went wide. "You found a fountain?" he said as he bounced up and down with excitement. "How will we evolve me? Maybe I'll get something that lets me turn into a ghost. Ghost Potato! Then I'll be able to walk through walls, or make myself incorporeal and dive through someone's chest. I'll make myself whole again and *bam*! I'll light them on fire from the inside!"

"We don't have any gold coins," I said. I looked hopefully at Geeta but she shook her head. "We're just here for the fountain's healing waters."

"Or maybe I'll get electric powers," Spud continued. "That would be cool. Electric Potato. And it'd make sense, right? Maybe I'll join up with the dwarves and they'll let me fight for them. I'll be their god. They'll want to execute you and Geeta, but I'll say, 'Nay, loyal subjects. For these bipeds doth please me, even if the big one reeks. Let them live, I say. And bring us your finest ham.'"

"We don't have any gold coins," I repeated.

"Oh," Spud said. The news dulled his enthusiasm. "That's fine, too. Let's get you healed, I guess."

With Geeta in the lead and Spud on my shoulder, I limped back to the Fountain of Wishes. Sure enough, within seconds of drinking its waters, my skin knit back together. Even when I moved my wrist around and flexed it, I could barely feel my injuries.

"You're looking much better," Spud told me. "Too bad you ruined our only ham. Those lampreys were really ugly creatures."

Once I was healed, we walked through the forest and stopped on one side of the bridge. The well-lit cobblestones glowed like a beacon. On either side of the bridge sat block houses and a walkway ran between them.

I looked at the nearest block house.

Dark City (Block House Alpha)

The first of twenty-four block houses on the Bridge of Advancement. Why twenty-four? One for each letter of the Dwarven alphabet.

The walls of Block House Alpha are made of reinforced stone and the door is made of ironwood. It's a fitting structure from which to launch defensive maneuvers against invading lampreys or winged imago.

"Where are the dwarves?" Geeta asked.

I'd had the same question. I pointed to the first block house. "Let's see if anyone is home," I said. "Spud, I hate to do this, but I need to put you in the pouch. Stay quiet until I call for you. You'll be our secret weapon. Can you do that?"

I was worried Spud might protest, but he said, "If I get to be a secret weapon, I'll sit in a sewer. Put me away, Crow!"

I dropped him into the pouch and looked at Geeta. "The *drughyr* honors you," she said. "You are lucky to have such a steadfast companion."

"Hear that, Crow?" Spud said from the pouch, his voice muffled by the leather. "Oh! I'm supposed to be quiet. Sorry!"

We stepped to the doorway of the first block house. As I suspected, a dwarven soldier sat inside. He was behind a desk, his hairy hands moving marbles across a board on its surface that I assumed was some sort of game. When he saw us in the doorway, the marbles dropped from his fingers and he took hold of the spear that had been leaning on the table beside him. He was on his feet in an instant, the spear leveled at Geeta's chest.

He's quick. Quicker even than Geeta. Something to be aware of if we encounter others.

"Easy," I said. To Geeta, I said, "Don't let him scare you."

It was my first good look at one of the dwarves. He was half as tall as me and stocky, his biceps poking from his loosely hanging white tunic. Each of his wide ears contained a gold stud driven through the lobes. Above a pair of black pants was a leather belt filigreed with silver wire. He had a sallow face and a pale scar that started at his right ear, ran across his cheek, and puckered at the right-hand corner of his mouth. His gray hair was tied back in a ponytail.

Dwarf Foot-Soldier (Rollag)

When the Insanity hit the first levels of Toroth-Gol, a single band of dwarves escaped the wrath of the giants by retreating to this plateau. A hundred years of separation from their ancestral lands

created its own type of insanity, which caused this group's holy circle to experiment with forbidden magics. One of these was electricity, which suffuses each member of this group. In addition to earning them the ire of local fauna, the use of electric magic gave this group the nickname "Electric Dwarves." Frankly, it's a stupid name, like something a bunch of writers who get together once a year for a writing retreat around the holidays might name their "band."

"*Ayar cin dun hi?*" Rollag said. I had no idea what that meant.

"Pull out the lamprey hide," I said to Geeta. I bowed as she removed the dead lampreys. To the dwarf, I said, "Honored dwarf, we come in peace. We would speak with your leader."

Rollag looked at the dead lampreys and then back at us. He asked another question in his native tongue, but we didn't know what that meant, either.

I tried again. "We were hoping for safe passage across the bridge," I said. I pointed in the direction of the Dark City, then pointed to us.

That registered. Rollag nodded. A second later, he pointed to us and held up a palm.

"*Sin,*" he repeated. "*Sin, sin.*"

Although we couldn't understand him, the sign for "wait here" was universal.

"I think he's telling us to sin," Spud whispered from the pouch. "Oh sorry. Quiet! I keep forgetting."

To my relief, it didn't seem like Rollag had heard. "We'll wait here," I said. I placed a hand on my chest, and then pointed to the ground. "Us, yes. We stay here. *Sin.*"

Rollag nodded. "*Sin,*" he said as he exited the block house and walked past us, his spear held menacingly.

"*Sin,*" I repeated, my hands raised. "*Sin.*"

With a final nod, Rollag turned and disappeared down the walkway between the block houses. *Perhaps there's some skill that triggers a mastery of dwarven language? Something to explore later.*

We'd only been standing there for a minute before we saw three dwarves walking toward us: Rollag and two others. Because of the way the block houses were set up along either side of the bridge, I didn't see them until they were about twenty feet away. But as soon as I did, I knew they were different than the foot-soldier we'd encountered.

"This must be leadership," I said quietly, a statement that would've been obvious even if it hadn't been corroborated by the text that appeared in my vision. The smaller of the two dwarves wore form-fitting silver armor with gold chevrons at each joint. A forked black cape hung from her shoulders, and she carried a two-handed greatsword so long that it bordered on impractical. The grip itself was as long as her forearm and the cross guard was formed from the same gold chevrons that covered each of her joints, one layered over another so that her top hand almost disappeared beneath them.

Dwarf Sub-Captain (Nona Sunsong)

When the dwarves fled through the thousand doors, the Mad Mage led a large contingent to the Dark City. One of those in his retinue was Nona Sunsong, daughter of Lyle and Patricia Sunsong and twelfth in line for the dwarven throne. Though the exodus has scattered the dwarves and many think the royal lineage is no longer relevant, Nona has proven the purity of her bloodline through martial prowess, rising through the ranks of the Mad Mage's army to become the right hand to Dietrich Warblade, the dwarf bridge captain.

Interesting. The blurb gave me a little more information about the plight of the dwarves. Not much, but it seemed like they were the ones who'd built the Castle of 1,000 Doors in an attempt to escape... *something.* The Insanity? I'd seen that referenced several times, though I still didn't quite understand it.

The other member of the party was the captain himself: Dietrich Warblade.

Dwarf Bridge Captain (Dietrich Warblade)

Previously a commander in the Great Dwarven Army, Dietrich Warblade elected to continue serving in the military after the exodus, taking on a role as one of three bridge captains. He doesn't like outsiders. But you're about to find that out for yourself, aren't you?

That doesn't sound good, I thought as I looked Warblade up and down. Whereas Nona's armor appeared ceremonial, Warblade's looked decidedly used. Though polished, it was battered, with deep scratches and dents along the interlocking chest plates. Instead of heavy metal boots, he wore leather shoes, though it seemed as if the toes had been dipped in steel. Unlike Nona, Warblade carried a spear. He had a red cape draped over his shoulders, clipped over his left breast with a pin in the shape of a lightning bolt.

The two approached and I got down on one knee, motioning for Geeta to do the same. Her scales scraped against the cobblestones.

As I stared at the ground, someone above me spoke: "You may rise." I couldn't quite place the accent. Then again, I'd never met a dwarf. "You are hunters from the castle?"

"Greetings, honored dwarves," Geeta said, her head bowed. "Our travels bring us through the—"

"Enough." With a word, Warblade cut her off. Geeta looked up, glaring at the bridge captain.

Please don't do anything stupid.

Warblade continued, saying, "Answer my questions or I'll cut you down where you kneel. You are hunters?"

I could tell it took Geeta a considerable amount of willpower to swallow her pride. "Yes."

"And how is it that you came to the Dark City?"

"A friend told us to find him here," I said. "We humbly request entry."

Warblade laughed. It was a cruel laugh, the type you'd hear if a dog told you that it'd learned the difference between a soup spoon and a dessert spoon and would like to be included at the dinner table. I knew that laugh from my time on the field. Even if I was the best lightball player in the world, I was still from the Dregs, and the nobles who ran the Empire had made sure I knew that. Everyone except Valentine. No matter how high I rose, there was always someone richer and more powerful to bring me down.

"Outsider insolence is strong this week," Warblade said, more to himself than anyone in particular, and then muttered something in dwarfish to Nona. The princess nodded but didn't say anything. She also didn't smile.

Warblade turned back to Geeta. "What do you have to offer, now that you've begged entrance to our city? What gifts do you bring that would make you worthy?"

Geeta held out the dead lampreys. "We bring you this," she said through gritted teeth.

"This?" I winced as Warblade sneered. "Some dirty lamprey hides? This is a joke. An insult. Remove yourself from this stone before we consider your presence as trespass and your lives as forfeit."

With that, he barked an order in dwarfish and turned on his heel. Nona moved to follow. We were about to lose our only shot at getting into the city.

"Captain," I said, getting to my feet. The guard we'd first encountered growled and leveled his spear, the tip crackling with blue electricity. "We weren't only looking for a friend. We were charged with a special mission. We were told to seek you, specifically. We have a message that can only be delivered to your ears."

The captain stopped. "Oh?"

I might not have known how to handle dwarves specifically, though I knew how to handle the self-righteous. This was a group that thrived on power, and they loved when you stoked the flames of their egos.

"If you but allow us the chance, we would see our duty through," I said. "In exchange for the privilege, we give you this."

I didn't actually want to give him the Clockwork Guardian's Club, but it was the only thing I had of value. *Act now, worry later*. I'd find another weapon.

The club appeared in my hand and I set it on the cobblestones before me. The foot-soldier jumped back, but Warblade stepped forward, his eyes widening.

"Where did you get this?" he asked, bending his knees to get a better look at the club.

I bowed my head. "It was given to me by my own captain. Taken from the body of Cravag, last of the giants, who we killed with our own hands. I bring it as an offering. A token of my respect and a gift to the great dwarves of the Dark City."

Warblade looked me in the eyes. At least, he tried. I kept my head bowed and wouldn't meet his gaze. Warblade handed his spear to Nona, then took another step forward and hefted the club, running his free hand along the scarred wood.

"Who is your captain?"

I glanced at Geeta. "May we talk in private?" I asked him.

I thought Warblade might bash in my head with my own club. Instead, he nodded. "This is a great gift," he said, making the club disappear into what I imagined was his own Inventory. "And if you've killed the last of the giants, you've done the dwarves a great service. Very well. We may talk in private. Nona, take their weapons."

Nona stepped forward and patted down Geeta. My friend stood stiffly, looking as if she might flinch and plunge her stiletto into the sub-captain's heart. Given what I knew about her history, I didn't blame her for any hesitation about going weaponless. But at least now we had a chance at getting past the bridge.

Nona found the Stiletto of Silence strapped to Geeta's thigh and withdrew it, staring down the hilt at the brown-black blade. Then she shrugged, placing the knife into her Inventory, and moved to me. I held out my arms as she ran her hands down my ribs and along my back. When she got to my waist, she opened the pouch and removed Spud. With his eyes closed and his mouth shut, he looked like an ordinary potato. She held him toward Warblade and said something in dwarfish.

"What is that?" Warblade asked, squinting at the object in her hand. "Is that a potato?"

"Captain." I averted my eyes. "It's silly, I know, but it brings me comfort. My wife was a potato farmer. This is all I have left to remember her."

Warblade said something to Nona in dwarfish. To me, he said, "You humans are odd. Even the giants made more sense than you." But he nodded at Nona and she handed back Spud. I put him in the pouch, silently thanking my lucky stars that he hadn't made a grand entrance.

Once Nona had given Warblade the "all clear," he motioned us into the block house. We stepped inside and Warblade closed the door behind him. As we'd seen from the doorway, the room contained a single table. The only ornamentations were glowing blue lamps that hung from the walls. There was an unlit fireplace with cords of wood stacked beside it, and beside that were shelves that held pickled vegetables and—lo and behold—*two hams*. Against another wall was a rack of spears; none of them were like the massive war spear that Warblade carried but were thinner, less-impressive weapons akin to the one carried by the foot-soldier. There were also several crossbows and a table heaped with bolts.

All in all, it was a cold room, little more than a hut from which to mount an effective defense. Arched windows faced the forest, and another set looked toward the bridge. A third set gave a view of the chasm. The floors were hard stone except for the part closest to the far wall, where the stone turned to iron grating that allowed one to see into the darkness of the chasm below.

Warblade crossed the room and sat, leaning his spear against the table. I joined him at the desk. Geeta took up a spot beside the door.

"What is it, then?" he asked, looking at us curiously. "What's your message?"

I opened my mouth to tell him... I don't know. Probably something dumb. Probably something that would've gotten us killed.

"So—" I said, and that was as far as I got before the winged imago attacked.

23

Here's a fact: winged imago are terrifying.

One of them appeared in the window that looked out over the chasm. It was about six feet long, with the paper-thin wings of a dragonfly and the pale, segmented body of a lamprey. Tiny forelegs writhed along its armored stomach and it had six small arms under its head. At its rear end, it had a half-dozen thin, segmented legs that curved at the ends like wicked fishhooks. The thing hovered outside the window and chittered, crossing and recrossing its arms.

Winged Imago

You ever pull open the shower curtain and see something in the tub with too many legs? Something that skitters into the drain as soon as it sees you? The winged imago is like that, except that it's six feet long, spits acid, and wants to eat your flesh. Especially if you use electricity. The breeding form of the lamprey, the winged imago is found in the forests surrounding the Dark City. If you're seeing this message, it means you've encountered one. Sucks for you.

Warblade turned to follow my gaze. When he spotted the winged imago, he jumped to his feet and hefted his spear. He tried to shout something, but Geeta had hit him with the Mark of Silence. I couldn't help but notice the look of grim satisfaction on her face.

As Warblade realized he'd been silenced, his eyes widened. Once again, he attempted to yell. But he was squarely in Geeta's sights and so his cry came out as a whisper.

The winged imago that hovered at the block house window moved aside, revealing a hundred more that came up over the side of the bridge. Geeta stepped to the door and flipped the latch, locking us inside. If I thought Warblade's eyes were wide before, they now threatened to pop from his skull.

"Give me back my voice," he said to Geeta. I could tell that he was trying to shout, but it came out as a barely audible whisper. He pointed at Geeta, his finger trembling. "Witch," he said. "I need my voice to command!"

From outside, Warblade's subordinates banged on the door. *Things are heating up.* I flipped the switch on my battery pack. "Spud, it's time."

The pouch at my waist popped open and Spud jumped into my hand. A flick of my fingers made him hover above my palm.

"Guess who it is?" the potato said, turning a pirouette in the air. The sound of his voice made Warblade turn toward us. "One wrong move and my buddy takes your head off. Spud Squad!"

It was a good entrance. I raised my hand toward Warblade, putting his head directly in my sights. "Put away your weapons," I said. "If you play this right, we all walk out of here alive."

Warblade looked from me to Geeta. At first I thought he might attack, but he only narrowed his eyes and set the spear back against the table.

"I don't know what you're playing at, but you're dead if you continue this charade," he whispered, his nostrils flaring. At the steel in his voice, I reconsidered my assessment of the captain. Undoubtedly, he was someone who enjoyed the power that came with a position of authority. He also struck me as someone who understood his responsibility. He cared about his city, the bridge, and its soldiers. While I could fault him for being rude, I couldn't call him a coward.

"We need to get into the city," I said. "As soon as we open that door, your soldiers will take us down. Give us your word that if we let you go, you won't harm us. You'll let us into the city and you and your people won't raise a weapon against us."

I stared at Warblade, watching the emotions twist on his face. On the one hand, he wanted to save his soldiers. On the other, he thought us the catalysts for the invasion, which was actually kind of flattering.

Agree to my terms, Warblade. The captain licked his lips and glanced toward the window. I followed his gaze. Through the aperture, I watched as one of the dwarves threw a spear at an airborne bug, piercing it through the stomach. The creature buzzed and sizzled, jerking spasmodically as electricity coursed through its body. Unable to keep its wings beating, it crashed to the stone. It was an impressive throw, but it left the dwarf without a weapon, and a second later, half a dozen winged imago darted toward it.

The bladed sparrowhawks flew from their cages to meet the enemies, but they weren't quick enough to save the dwarf. The dwarf, overwhelmed by winged imago, drew a dagger from the sheath at his belt and, to my horror, slit his own throat. The winged imago fell on him anyway, their hooked back legs pumping like pistons as they punched their hind hooks into his body.

"Your word," Geeta growled. "Your word, and I will add these insects to my own list of enemies."

From outside, the captain's subordinates continued banging on the door. The panic in their voices made me want to be sick.

"I give you my word as captain of these forces," Warblade whispered. "Open the door and you will not be harmed."

At that, Geeta flipped the latch and pulled open the door. Nona and the foot-soldier spilled inside, nearly tripping over one another as they scrambled toward safety. They were just in time. No sooner had they entered than a winged imago slammed into the ground where they'd been, its hooked hind legs scoring the cobblestone.

"Hold!" I shouted to Geeta. This was one of the exercises we'd practiced while waiting for Spud to return. As she maintained her position, Spud rocketed from my hand, screaming as his body blazed. He hit the winged imago with a sound like crunching bone, and then I caught him in the cone of magnetism from my right glove. I pulled my arm back in a reverse throw and yanked him back into the safety of the block house. "Close!"

Geeta slammed the ironwood door and flipped the latch.

Warblade stared at me, his mouth hanging open. Then he stormed toward the window that overlooked the bridge.

I couldn't catch the curse he was hissing as he assessed the chaos, though his voice had returned to normal. Nona, who had recovered from diving into the block house, spoke in dwarfish to the captain, but Warblade ignored her.

"What can we do?" I asked, joining him at the window. Several groups of soldiers had released bladed sparrowhawks from their cages on the roofs of the nearby block houses. The metal birds circled the air above the bridge, trying to harry the winged imago, but most of them weren't able to do much before the flying carnivores batted them out of the sky.

"This is a coordinated attack," Warblade said. "I need to get back to the Core Command Center and activate the bridge's defenses."

"Where's that?"

"The far end of the bridge."

Of course. That makes total *sense. The only way to activate the bridge's defenses against flying, predatory bugs is to cross a bridge infested with flying, predatory bugs.*

His course decided, Warblade turned on his heel and stormed across the room to a horn that hung from a nail beside the door. After lifting the latch, he threw open the door and placed the horn to his lips, his voice ringing across the bridge. Although his words were in dwarfish, I could tell that he was rallying his troops. Outside, the surviving dwarves cheered.

When he was done, Warblade closed the door, hung the horn back on the nail, and pointed toward me. "Your message."

"What?"

"The message. The one given to you by your captain who slew the last of the giants. What was the message your captain gave you?"

"Oh." My mind raced. *I guess he didn't understand that had been a ruse? Maybe that's a good thing. Captain's word or not, I don't think he would've been very happy if he learned we'd been lying.*

"He, uh, he wanted me to warn you about this attack, though he didn't think it would come so soon," I said. "He thought you'd have another few days at least."

Warblade narrowed his eyes but nodded. "Very well. If you see your captain again, thank him for his warning." He nodded at Nona and the foot-soldier, then spoke in his native tongue. I couldn't understand him, but I imagined he said something like, "Now, we fight. For the dwarves of Dark City!"

Warblade ran from Block House Alpha. At his heels were sub-captain Nona Sunsong and the foot-soldier.

"Come on," Spud said, straining at the field that kept him hovering above my palm. "After them. To battle, Geeta! To war, King Crow! We put our lives on the line for the dwarves of the Dark City!"

Geeta glanced over at me. "Do we follow?" she asked.

I shook my head. "We hold. Stay inside."

She nodded her understanding. A second later, it proved to be a wise decision. No sooner had the soldier taken half a dozen steps than a winged imago dropped atop him, piercing his torso with its hooked hind legs. The soldier screamed, causing Sunsong to turn. With her sword, she neatly skewered the insect through its abdomen.

She hadn't been quick enough to save the foot-soldier. Both the dwarf and the winged imago collapsed just beyond the doorway. Nona spared the foot-soldier a pitying glance before she was off, black cape streaming behind her as she followed her captain down the bridge.

With the door open, the sounds of battle had grown louder. The screams of dwarves, the hum of electricity, the screeching of bladed sparrowhawks. The chittering of the winged imago gave me goosebumps. Beyond the doorway, the dying foot-soldier moaned softly and muttered something in dwarfish.

I nodded to Geeta, who pulled the dying foot-soldier inside before shutting the door and throwing the latch. We really were hitting that "know-what-your-partner-is-thinking-before-they-need-to-say-it" groove. For Spud's sake, I said what we were *both* thinking.

"We should let them handle this one," I said. "We'll go outside when the battle is over."

24

There's a time for heroics and a time for survival. This was a time for survival.

Over the course of the next half hour, Geeta and I did what we could to make the dying dwarf more comfortable. We couldn't save him. But I sat with him until he took his last, ragged breath.

"That's that, I suppose," I said once he was gone. At least we'd helped him go with dignity. I used my fingers to close both of his eyes. Then I joined Geeta in loading the contents of Block House Alpha into my Inventory.

I took the ham—obviously—and, despite Spud's advice to the contrary, topped off my collection of pickled vegetables.

"You're like a brother to me, which makes this cannibalism!" he shouted from where he sat on the table. "At the very least, it's vegetable cruelty."

I didn't argue and took the food, doing my best to ignore him. When I moved onto the weapons, the dungeon gave me a description.

Ironwood Spear (Electric)

Dwarves love poking things with sticks. For the electric dwarves

of the Dark City, this ironwood spear makes a two-for-one special: poke things with a stick and blast them full of magical electricity. To activate the spear's electric features, cover the rune on the shaft.

The spear was about six feet long. I lifted it and found it to be surprisingly heavy, the shaft made from the same dense ironwood as the block house door. Per the description, I found a rune carved into the shaft about a third of the way down from the head. When I covered it with my palm, the point crackled with electricity.

"Are you replacing me?" Spud asked, angrily bouncing on the desk. "I thought you were my friend. My one-and-only. My ride or die. This is a wild breach of trust, Crow. What happened to the Spud Squad?"

"We need to think strategically," I said, loading the spear into my Inventory. "You're great for distance, Spud, but I need a contingency weapon. Warblade still has my club, and if I lose you, I'm defenseless."

"I have seen Crow defenseless," Geeta said. "When I brought him through the portal to the Dark City, he did not have anything he could have used as a weapon. I could have slit his throat with ease. Then what would you have come back to?"

It was enough to make Spud fall still. "I wouldn't have come back at all," he whispered, a shiver running through him. "I would've been stuck in Potato Hell forever."

I put another spear in my Inventory. Waste not, want not. "I could also sell or trade these. You saw how helpful it was to have the club. Without that, we wouldn't have gotten our private meeting with Warblade. No one is replacing you, Spud. You're my one-and-only. My ride or die."

That cheered him. At least, it stopped him from complaining while we continued ransacking the room. Just for good measure, I took another spear. Geeta, who had the short-range options covered but needed a more practical long-range weapon, took a crossbow and fifty bolts, which was all she could carry. Since I had plenty of weight to spare, I added another hundred bolts to my Inventory.

When we finally left Block House Alpha, our Inventories were laden with both food and weapons. The battle had stopped. The dead and dying lay everywhere, the red blood of the dwarves mixing with the green and brown fluids that leaked from the corpses of the winged imago.

"Stay alert," I growled, my eyes scanning the bridge for any sign of danger.

As we made our way to Block House Beta, cogs and gears from broken bladed sparrowhawks crunched underfoot. When we got closer, I received the same description that I'd gotten from Block House Alpha—only this one was titled "Block House Beta." The second block house on the bridge had the exact same layout as the first, but when we pushed open the ironwood door, we found four hammocks strung up inside. There was more ham—which I took without hesitation—and more bolts, which I also took.

The third block house, Block House Gamma, contained a live dwarf. He sat with his back to the wall and had a crossbow in his lap. He was missing his left leg below the knee, the wound so fresh that it bled freely. Tears left tracks on his dirt-stained cheeks. As we entered, he looked up, his eyes glistening, and tried to lift the crossbow. When he couldn't, he drew a belt knife and moved it toward his own throat.

"Stop!" I said, running into the room. It was too late. Blood sheeted down his tunic as he drew the knife across his neck. He smiled at me with blood-stained teeth before he went limp, slumping over his own legs. His fingers relaxed and the belt knife slipped from his hand to clatter onto the stone floor beside him.

"What's with these guys?" Spud said. "Why do they keep doing that?"

"Better dead than victim to the enemy," Geeta murmured. "I have seen this behavior in some of the southern tribes."

"But we're not the enemy," Spud said. "Though I guess they don't know that."

I nodded. When I'd played lightball, there was a southern team in our league that had a similar "go-down-with-the-ship" mentality: the Crescent Necromancers. During every game we played, if it looked like we'd beat them, they'd stop going for the ball and focus on injuring us. It wasn't just the enforcers, either—even the keeper tried to hurt us. If you've ever been hit with the fan from a keeper, you know it's not a joke. That style of play infuriated our team, but it was the southern way.

Thankfully, as we continued down the bridge, we didn't encounter any more suicidal dwarves. We saw a lot of terrible things, but not that. Block House Kappa and the bodies that surrounded it were on fire, and the air was so hot and filled with soot that I had to pull my jumpsuit over my mouth and nose to run past. The ironwood door of Block House Mu hung from a single hinge, and there was the body of a dwarf across the threshold.

With the exception of the lingering flames from Block House Kappa and our footsteps, the scene was eerily quiet. We passed several more block houses, but after checking the first dozen and finding nothing of value beyond what we'd already discovered, we headed straight toward the other side of the bridge.

"Where do you think everyone is?" I asked.

Geeta shrugged. "Maybe they ran for safety. Or maybe they killed each other off."

Just beyond Block House Rho, we found the body of Dietrich Warblade. He lay face-down in a puddle of blood surrounded by no fewer than fifteen winged imago. Two of them still lived. The first, which was missing its wings, chittered as we approached and crawled toward us. The second had guts spilling out of its pale abdomen, yet it also tried to reach us.

I pointed to the bug with the hole in its stomach. "You go for that one. Practice your aim. I'll take the bug without its wings."

With her new crossbow, Geeta put a bolt through the head of the winged imago I pointed out while I used Spud to end the other one.

"Nasty creatures," Spud said, spitting out green ichor as I brought him back to hover over my palm. "But dang if Warblade wasn't a fighter after all. Good thing these bugs arrived before we had to fight him. He would've beaten both of you to a pulp."

I stepped over the bodies of the winged imago, making my way toward the dead captain. Nona was nowhere to be seen, and neither was the captain's mighty spear.

Text appeared, asking me if I wanted to take back my club. *Yes.* Immediately, the club appeared back in my Inventory. I also had the option to loot a set of armor.

Sunsong Bridge Captain's Armor

The fabled battle armor of bridge captain Dietrich Warblade. An heirloom passed through five generations of Sunsong rule and gifted to Warblade when he assumed the position of captain on the Bridge of Advancement. Sunsong Bridge Captain's Armor protects its wearer from poison.

WARNING: This armor has been imbued with an active debuff called "Enemy of the Dwarves." If you're not bridge captain Dietrich Warblade, wearing this armor will cause dwarves to attack you on sight. Debuff can be removed by an armorer with the requisite skill.

Loot? Yes or No.

Taking the armor was a risk, but I mentally selected "Yes." I didn't think we'd seen the last of the dwarves, though it wasn't like I had to put it on right then.

"So long, Warblade," I said as I put the armor into my Inventory. "You died bravely."

I gave a silent nod to the dead captain. I hadn't liked him, but he'd fought to the last. In my mind's eye, I saw an image of him and Nona pressed back-to-back, surrounded by the chittering winged imago. Perhaps they'd been overwhelmed. In that case, Warblade almost certainly would've done the valiant thing, sending Nona to the safety of the command center while he made a final stand. Maybe he'd thrown his spear at a winged imago that had been trying to pursue Nona, spearing the bug through the chest but losing the weapon.

We continued down the bridge. Between Block House Phi and Block House Chi, we found the dead body of Nona Sunsong. She lay on her back, her gray eyes staring at the starless sky. The spine of a winged imago protruded from her forehead.

"Unlucky," Spud said as we approached. "She was a princess, right? Does this end the line of succession?"

I was about to reply when text appeared.

Sunsong Royal Armor of Advancement

Armor crafted from wyrm hide overlaid with steel. An heirloom passed through six generations of Sunsong rule and gifted to Nona Sunsong when she assumed the position of sub-captain on the Bridge of Advancement. Sunsong Royal Armor of Advancement protects its wearer from poison and curse.

Loot? Yes or No.

"That's all yours," I said to Geeta.

"I will take this," the reptilian said in that strange, halting pattern of speech. She pulled the bloody armor into her Inventory and we continued.

The final block house sat like a bulbous toad in the center of the bridge. Behind it, the city walls rose sixty feet into the air, looking even more impenetrable than they had from a distance. Unlike the others, Block House Omega was four stories tall, and the outer walls of the second, third, and fourth stories were embedded with arrow slits. On the roof were cages for the bladed sparrowhawks.

We reached the far end of the bridge without a problem. Before Block House Omega, the cobblestones of the bridge were replaced by two metal panels, their surfaces weather-worn and corroded. From front to back, they were each about twenty feet long. Where they met in the middle, there was a thin black line, as if the panels could open independently of one another.

There was no going around them. "Do you think it's a trap?" I asked, standing at the edge of the corroded metal. But I already knew the answer. There was something similar on the ramps in Steel City that led up from the Dregs. The ramps were constantly patrolled by watchful soldiers of the Empire, who only provided access at specific times of day—and even then, only if you had the right paperwork. When crossings weren't available, the soldiers could pull a pin that caused the panels to fall away, leaving a massive gap in the center of the ramps.

"I'm going out on a limb by saying yes, those are *definitely* traps," Spud said.

Tentatively, I stepped on one of the panels. It held my weight. If the panels could fall away to prevent enemies from accessing the final block house, the latch that secured them was firmly closed.

"Solid," I said. I crossed quickly, not wanting to test my luck. Geeta waited until I'd made it across before joining me on the other side.

Instead of the single door of the other houses, Block House Omega had two massive ironwood doors that, when opened completely, would've allowed my entire lightball team to walk through arm-in-arm. One of the doors was closed but the other was open. Not all the way, but enough to let me, Spud, and Geeta slip inside.

"What's our approach?" I asked.

"Peek-a-boo?"

I nodded. Geeta's crossbow disappeared into her Inventory. The move required stealth, speed, and dexterity, and carrying the clunky wooden weapon would only slow her down.

"Peek-a-boo on three," she said, lining up with the crack in the door. "One... Two... Three."

She ducked through the doors. I waited with Spud hovering above my left palm, ready to rush inside and shoot at the slightest sign of danger. But a few seconds later, Geeta ducked back through the crack between the doors and nodded.

"All clear," she said. "The path to the city is just beyond."

25

If the Dark City had ever been described as lively, those days were long since past. As I stood on a hazy street, I realized that most of the houses around me were abandoned. Half-built scaffolding clung to the sides of buildings that were missing doors and windows. The cobblestone streets were choked with fog, which did nothing for visibility. The murk was thick as chowder.

I ducked as something small and dark darted past my head. I thought it was a bat until it screeched and I recognized the call of a bladed sparrowhawk.

"I gotta be honest, Potato Hell isn't the greatest, but I don't think I'd ever come here for vacation," Spud said. "At least in Potato Hell, we've got mini-golf."

"What is a mini-golf?" Geeta asked.

Spud must not have heard her, because he continued, saying, "Maybe people could have a nice time exploring the empty buildings? But that seems like a really good way to get a splinter. Or tetanus. God, why is this place so *wet?*"

I agreed with the sentiment. When I'd lived in the Dregs, I'd had two entire levels of city above my head, which did wonders to keep out the rain. We didn't get any sun, either, but the heat lamps helped with that. After I experienced rain for the first time, I realized I didn't love it. Rain was so dreary. I wouldn't go back to the Dregs for anything, though if I had to choose between "rain and cold" or "dry and heat," I'd take "dry and heat" ten times out of ten.

I peered into the soupy gloom, but I could only see a hundred feet in front of me. Another bladed sparrowhawk flitted through the air overhead.

"Let's get a sense of where we are," I said, pulling up my Map. The wide thoroughfare on which we stood provided a straight path to our destination. But there were other, less-conspicuous paths, including a dozen smaller streets and alleys. I identified them quickly; you don't spend fifteen years in what's functionally a maze without the ability to find clear, efficient paths to a destination. It's one of those skills you never really lose. "We have choices. Do we take the main street? Or do we go with another option?"

Although Geeta couldn't see my Map, she had her own, so I walked her through the routes I'd identified using common points of interest.

"It's all the same to me," she said. "Unless we scout, we don't know if one of these paths is better than another."

"Do we have time to scout?"

Geeta shrugged. "I do not know." The timer in the upper right-hand corner of my vision showed that we had under two weeks to beat the level. "I do not know how long it will take to get out of the Dark City."

I peered into the gloom. "Let's push for it," I said. While I hadn't forgotten the Core's warnings, the streets really appeared to be empty. "You game? If we get split up, we can meet at Block House Omega."

Geeta nodded. As we walked, I kept an eye on the surrounding buildings. Other than the occasional bladed sparrowhawk, we didn't see so much as a hint of movement. There were no dwarves. Nor any winged imago.

This part of the city was dead.

If the Map hadn't made our destination obvious, we would've known where to go from the lights. After a bit of walking, they appeared on the horizon, hovering over the side of the plateau that dropped away to the sea. We trudged in silence, my thoughts interrupted a few minutes later when Geeta's scaled hand landed on my shoulder. I stopped in my tracks, glancing over at her. She pointed into the gloom.

At first, I couldn't see what she was looking at. Then I realized that something sat in the middle of the street. It was maybe twenty feet tall, its color so similar to the darkness that I'd looked past it half a dozen times.

Without a word, I dropped into a low crouch, yanking Spud from my shoulder and bringing him to hover above my palm. When his face came into view, I could see that he was trying to talk. Thankfully, no sound came out—Geeta had had the foresight to hit him with Mark of Silence.

I held a finger to my lips and he shut his mouth. Then I motioned to Geeta and she dropped the Mark of Silence.

"Can you tell what that is?" I whispered.

Geeta shook her head. "I need more light," she replied.

"Oh! I can help with that," Spud said. "I'll activate my flames and you can send me toward that thing. Then we'll all be able to see."

"Except you scream when you're on fire and we're trying to remain inconspicuous," I said. That gave me an idea. "Geeta, can you hit Spud with Mark of Silence?" I said. "That way, we can set Spud on fire without the noise."

Geeta nodded and flashed me a thumbs up. I activated Spud's lowest flame setting and was pleased to see that my plan had worked. Although Spud was clearly moaning, we couldn't hear a sound.

Carefully, I rolled Spud toward the object. I didn't want to risk shooting him. If I sent him too far and Geeta lost her line of sight, his moans would fill the street.

Let's avoid that if we can help it. I squinted into the gloom. Spud's light fell on the object.

Doomsday Construct, I of III (Metalhawk)

One of three Doomsday Constructs created by the Mad Mage to

protect the Dark City. Senses prey using thermal vision. Loadout includes dual mounted shoulder guns, heat-seeking rockets, and the powerful desire to destroy anything it perceives as a target.

PS - that's you!

I pulled on Spud and he flew into my palm. With a thought, I extinguished his flames. Then I nodded to Geeta and she dropped Mark of Silence.

"We should back away very slowly," I said. "I don't want to fight anything called a Doomsday Construct."

"Maybe it's friendly?" Spud suggested.

As soon as he finished speaking, the streetlights snapped on, and the object before us moved. One moment, it was an inert sculpture; the next, it had wings. I've seen some fearsome things in my life, but few were as terrifying as that twenty-foot wingspan.

"Uh, Crow?" Spud whispered. "What should we do?"

A second later, the object had finished transforming into a giant metal bird with wings covered in silver blades. The ones that hung off the edge of its wings were almost two feet long.

Metalhawk. Now the name makes more sense.

Before us, Metalhawk lifted one piston-driven talon and drove it into the ground, scoring the stone. Its eyes lit with red light.

"Targeting organic life forms," Metalhawk said in a voice buzzing with electricity.

"You're a bird guy, right Crow?" Spud stammered. "It's in your name. Maybe you can make friends with it?"

The red light of the construct's eyes moved into the guns mounted on the creature's shoulders. Metalhawk shook, and its blade-like feathers rang as they rattled against each other. The construct shrieked. The sound cut the quiet night like a fork against glass. The creature's beak clicked closed and it looked at us with unmistakable animosity.

"Get down!" I said as six rockets shot from the bird's wings and arced toward us. But even before I yelled, Geeta had started running toward a nearby building. I dove the other way, firing Spud even as I fell.

"*Agh!*" he screamed as he activated Hot Potato on his own. "It burns so good!"

Spud's voice faded as he flew into the distance, taking the heat-seeking rockets with him. Plumes of exhaust trailed behind the foot-long projectiles as they followed the potato into the sky. Getting to my feet, I activated my glove and pulled Spud back toward me. The sudden change in the direction of their target caused two of the rockets to slam into each other. The explosion they made took out the other four projectiles, though the resulting concussive blast knocked me back to the cobblestones.

Spud, still screaming, burst through a mass of white smoke, hurtling toward me. So did Metalhawk. The bird screeched while it thumped down the street, charging me like a bull.

"Do something, Crow!" Spud yelled. He turned off his own flames so that I wasn't burned when he smacked into my palm. I got to my feet again, held out my other hand toward Metalhawk, and activated the magnets. The bird was metal; in my panic, I tried to push it away, though I might as well have tried beating the thing with a flyswatter. Metalhawk wasn't deterred for a second.

I might've died that night, if not for two things. The first was Spud, who I shot right into Metalhawk's broad forehead. That was enough to interrupt the bird in the middle of its lunge. It stepped backward, more shocked than hurt, and its beak closed on empty air instead of my torso. Spud spun away and rolled behind a pile of masonry. I lost sight of him, but at least I knew he was safe.

The second was Geeta, who leaned out the second-story window of a building some fifteen yards away and shot Metalhawk with her crossbow. The bolt clanged harmlessly off an armored wing, not even leaving a scratch, but once again the distraction bought me time. In the time it took the massive construct to glance toward Geeta, I slipped through the doorway of a nearby building.

Although that building didn't have working lights, I could see plenty thanks to the outside street lamps, which had come on a few seconds into our battle, as if intentionally. Their blue light cast the room in an eerie glow. At one time, someone had used the building as a party-supply shop, as evidenced by signs that said, "Candy Here!" and, "This Station Makes Balloons!" as well as the piles of dusty candles that littered the floor.

Outside, Metalhawk screeched. The doorway was too small for the bird to fit inside, but I knew it was only a matter of time before the construct battered its way through the stone walls. I ran, heading to the staircase at the back of the store in hopes of finding an exit. I'd just mounted the first step when someone spoke from behind me.

"Crow? You in here?"

It was Spud. He sat just inside the threshold, peering into the dark store.

"Back here," I whispered. "Get over here!"

Spud turned, his white eyes finding me, and started rolling over. I activated my glove and brought him the rest of the way.

"You saved my hide back there," I said as he smacked into my palm. "Nice work."

"Talk about excitement!" Spud said. "I could sure go for a margarita right now."

With Spud in hand, I continued up the stairs. "We should try and find Geeta," I said. "See if we can come up with a plan. I just saw her in that building on the other side of the street."

"How will we get across?"

I shook my head. "I don't know. Let's see if we can get a better view."

We reached the top of the staircase. The room in which we stood contained tables and chairs set out in a horseshoe shape, and the tables were covered in cloth so dusty that I couldn't make out the pattern. One of the tables even held a drooping cake.

But it was a table covered in presents that had caught my attention. One of the wrapped packages had been ripped open and coins spilled from the side.

"Coins for the Fountain of Wishes," I breathed.

Gold Coin (x23)

See those coins there? Yes, those ones. You hereby have permission to take THREE. Spend them, bite them, bake them into a chocolate cake and serve them to your friends. It's your party! But if we're being real, you should probably throw them into a Fountain of Wishes.

I was about to take a step forward, though I froze. Near my shins was the glinting yellow light of a rope trap. I followed the thread with my eyes and spotted another trap, and another. They looked like the trap I'd seen guarding the doorway to the Fountain of Wishes, but instead of a single trap, this room contained dozens of them. In fact, there were only a few square feet at the top of the stairs without traps. Otherwise, they covered nearly every square foot of the room. Not even Spud could've reached the table without touching one.

Thank goodness Geeta pointed that trap out to me near the Fountain of Wishes. Otherwise, I wouldn't have known what these were.

"Okay," I said to Spud. "New plan. We're going to—"

That was as far as I got before Metalhawk crashed through the second-story windows, setting off every single trap in the small space. I had just enough time to think, *If I'm going to die, I hope I take that bird with me,* before the floor opened beneath me.

26

I awoke on my back with my whole body aching and my mouth tasting of plaster. But I was alive. At least, I thought I was. I sat up, wiping at my mouth with the back of my hand, and realized that I'd been lying on a thick wool carpet.

Where am I? The last thing I remembered was falling, and then I was… here.

I looked around. Strangely enough, the room felt familiar. At first, I couldn't quite place it. I noted the soft carpet, the tasteful lamps, and the shelves stacked with books. The room looked like a wealthy person's library.

Suddenly, I knew *exactly* where I was.

"No," I said. "No, no, no. No way. I'm not doing this again."

Secret Area of the Pitiable Unfortunate

Oh, you thought you were doing well? The fact that you're still alive is an absolute anomaly. That's why we're giving you a chance to even the odds. A little boost, so to speak. Either that or certain death. Good luck!

"I *really* don't want to do this," I said.

"Do what?" Spud asked from where he sat on the carpet beside me, yawning like he'd just woken from a long nap. "Wow, I just had the weirdest dream. When that floor collapsed, I thought we were goners. But now we're here! Nothing is wet, the light is decent, and this carpet is super plush. I can't believe our luck, Crow. This is great!"

"You weren't around the first time I was in a room like this," I said. I told him the story.

"But that was how you got the upgrade that made me, right?" Spud said. "I mean, without that wheel, we wouldn't be together. So how bad could it be, really?"

I rubbed a hand across my head. "Other than the sections that will kill us?" I said.

"Sure, but you didn't land on those," Spud said. "Look at the situation! We could be stuck under a million pounds of rock, but instead we're in a warm library with a chance to snag a boon from the dungeon itself. I'll be honest, Crow: you sound a bit ungrateful."

I sighed. "Let's go see what the dungeon wants."

I set Spud on my shoulder and walked into the vestibule. It was similar to the last one, though instead of a stool, this one contained a waist-high well. The stone well was covered with a sheet of tarnished copper that had a seam running down its center. On the far side of the room were two stained-glass windows that featured scenes from the Dark City: the one on the left was illuminated by the glow of the smaller, redder moon, while the window on the right featured the blue one. The final difference between this room and the similar one in the Secret Area of the Beaten Unfortunate was the oil painting that hung between the stained-glass windows. While the last one had featured three balloons, this one showed bare, spindly trees lining a gray street.

You've found the Prize Room! To unlock Water Shot, you must answer a riddle. Failure to answer the riddle within the allotted time will result in certain death.

When you know the answer, speak it out loud. You may guess as many times as you'd like before time runs out. Ready?

Yes.

"The test was different last time," I said. "But this one unlocks something called Water Shot."

The news didn't bother Spud. "Duh," he said. "It's a different room. You want the dungeon to get stale?"

Frankly, I didn't care one way or the other, but I didn't think it wise to antagonize the dungeon before I gambled with my life. "Ready?" I said to Spud. "I'm going to start the timer."

"I was born ready," Spud said. "Is that cliché? Probably. Anyway, I'm ready."

I clicked "Yes," and new text flashed across my screen. Once again, I had thirty seconds to answer.

What can go up a chimney down but not down a chimney up?

Up. Down. Chimney. The words were confusing. I tried breaking the riddle into parts. *What can go up a chimney down? But that doesn't even make sense. Down a chimney up? That doesn't make sense, either.*

"An umbrella," Spud said.

"What?"

"That's the answer. An umbrella. You know what an umbrella is, right?"

"Sure. But—"

Spud ignored my protests. "See, if an umbrella is *down*, you can stick it *up* a chimney. So what can go up a chimney while it's down? An umbrella. But if it's *up*—like, if it's open—you wouldn't be able to pull it *down* a chimney. See?"

I needed more time to think about it. "I'm not—" I started to say, but again, Spud interrupted me.

"Just say it," he said. "Umbrella. That's the answer. You can work it out for yourself in your own slow brain later."

"Umbrella," I said, and the timer stopped.

Fourteen seconds. That was close. And I definitely wouldn't have gotten it without Spud.

I glanced over at him. The potato stared back at me with a self-satisfied grin on his face. "Riddle Master of Potato Hell for three years running," he said proudly.

"That was brilliant," I admitted. "But let me work this out. You're saying that when an umbrella is down, you can fit it *up* a chimney, but when it's up, you can't fit it *down* a chimney. Huh. Actually, that makes—"

This time, I was interrupted by a rumbling from the well. Both Spud and I looked to the source of the sound. A second later, the copper panel that covered the well parted along the seam, each side opening up and out to reveal a dark hole. A gun mounted to a stone base rose through the newly created gap and settled into place with a click.

The gun wasn't like any other weapon I'd ever seen. It was about two feet long and sat on a mount that allowed it to swivel. At the base of the mount was a red button similar to the one I'd pushed to start the Gambler's Wheel.

Water Gun of the Pitiable Unfortunate

Push both triggers to start the flow of water. Aim for the center of the red target.

Win and receive an Ophthalmic Augmentation. Lose and receive certain death.

"The red target?" Spud said. "What red target?"

"I imagine the target will become clear when we press that big button," I said.

Spud considered this information. "Hmm," he said. "Well, you get both hands on the gun, and I'll press the button."

As far as attack plans went, it certainly wasn't a bad one—mostly because we didn't have another choice. I gripped both handles of the gun, the metal cool beneath my palms. My thumbs rested on the triggers. When I gave the gun an experimental twist, it pivoted smoothly on its mount.

"Ready when you are," I said, looking down the barrel. There were sights on the top of the gun that allowed me to line up my aim. I took a deep breath. In the Secret Area of the Beaten Unfortunate, I'd played a game of chance.

Will this be similar? Or is this a game of skill?

I wracked my brain, but "Water Shot" wasn't a game I remembered from the arcade in the Pleasure Gardens. Then again, every time I'd been in the arcade, I was too drunk to fully know what I was doing.

"Here we go," Spud said. My palms felt slick against the handles of the gun. "I'm pressing the button in three… two… one."

Spud jumped on the button. Instantly, both stained-glass windows shattered, the colorful pieces of glass spilling to the floor like handfuls of gemstones. I swiveled my gun to the right. Behind the now-shattered window was an alcove that contained a large blue target with a black hole at its center the size of an Empire mark. Above the target was a glass tube, perhaps three feet tall, marked with lines that denoted percentages. Twenty-five percent, fifty percent, seventy-five percent. The top line didn't say one hundred percent and instead listed "Winner!"

"That's the blue target," Spud said frantically. "You want the red one. Aim to the left!"

I swiveled the gun to the left and found the red target. The setup was similar to the one on my right, except that the red target was a fraction of the size of the blue one, with the hole at its center only about the size of my thumbnail.

"Why are you waiting?" Spud cried. "Shoot, Crow! Shoot!"

Spud's voice snapped me into action. I lined up the barrel of my gun with the center of the target and pressed both triggers with my thumbs. As I did, a stream of water shot from the barrel.

"Go, go, go," Spud said. The tube above my target started filling with water. To my horror, I noticed that the tube above the blue target was filling as well.

A race. Me and Spud against the dungeon. That's the game. First one to fill their tube wins.

From where he sat at the base of the gun, Spud continued to offer his thoughts. "Faster, Crow," he said. "You're not shooting fast enough."

I pressed down harder, but it didn't seem to make the water come out any faster. "I'm shooting as fast as I can," I said. "This game is rigged!"

"It doesn't matter," Spud said. "We have to try. The other tube is already twenty-five percent full!"

I wanted to look at the other meter, yet I couldn't afford to take my eyes off my own target. My stream was perfectly trained. If I moved, I might upset a delicate balance.

"By the Dregs, come on," I whispered, my eyes locked on the center of my target. "Go!"

Water shot from the barrel. Slowly but surely, my tube filled. On the lightball field, players talk about a phenomenon called "flow state," where you get so invested in the outcome of your actions that everything else falls away. When you're in a flow state, your rational mind overrides the emotional one. You lock in. Time loses its meaning. You don't see, hear, or feel any distractions. You're completely focused on the goal at hand.

At some point during my game of Water Shot, I entered that flow state. Dimly, I was aware that the other meter was still filling. I knew Spud was shouting at me. But I only had eyes for my target. My entire existence shrank to three things: the Water Gun of the Pitiable Unfortunate, the stream of water that shot from its barrel, and the thumbnail-sized center of that tiny red target.

In the end, it was Spud who saved us. While I was focused on my target, he threw himself at the other tube until he managed to crack the glass. The crack wasn't huge, but it was enough to make the tube start leaking. Enough to give us a fighting chance.

Only when my tube was full and I took my hands off the gun did I realize what he'd done to help us. "You beautiful potato," I said as the water level in the other tube decreased. "You've saved the day yet again."

"Ain't no thing," Spud said. "I figured that if the dungeon was allowed to cheat, we could too."

A second later, text flashed across my vision.

You beat the odds! You've earned an Ophthalmic Augmentation, which allows you to upgrade your ocular implant. Ophthalmic Augmentation can't be stored. You have one option. Choose now?

Confirm.

Only one option? I suppose I know better than to hope it's a good one. I'll have to roll with the punches.

I selected "Confirm." New text appeared in my vision, outlining my new upgrade.

Ophthalmic Augmentation: Mission Critical

They say that if you're heading into a maze, you should bring some string or a bit of flour to mark your path. But goblins love to cut string and flour attracts blood gnats, so that's pretty terrible advice.

This upgrade allows your Map tab to show which rooms you've visited and which remain unexplored. The upgrade also allows you to place up to three pins on the rooms of your choice.

Note: this upgrade only works after you've unlocked the floor map, and it only works on your current floor.

Well, I'll be, I thought as Spud and I looked at each other.

"Huh," he said. "That's surprisingly awesome!"

27

The portal out of the Secret Area of the Pitiable Unfortunate put me and Spud in an underground chamber. Veins of pulsing blue energy ran through the walls, and mushrooms grew from the stone. They were each about an inch high, grouped in clusters of thirty or forty, with thin gray stems and delicate caps. As I looked at them, text flashed across my vision.

Subterranean Cave Mushroom

There's a fungus among us! The electrical energy that pulses in the walls of the tunnels beneath the Dark City catalyzes the growth of this special type of mushroom. Are they edible? Will eating them give you superpowers? Will that open the door to an excruciating death? Try 'em and see!

We've heard mushrooms don't grow on rocks, but then how do you explain *this*? We say, "Get lost, mycologist. That's a dumb job anyway."

"Don't try them," Spud said as I finished reading the text. "Mushrooms are gross. The sworn enemy of all potatokind."

"Thanks for the advice," I said.

After making sure nothing was about to attack us, I opened my new Map. Immediately, I could see that it was vastly superior to the old one. Instead of a top-down, two-dimensional view of my current level, this one showed a three-dimensional view of the Dark City, as if it were a cross-section. With a thought, I could move the map around, zooming in and out or even rotating it to get a better look at certain chambers or pathways.

I found the corridor in which we stood, a subterranean passageway beneath the city. The entire plateau that supported the Dark City contained more passageways, chambers, and rooms than an anthill. Many of the passages opened onto beaches at the plateau's base.

"Look at that!" Spud said. "We could've reached the fortress through these underground tunnels instead of trying to cross the bridge and walk through the city. That would've let us avoid Metalhawk!"

I saw what Spud was talking about. "No sense in worrying about it now," I said. "Also, whatever lives in these caverns might be *worse* than Metalhawk."

"Right," Spud said. "Because bugs make tunnels like this. Big bugs. On second thought, let's get out of here!"

I nodded and closed out the Map. The only thing worse than coming across a winged imago would be doing it underground. "Geeta and I said that if we got split up, we'd meet back at Block House Omega," I said. "I say we grab her from there, and then we can decide on a plan."

"Sounds like a plan to me," Spud said. "Let's do it."

I set Spud to hover above my left palm and started down the tunnel. The blue energy that pulsed through veins in the tunnel walls gave us enough light to see, so I didn't need to activate Spud's flames. I knew he couldn't help his moans, but until I knew what lived in these tunnels, I didn't relish the idea of letting Spud alert everything within several hundred yards to our approach.

The path back to Block House Omega was easy. The shortest route was down several hundred yards of tunnel and through a massive, central cave, then up a ladder. That worried me, as it seemed like just the place the dungeon would drop something dangerous, but I kept my eyes open as we approached the cave entrance.

"We go quietly," I whispered to Spud. "Yes?"

"Obviously," Spud said. "I'm not trying to get eaten any more than you, even though I definitely taste much better."

I stepped into the cave, my eyes darting from strange rock formations that rose from the ground to the glowing blue crystals jutting down from the ceiling high overhead. The crystals were massive, the size of Steel City's Spire, each one large enough to crush a neighborhood should it happen to release its hold on the ceiling.

"This place is huge," Spud whispered, a note of awe in his voice. "You could fit a hundred thousand potatoes in here!"

If there was one advantage to the layout of the giant cave, it was that the stalagmites that grew from the ground provided ample coverage. I moved between them, my ears attuned to any sound other than the drip of water and the scuffing of my feet on the slick rock floor. But the only thing I heard was Spud, who said, "But what in the name of holy carbohydrates is that?"

The creature before us was so big that I'd first mistaken it for a rock formation. It was easily three hundred feet long, its thick body perhaps forty feet high, with jagged stone spikes along its back that gave it at least another five feet of height.

"I'm not quite sure," I said, running my eyes down the length of the creature's body. Its face looked like a flower, the petals made of stone and the center a black maw framed by rows of jagged teeth.

If the Empire had anything like this in their armies, they could end the war with the Thuins in seconds. A second later, another idea struck me. *Forget hypotheticals. If that thing sees us, it could end us in seconds. Good thing it's sleeping.*

Subterranean Wyrm Queen

Wonder where lampreys come from? They don't get dropped by a stork. Nope, they pop out of this thing. Also, if you've been wondering why the lampreys and winged imago are pissed at the dwarves, it's because the dwarves chained up their mother—aka this thing—and are using her energy to keep the portals behind the thousand doors open and stable. Imagine how you'd feel if someone enslaved *your* mom.

The next time you feel sorry for yourself, think of the subterranean wyrm queen trapped beneath the Dark City.

"I don't like this," Spud moaned in a whisper. "Crow, get us out of here."

As I'd learned from my battle with Cravag, if you run into something way bigger, stronger, and more powerful than you, don't run *away* from the exit—go toward it. I started to walk backwards, acutely aware of the water-slick rock beneath my feet. With my luck, I'd slip and dislodge a stalagmite, or accidentally trigger some sort of alarm.

We made it back into our tunnel without waking the beast. I'd never been so thankful to have walls of dripping rock surrounding me.

I pulled up my Map. "We go the long way?" I said, already mapping the route.

"Any way but the way that puts us nose-to-nose with the subterranean wyrm queen," Spud said. "What *was* that thing?"

I only knew what the dungeon had told us, but it was enough to put together the pieces of the story at play in the Dark City. "You read what I did," I said. "That's where the winged imago come from."

"The dwarves couldn't have found *another* source for their energy?" Spud said.

"I don't know," I said. "Let's find Geeta."

It took us another hour to find an alternative route, but we finally emerged from a trapdoor in the floor of Block House Omega. It blended in with the stone so cleanly that we simply hadn't noticed it before. No sooner had I climbed into the house and closed the door behind me than someone spoke my name.

"Crow."

I looked up. Geeta crouched on a nearby platform, a loaded crossbow held to one shoulder.

"Geeta!" Spud shouted. "You're alive!"

Geeta put the crossbow into her Inventory and slid down the ladder, joining us on the ground floor of the block house. I noticed there wasn't so much as a scratch on her ruby scales.

"Are you okay?" I asked her.

Geeta nodded. "The machine never even attacked me," she said. "It was more focused on you and Spud. After you went into that building, I tried to keep it in my line of sight, but I could not find it until that explosion." She eyed us up and down. "I am glad to see the two of you are alive. I thought you were goners."

"Booby-traps," Spud said. "The upstairs room was *filled* with them. When the construct came through the windows, it triggered all of them at once."

"Did the explosion take out the bird?" I asked.

Geeta shook her head. "No. I think you injured it, though. I saw it limping out of the rubble. I was going to try and take it out myself, but the explosion attracted the dwarves. I did not know if they would be friendly, so I hid. When the dwarves left, they took the bird with them. That is when I looked for you, but there was too much debris. Where did you go?"

"We fell through the floor and ended up in a creepy library playing a life-or-death carnival game," Spud said excitedly. "Crow won an Ornithological Augmentation, and then we got sent beneath the plateau where there are tunnels and a giant cave holding something called a subterranean wyrm queen. It's a monster as big as the freakin' city!"

Geeta looked at me curiously. "You won an augmentation that lets you see birds?"

"Ophthalmic Augmentation," I said, correcting Spud. "It upgraded my Map. I see the whole thing from the side now, which lets me view all the layers of a level at any given time. There's a tunnel complex beneath the plateau—that's where we just came from."

Geeta glanced toward the segment in the floor that had slid to one side. "That was there this whole time?"

I nodded. "The tunnels run to the fortress, but we can't use them unless we want to risk waking the subterranean wyrm queen."

"Spud mentioned that creature," Geeta said. "What is it, exactly?"

How to describe it? "It's a monster that makes Metalhawk look like a kitten."

"So we would not be able to kill it?"

"Us? No way. Just one of its teeth is probably bigger than you. But I don't know if we'd even want to kill it. When I looked at it, the dungeon text told me that the dwarves are using its energy to keep the portals behind the thousand doors open and stable."

"Hmm." Geeta tapped her scaled chin in thought. "So we can avoid it?"

I nodded. "Sure. It just means going back through the city."

"Which might mean another battle with Metalhawk," Spud said.

He was right.

I ran a hand over my head as I considered the best way to handle the predatory construct. "We should try to avoid Metalhawk at any cost. But in a worst-case scenario, I'll use Giant's Roar and my club. Once I activate the special skill, I'll only have thirty seconds to take down the machine, which isn't a lot of time. If it takes to the skies or avoids me during that period, we're going to be in trouble. So we'll have to catch it while it's distracted."

"Something tells me that *I'm* going to be the distraction," Spud said.

I raised a finger. "Only if Metalhawk catches us by surprise. But if we get the drop on the construct, I have another idea." I nodded to Geeta. "You're cold-blooded, right? That's why you wear the collar?"

Geeta's hand went to her neck. "That is right."

"Metalhawk sees through thermal vision," I continued. "The dungeon's description told us as much. Which means that if you take your collar off and match the ambient temperature, it won't be able to see you."

"I also will not be able to move," Geeta said. "If my internal temperature gets too low, I will freeze in place."

"But you'll have a window of time before you become immobile?"

"Yes."

"That's it, then. If we find the construct and can't get around it, Geeta will turn off her collar and become functionally invisible. Once she gets around it, she can start her collar back up. When Metalhawk turns to fight her, Spud and I will sneak up behind it and bash it with the club."

There was silence as the other two digested my plan.

"It's not your best idea," Spud said. "But I'm not sure what other choice we have."

Geeta sighed. "Agreed. Our first choice is to avoid Metalhawk entirely. But if we cannot, I will serve as the distraction."

We exited the block house, once again finding ourselves on the dark, deserted streets of the Dark City, and made our way toward the fortress. This time, we took a side route, Geeta scouting ahead while I moved with Spud. At some point during our trek, it started raining.

"When I get out of here, I'm not going to do anything but sit on the beach for a week," Spud whispered to me. "Make that two weeks. Maybe three."

I nodded. "I might even join you for that."

In the foggy murk, our destination blazed like an electric bonfire. Blue light glowed from behind each window and electricity danced in the lanterns that hung from the outer walls.

Dark City (Electric Fortress)

The stronghold of the dwarves in the Dark City. After years of fighting the lampreys and winged imago, the dwarves have retreated here, where the strongest among them prepare for their final stand.

"Final stand," I whispered. "That definitely doesn't sound good."

In the yard before the fortress, several dwarves stood behind concrete barriers. They hardly seemed to notice the rain that came down in sheets, but they noticed us. As we approached, one of the soldiers ran into the castle behind him while the others leveled their crossbows at us.

At least we didn't run into Metalhawk again. Cheers for small blessings.

Over a clap of thunder, one of the crossbow-wielding soldiers called to us. *"Drakor sicha,"* he said. *"Likrag'ach."*

I stopped and held up my hands. "We don't speak your language," I said. "Do you speak the Empire tongue?"

"Yes," the soldier said. "Halt. Keep your hands up." Like Warblade, he spoke our tongue with a heavy accent. But at least he understood us.

"We'd like to speak with the leader here," I said.

The soldier didn't bat an eye. "You wait. Stay right there or we shoot."

"Sounds like we wait," I murmured to Geeta and Spud.

We didn't have to stand there for long. Perhaps a minute later, the soldier that had entered the castle came back with someone else in tow.

"Let's definitely not mess with this person," Spud whispered.

Their head was shaved to the stubble, and numerous hoop earrings ran through the cartilage of their left ear. Although they were missing a helm, they wore a full set of armor rivaling the Sunsong bridge captain's armor I had in my Inventory, complete with spike-capped pauldrons polished to a high sheen.

Fortress Commander (Filen Blackhand)

One of the original dwarves who entered the Dark City with the Mad Mage, Blackhand has committed their life to protecting the Mad Mage. If you hadn't guessed from the shaved head and the respect Blackhand commands from their subordinates, they're one

of the most dangerous dwarves in the city. If you want to test your luck, insult the Mad Mage or tell a bad joke in their presence.

"State your business," Blackhand called over the storm.

Time for another lie. I hope this doesn't become a habit.

"We're here by orders of bridge captain Warblade," I said. "The Bridge of Advancement has fallen, but the gate is secure."

Blackhand looked at us suspiciously, their gray eyes taking our measure. "At ease," they said finally. The soldiers relaxed, lowering their crossbows. "You're a friend to the dwarves?"

"Yes. We fought winged imago with them a few hours ago. And before we came here, I killed the last of the giants, which I know are a sworn enemy of dwarves."

That got a raised eyebrow from Blackhand. "The Mad Mage will want to meet you. Come."

They turned on their heel, motioning for us to follow. We didn't need another excuse to get out of the rain. We followed Blackhand up the stairs behind them into a wide tunnel. As we came out the other side, I realized that the building we'd just exited was a defensive structure situated outside the main fortress. The *real* fortress sat on the other side of a massive yard, the curtain wall thick and imposing.

In the yard around us were soldiers sparring or shooting crossbow bolts into distant targets. I watched them train despite the weather, silently thanking the gods we hadn't entered the fortress by force. Even if there'd only been a quarter the number of soldiers, it would've been folly.

It was a testament to the discipline of the dwarves that not a single soldier interrupted their training to watch us. If anything, they fought harder in our presence.

Not our presence, I thought as we crossed the yard. *They're putting on a clinic for Blackhand.*

I knew it wasn't easy to earn respect. I nodded appreciatively, then continued following Blackhand across the stone pathway and through a portcullis that led inside the actual fortress. The entrance was grand and imposing, with stone pillars that supported an arched ceiling high overhead. Each pillar held a lantern that contained the same blue electricity we'd seen outside.

"Are you with the others who arrived here recently?" Blackhand said, interrupting my thoughts.

"Others?" I said curiously.

"The Undead Librarian?" Blackhand said. "The Mechanic? The Grass King?"

"Perhaps," I said. "We're looking for our friends and heard they'd be here."

"You'll meet them soon enough, I'm sure," Blackhand said. "The Mad Mage has a plan, and that plan has a role for all hunters. The Mad Mage will explain when you meet him."

We followed Blackhand as they led us along a thin red carpet that ran to a statue on the opposite side of the room. My heart skipped a beat when I spotted the fountain that surrounded the statue, as I thought it might be a Fountain of Wishes, but then realized it was just a regular fountain.

Anyway, you didn't have gold coins. I wonder what happened to the ones from the party-supply shop...

My thoughts were interrupted by Blackhand. "We had many years where the city thrived," they said as we walked. "But recent years haven't been as kind. We now live in a harder, darker place."

In another context, it might've come off as dramatic. But we'd seen the horrors the dwarves had faced.

"Why is that?" I asked. "What happened?"

Blackhand shook their head. "The Mad Mage will explain."

We climbed a set of stone steps that led to an elevated landing, then followed Blackhand down a corridor. Along the way, we passed several armored dwarves, each of whom gave Blackhand a crisp salute. Soon, we stopped in front of a door.

"Stay here until the Mad Mage calls for you," Blackhand said, their hand on the knob.

"Thank you," I said. "But I thought..."

I trailed off as they pushed open the door. Behind it was a room fit for royalty, made even grander by the hard fighting I'd experienced.

While the rest of the fortress was austere, the room before us was warm and inviting. Sumptuous carpets covered the floor and pillows and blankets lay piled atop the collection of nearby couches. Tapestries hung from the walls and banners draped from the ceiling. A fireplace on the far side of the room contained actual flames, not just the cool blue electricity that lit the lamps outside.

"You will wait until the Mad Mage calls for you," Blackhand repeated, and their voice brooked no argument—not from me, at least. Geeta looked like she might disagree, but I put a hand on her shoulder.

"Very well," I said. We stepped into the room. Blackhand nodded, saluting curtly before shutting the door behind us.

"I did not like their attitude," Geeta growled, her yellow eyes still fixed on the door. "I am debating whether or not to add them to my list. I think a battle between us would be interesting."

Speed and stealth versus strength and technique. "I have no doubt," I said. "But we're on their turf, so let's not antagonize the whole castle, eh? Not when we could be enjoying a fire."

After the Fountain of Wishes, modesty wasn't really on the table. We stripped off our wet clothes, spread them on the stone to dry, and wrapped ourselves in the warm towels someone had left on a nearby chair. One around the waist, one over the shoulders, one tied turban-style around the head. Geeta matched me. Then we collapsed onto the couches.

"It ain't a beach, but I guess it's pretty nice," Spud said from where he sat on the coffee table. "Whatever the Mad Mage wants, let's give it to him. As long as we get to stay here a few more hours."

We'd only been lying on the couches for about an hour before someone knocked on the door.

Geeta groaned. "I am too comfortable to move. If you get it, I will give you the next piece of rare treasure I find."

"Let Spud get it."

Geeta glanced at the table, where Spud was sleeping deeply. "Wake him up, then. But he does not have hands."

"Fine. But I'm holding you to that thing about the treasure." I stood from the couch and started toward the door. Someone knocked again. "Coming! Give me a second."

When I reached the door, I threw the latch and pulled it open. On the other side stood a familiar face. The green tunic and cloth trousers were new, as were the hawk feathers in his hair and the simple gold diadem that hung over his forehead. So was the long sword that hung from his waist.

I knew who it was even before text flashed across my vision.

"Hey there, *pacho*," Jocko said. "Good to see you again."

28

"**Y**ou!"

Jocko wrapped me in a hug. It was the most comforting contact I'd had in a long time, and it felt good. Even though I didn't know him that well, I returned the gesture.

Grass King (Jocko)

Born to the Koa'tan Tribe, Jocko started his military training at the age of four, eventually becoming a high-ranking member of the Thuin armies. During his military tenure, he was confirmed as having fought on the front lines of several of his people's most significant victories. Jocko was captured during the Night of Traitorous Blades and sentenced to Toroth-Gol.

"How are you alive?" I asked. "What are you doing here?"

"I could ask the same about you!" Jocko said. "We should talk, *pacho*. May we come in?"

Behind him stood a small woman with unruly hair that poked through a blue bandana in two puffs. She wore a leather apron, which had a variety of small tools sticking from a pocket in its center. Her right hand was dyed black.

I glanced up to the woman's face to see her grinning at me.

Flight Mechanic (Brynn)

Born with a congenital limb defect, Brynn was left in the desert to die by her parents, a pair of nobles from the Crescent. She was found by a Thuin tribe passing through the area and adopted as one of their own. Although not a Thuin by birth, Brynn considers herself a member of her adopted tribe and has joined them in their fight against the Empire. A brilliant engineer and military tactician, Brynn was captured during the Night of Traitorous Blades and sentenced to Toroth-Gol for treason.

Jocko cleared his throat to get my attention, and I realized that I hadn't answered his question.

"My apologies," I said. "Come in, please."

I stepped away from the door and Jocko slipped past me. As he did, I realized he and Brynn had a third person in their party: the woman I'd defended on the rail car. She looked much like she had when I'd seen her the first time, though now she carried a satchel slung over one shoulder.

Undead Librarian (Rayne)

No one remembers exactly when the mysterious Rayne joined the Thuins. When she did, her martial prowess and sound strategic advice helped her rise in the ranks of the Thuin military. After helping the Thuins emerge victorious in multiple battles against the Empire, Rayne was captured during the Night of Traitorous Blades and sentenced to Toroth-Gol.

Geeta came to stand next to me, her hand around the hilt of her stiletto. "You know these people?"

I put a hand on her shoulder. "These are friends," I said. I didn't know if that was true, exactly, but I didn't think Jocko would hurt us. I turned to face him. "Why don't we sit down?" I said. "I'd love to catch up. I'm sure we have a lot to talk about."

"Excellent idea," Jocko said. He motioned to the couches. "Ladies?"

Brynn and Rayne brushed past me, Brynn with a cheerful nod and Rayne with a grunt and a shake of the charms tied into her dreadlocks. Jocko closed and locked the door, then followed them toward the couches.

"Steady," I said to Geeta, who still hadn't taken her hand from the hilt of her blade. "I trust these people."

She nodded. "Then I will trust them, too. But what are they doing?"

As we watched, Jocko and his companions crossed the room and marked each of the four corners around the sitting area with white, pill-shaped cylinders.

"I'm not sure," I said to Geeta. To Jocko, I said, "What are you doing?"

Jocko turned. When he saw me looking at him, he put a finger to his lips. Then he motioned me inside the invisible square formed by the cylinders.

"Stay calm," I said to Geeta as I felt her tense. I approached Jocko and joined him inside the square. Geeta came to stand beside me. Jocko gave us a thumbs up and nodded to Brynn. Around us, a cube of pink light crackled into existence.

"There we go," Jocko said. "Aural Containment Field." He flopped onto the couch. "Nice little piece of tech Brynn invented for us back in the desert," he said. "Not part of the standard loadout. You wouldn't believe how we got that in here, *pacho*. That wasn't fun for me. Or Brynn, I imagine. *Now* we can talk freely."

"I had to pull it out with these," Brynn said, lifting a pair of tongs from the pocket of her apron.

The cube covered us completely, each corner touching one of the cylinders. "Any chance you have some whiskey?" Jocko said. When I shook my head, he sighed. "There's never any whiskey. I should bring some next time. Don't know where I'd hide it though."

Brynn flashed a wicked grin. "I'm sure we could think of something."

Jocko scoffed. "Sit," he said, patting the couch beside him. "Make yourself comfortable."

We sat. I still had no idea what was going on, but I had a feeling I was about to find out.

"Okay, *pacho*," Jocko said. "Where to begin? Remember on the train, when I said that you didn't need to protect Rayne? I didn't mean you should avoid picking fights with guards—though that's a good idea in general. I meant that Rayne could take care of herself. You see, she's the second highest-ranking member of the Thuin army."

I glanced over at Rayne, who sat just like she had been on the train. She was completely still, her dreadlocks hanging over her face. The golden charms in her hair contained more than just colored stones. One was carved into a tiny sword, another was shaped like a spear. There were also multiple skulls.

"Her?" I was skeptical. "I don't mean to be rude, but can she even hear us?"

If Rayne *could* hear, she didn't respond.

"She can hear you," Jocko said. "She's just thinking about other things." He tapped a tan ear. "She can hear ghosts. Could do it even before we got here. They tell her things."

"Things?" Geeta said.

"It's how we know about what's down here," Jocko continued. "How we knew about the Dark City too. I lied to you, in the car. I told you I was here because I killed a man who disrespected my sister. But I'm here because the only person above Rayne in the Thuin army is me."

"You," I responded.

He flashed me a smile. "Yup."

"*You're* the Desert Blade?"

"Always loved that nickname. At your service. Let me explain."

Before he could continue, Spud awoke. He'd been so quiet I'd forgotten he was on the table. Now he yawned, rotated to face me, and blinked the sleep from his eyes. When he saw Jocko sitting next to me, he said, "Hiya, stranger! I'm Spud!"

What happened next can only be described as chaos. Jocko stood, a sword appearing in his hand. I hadn't even seen him draw it. Brynn was also on her feet; a translucent blue shield had popped into existence around her and she held a baton, the tip crackling with electricity. Geeta seized Brynn's wrist, another hand extended toward Jocko, and she was yelling, "Stop! Stop!" Spud was screaming. Only Rayne and I hadn't moved: Rayne because she didn't seem bothered, and me because everything had happened so quickly I hadn't had time to react. The crinkle of a smile peeked out from behind Rayne's dreadlocks.

"What in the name of a desert lizard's underbelly is *that?*" Jocko yelled, looking down at Spud.

"Uh, rude," Spud said. "I could say the same thing about you. What's a Grass King?"

"Everybody calm down," I said, holding up my hands. "This is Spud. Uh, Spud is my primary weapon. He's a sapient, electromagnetically charged potato. With elemental powers. Spud, this is Jocko, Brynn, and Rayne."

Jocko squinted at Spud. "That's interesting," he said. "Apologies if we got off on the wrong foot, *pacho.*" He sheathed his sword and sat back down. His movement broke Brynn from a spell, because almost at the exact same time, the translucent shield disappeared and she placed the baton back in a holster at her hip. Then she sat down, too.

"An honest mistake, I'm sure," Spud said. "A pleasure to meet the three of you."

"Uh, where were we in your story, *majoré?*" I said to Jocko. "I think you were telling us that you're the Desert Blade?"

Just saying the words out loud made my head spin. Supposedly, the Desert Blade was the bane of the Empire's existence, a peerless general who'd led the Thuins in their guerrilla tactics. To be honest, I'd always assumed the Desert Blade was an invention of the Empire, a scapegoat created for citizens to curse and burn in effigy. Now, the long-limbed swordsman who'd sat beside me on the rail car—and who was sitting next to me in Toroth-Gol—was claiming the name for himself.

"That's right," Jocko said. From anyone else, the words would've been crazy. But there was something about the way Jocko carried himself that made me want to hear him out. "I'm the Desert Blade, as my father was before me."

"But you got captured?" Geeta said.

Brynn laughed, then said, "In a sense. We put ourselves here on purpose, based on information that Rayne got from her communion with the spirits."

"On what?" I said. "Why?"

Brynn raised an eyebrow at me. "You know the rules of this game?" she asked. "Ten levels, grab the Heart of the World, and you go free?"

I nodded. "Of course."

"Do you know what the Heart of the World *is*?"

I rubbed a hand over my head. "Not really. I assumed it was a jewel. A piece of treasure or something."

Now it was Brynn's turn to nod. "It's both of those things. But more importantly, it's the source of magic. The source of the spirits that Rayne hears. *That's* why the Empire wants it—whoever controls the Heart of the World controls magic."

That didn't add up. "The Empire hates magic," I said.

"Because they can't control it," Jocko said. "If they could, don't you think they'd use it?"

I thought about my father's mines, and the millions of pounds of ore that enslaved prisoners dragged out of the ground to produce the Empire's great war machines. I remembered the great fortifications and cannons we'd seen strewn throughout the Wastes on the ride to Toroth-Gol. The Empire used metal because it was convenient. But I knew that Jocko spoke the truth: when it came to expansion, control, and dominion, the Empire would use any tool at its disposal.

Now Geeta jumped in. "Let us say you are right, and that the

Empire wants the Heart of the World. That makes the dungeon... what, exactly? A defense mechanism?"

"Yes," Jocko responded. "It ensures that only the strongest have a chance at taking the Heart of the World. Because you need to be strong to wield the source of magic itself. The Empire knows this, so they send their prisoners after it. Most likely, the prisoners die in their quest. Not only does the Empire solve a big problem, but they also get some great content. And if a prisoner *does* happen to make it through, they come out of Toroth-Gol with the Heart of the World—which the Empire will promptly take."

"But Thuins want the Heart of the World, too," I said.

"Of course," Jocko said. "We're losing the war, *pacho*. Every season it drags on, the Empire pushes my people farther into the Wastes. Now they have camps for us. There's infighting among our tribes for the first time in centuries. So, we took a risk. We put ourselves in Toroth-Gol. And we brought a secret weapon."

Geeta fixed him with her yellow gaze. "What is that?"

Surprisingly, instead of responding to her, Jocko looked at me. He drummed the fingers of one hand against his muscular upper arm. "Do you know?"

I shook my head. "Me? What are you talking about?"

Jocko sat up and leaned forward. "I'm going to tell you both something a little odd. Have you ever heard the name Jaguar?"

"Jaguar?" I looked to Geeta, but she shook her head.

"Leader of the Empire," Jocko said.

"August Morgan is the leader of the Empire," I said. It was impossible to walk the streets of Gomindor without seeing his face plastered on a hundred different screens and posters. "Is Jaguar his nickname?"

"Nah," Brynn said. "Morgan is Prime Minister. Jaguar is Jaguar. Who do you think put Morgan in his position? *Jaguar* is the one behind the Empire. The brains behind the whole stinking operation."

I'd never heard of anything like that. Before I could say as much, Jocko said, "You're going to tell me you've never heard of Jaguar. But isn't that the point? If you were the *actual* leader of the Empire, wouldn't it make sense to stay in the shadows?"

I had to admit that he was right. If I knew people were gunning for me, I'd try to stay behind the scenes.

"Jaguar, then," I said. "I'll play along. What about him?"

"He's my enemy," Jocko said. "*Our* enemy. Your father's enemy, too. Your father was a traitor to the Empire, *pacho*. He's been working with the Thuins for three decades."

My stomach dropped and the skin of my arms prickled with gooseflesh. "My father would never betray the Empire," I said, speaking the words automatically. But even as they left my lips, I knew they weren't true. How many times had he told me about the future his late wife had imagined for Steel City? A free society with all classes free from the tyranny of enslavement? Despite the words he spoke in public, my father had no love for the Empire. His allegiance was with society's underdogs.

Brynn stared at me. "He knows it's true. I see it in his eyes."

I couldn't speak. I swallowed and tried again. "Let's say that you're right. So what? What does it mean?"

"Your father has been my people's most valuable source of information about the Empire's movements for the past thirty years," Jocko said. "He was my father's closest confidant, and when my father died, that relationship passed to me. It was Sal Valentine who came up with the idea for this plan."

"Plan?" I said.

"If we were ever getting beaten so badly that it looked like we'd lose everything, we needed to take drastic action," Jocko continued. "One final push for the Heart of the World. We'd stack the dungeon with Thuins—and our secret weapon. A sleeper agent with no love for the Empire, pulled from the Dregs and trained by Valentine himself."

The implications of what he'd said hit me. "You're talking about me."

"Of course," Jocko said. "Your father knew Lucca Bert was trailing him. He knew that it was time. He met with us and let Lucca take pictures. Made Lucca think he'd discovered a secret Thuin plot. At the same time, we let the Empire's soldiers follow us back to the desert. Three days later, they rounded us up like sheep."

I shook my head. "I don't understand. You couldn't have been sure they would send you to Toroth-Gol instead of killing you on the spot."

Brynn shrugged. "It was either take the risk or die. We took the risk."

I looked from Jocko to Brynn, and from Brynn to Rayne. *These people are insane.* And yet, most of what they'd said made sense. *Everything except the part about me.*

"I still don't understand how I fit into the picture," I said. "I'm nothing special. You're saying that my whole life has been some sort of contingency plan?"

"Crow, look at yourself," Brynn said. "You're a super weapon. Your aptitude tests are off the charts. You've been trained to defend yourself since you were ten. You've spent the last decade honing your body and practicing leadership on the field. And what's more, you have no more love for the Empire than your father. You might not have much experience with magic, but you have more raw talent than anyone else in here. That's talent we can *train.*"

"Train?"

Jocko sighed. "We don't know where your father is now, and I'm sorry he never told you the truth. But you're not here by accident. We're after the same thing. All of us. The Heart of the World. The end of the Empire. We'll find your father, or we'll avenge him. And Geeta, whatever you're after—"

"I will take care of that myself," she said. "Until then, our interests are aligned. I will help your cause."

Jocko nodded, then looked at his engineer. "Brynn, are you done aligning those devices for them?"

"Just about." A spark zipped from the tip of her gold index finger to an object she held in her other palm. "There's one."

She tossed the object to me and I caught it, realizing that I now held a metal disc about the size of an Empire mark. But instead of August Morgan's face on one side and the Helios city skyline on the other, this disc was smooth as glass and the color of quicksilver.

Brynn's Radio Frequency Interference Device

A proprietary technology developed by the Thuin engineer Brynn, this disc has the ability to restrict the feed that runs from your ocular implant to the Empire's media groups for thirty seconds. To use it, simply remove it from your Inventory and think *activate*. The device can be used once every hour.

I glanced up at Brynn and she winked at me. "Put that in your Inventory," she said, and I made it disappear. "Same goes for you, Geeta. Here, I've got one for you too."

Another spark left Brynn's finger and she threw a second disc to Geeta. The reptilian snatched the disc from the air and made it vanish.

"What's the plan, then?" I said. "What do we do?"

"Now we find the door to the next level," Jocko said. "And we fight for our lives. Maybe we'll even beat the thing. Eight levels after this one, we're out of here. Eight more levels and we can destroy the Empire. You in?"

It wasn't even a choice. "Let's destroy the Empire," I said.

29

From our room, Jocko and his crew led us to the basement of the castle.

"What we've managed to uncover is that the door to leave this level is in the tunnels beneath the fortress," he said as we walked. "It's guarded by something called—"

"The subterranean wyrm queen!" Spud said excitedly. "Crow and I were down in those tunnels. We both saw it!"

"Then you know we're not just going to walk past it," Jocko said. "That thing could crush us all without even waking up. Which is why we've been working with the Mad Mage on an alternative solution."

"Oh?" I said.

We stopped in a circular vestibule and Brynn put a hand on the knob of the door in front of her. "The Mad Mage's laboratory is just on the other side of this door," she said. "He'll want to invite you in himself, which is a good thing. In dwarven culture, an invitation of hospitality is sacrosanct. It means he won't harm you. When you meet him, uh... well, the Mad Mage is particular. You'll see what I mean. But he's brilliant. An absolute genius. So just go with it, okay? Just listen and don't say anything to upset him. Yeah?"

"Uh, okay?" I said.

"Great," Brynn said. "I'll be right back."

With that, she disappeared through the door. I looked to Jocko, who met my gaze. He shrugged. "He's a little eccentric, is all," he said. "Just let him talk. You'll be fine."

The door opened again, and Brynn came back into the vestibule with a dwarf in tow.

"Crow, Geeta, Spud," she said. "This is the Mad Mage."

I'm not sure what I'd expected. From the name, maybe someone with a pointy wizard's hat. But the Mad Mage looked more like an engineer than a wizard. He was a dwarf; similar to Brynn, he carried a variety of tools, though he kept his in holsters wrapped around his thighs. The top of his head was bald and wrinkled like a baby bird, with liver spots giving an indication of his age. His bushy white eyebrows ran almost all the way over to his ears. He had a full mustache and beard, and the mustache was dyed brown above his mouth with the type of stain that could only come from decades of smoking pipe tobacco. His beard was separated into two braids, each held together with a gold ring.

Artificer (Mad Mage)

Once the king of the dwarves, the Mad Mage's experiments with interdimensional travel accidentally unleashed the Insanity upon the world. To save his people, the Mad Mage created the Castle of 1,000 Doors, which allowed dwarves to flee to all corners of the multiverse in an event known as the Great Exodus. For the last hundred years, the Mad Mage has worked to undo his accidental crimes and create a safe passage for his people to return to their home world. He's one of the most brilliant engineers and tacticians in all of the many worlds.

The Mad Mage grinned at us, his teeth as stained as his mustache.

"Greetings, friends," he said. "Call me the Mad Mage. Everyone does." He gave a cackling laugh. "I've heard you're going to help with the wyrm. I'd like to invite you inside. You're just in time to witness our final preparations."

He stepped through the door and our group followed him into his laboratory. Wires dangled from the ceiling and cables ran along the walls. There were scorch marks on the floor. Broken beakers and spilled chemicals sat under acid-eaten tables. In one corner of the room, a desk was piled high with books, many of which had been pushed off and now lay on the floor. In another, a massive ball hung from the ceiling by a coiled tube, spitting arcs of electricity to smaller balls on the top of several tanks.

As I looked around, a description of the lab popped into my vision.

Dark City (Thaumaturgic Laboratory)

Located in the bowels of the Electric Fortress, the thaumaturgic laboratory is the dominion of the Mad Mage, the former dwarf king and artificer who accidentally unleashed the Insanity and built the Castle of 1,000 Doors. From this lab, the Mad Mage has created many of his most enduring inventions.

"Let me show you some of my creations," the Mad Mage said as he led us toward a small mountain of metal. "No need to fear them, as you're my guests. Beast! Reveal thyself."

To my surprise, the mountain of metal before us moved, the silver plates unfolding like a flower in bloom. I stepped back as they took the shape of a bear, fifteen feet tall and covered in armored plating. It stood on all fours with its head bowed. "Beautiful, isn't it?" the Mad Mage continued. "My second experiment with constructs. I call him the Beast of Ending. Beast, for short."

The bear had channels that ran from its eyes to a circular sigil on its chest. As I watched, the sigil glowed with blue light that spread through the channels to its torso, and then to its paws and eyes. Its eyes glowed blue, and it lifted its head to face us.

Doomsday Construct, II of III (the Beast of Ending)

One of three Doomsday Constructs created by the Mad Mage to protect the Dark City. In addition to savaging enemies with its massive claws and teeth, the Beast of Ending can shoot beams of superheated plasma from its eyes.

"Greetings, human," Beast said. "Greetings, reptilian. Greetings, tuber." The metal bear grinned.

This must be Metalhawk's younger brother, I thought as I looked into its glowing blue eyes. I could tell that its grin was an attempt to scare me, but I wouldn't show fear—at least, not outwardly. On the inside, my stomach felt queasy and it took all the willpower I possessed to stop myself from turning on my battery pack.

As terrifying as the Doomsday Constructs were, I couldn't help but wonder what type of threat an army of them would pose to the Empire. In the desert outside Steel City, I'd seen the machines the Empire had built with metal from my father's mines to wage war against the Thuins. While they were impressive, they weren't nearly as powerful or versatile as Metalhawk. And from Beast's description —not to mention the personal view of the construct I had from ten feet away—I could tell that it'd be as fearsome of a fighter as its brother.

Two hundred Beasts of Ending and a hundred Metalhawks would be enough to take Steel City. Is it possible to reproduce these machines outside of the dungeon?

"Hello, Beast," I said, still forcing myself to maintain eye contact. To the Mad Mage, I said, "How are the constructs made? Is it a laborious process?"

"Hmm," the Mad Mage said. "Ordinarily, I wouldn't reveal a secret like this. The baker never gives a recipe to his neighbor, eh? But I respect your intellectual curiosity, so I'll tell you: the creation of the constructs requires a magically-augmented technology known as soul transference. For better or worse, the process is no longer viable. It's possible to create a construct, but the knowledge required to keep it under control was lost with the giants." He shook his head as if lamenting the loss to the scientific community. "With enough time,

I'm sure I could rediscover it," he said. "Though lately, I've been a bit preoccupied."

So much for that idea. But maybe it was for the best. Fiction was littered with tales of worlds in which technology like the Mad Mage had described was accessible, and none of those stories ended well.

The Mad Mage seemed to have complete control over the weapon that stood before me. He waved a hand at Beast and said, "Back to sleep, my pet." Immediately, the light faded from Beast's eyes and the construct sat back on its haunches, its armored plates rearranging until it once again resembled an inert mountain of metal.

"Whoa," Spud whispered. "I was thinking it'd be cool to ride one of those into battle, but maybe some technologies are better left to history."

The Mad Mage continued his tour, leading us past Beast and around the tanks. "Beast has two brothers," he said as we walked. "One of them took some damage in the recent excitement. Not as much as poor Metalhawk, but enough to put him down for the count. We're fixing them both up right now."

As I came around the tanks, I stopped in my tracks. Behind them, Metalhawk lay on a stone slab like a dead body at a morgue, its great wings taking up half that side of the room. When I looked at it, I saw the same text that had appeared when I'd seen Metalhawk for the first time in the streets of the Dark City.

Beside Metalhawk, a second creature hung from chains that dangled from the ceiling. Unlike Metalhawk and the Beast of Ending, this creature was sleeker. It was perhaps fifteen feet tall and shaped like a human. Instead of a head, its neck ended in a pointed spike. Beneath the neck, transparent plates gave a view into the creature's inner workings, which even now pulsed with yellow light.

"What a strange family," Spud said.

I wanted to reply, but I found myself speechless. *Technology that's best left to history, indeed.* With the ability to mass produce the constructs, someone with twisted intentions would *absolutely* take over the world. As I watched, robotic arms moved around the humanoid creature, throwing off sparks as they sealed rivets and massaged the smooth mesh that formed the connections between its armored plates.

Doomsday Construct, III of III (Ramzoid)

One of three Doomsday Constructs created by the Mad Mage to protect the Dark City. Ramzoid is the most melee-focused of the constructs, capable of covering vast distances in a short amount of time and goring opponents with its massive spike.

"My third baby is named Ramzoid," the Mad Mage said. "Say hello, Ramzoid."

At the sound of its name, the creature turned the spike of its neck toward us. I couldn't see any eyes, yet I knew Ramzoid was watching us, somehow. A screeching rose from inside the creature's body and I immediately had to clap my hands to my ears.

That's almost worse than Cravag. Luckily, the screech was short lived.

The Mad Mage, who had also covered his ears, lowered his hands and smiled bashfully. "Like I said, getting some repairs. Come along."

The Mad Mage led us to a table in one corner of the room. There were eight seats, so each of us took one, with Spud taking a spot on the table and the Mad Mage sitting at the head. Once we were seated, the Mad Mage leaned forward and lifted a pitcher, pouring crimson liquid into nearby glasses. When the liquid hit a glass, it started to glow.

"Are you a scientist, Mr. Crow?" the Mad Mage asked, handing me a glass. I lifted it to my nose; it smelled like cinnamon and cloves. I set the glass back on the table. Although I trusted the Mad Mage's hospitality, I'd long made a point of avoiding unidentified liquids. It was a tenet that had served me well throughout my life, especially during the years I spent playing lightball with Grog, who'd frequently brought his god-awful home brew into the locker room.

Grog. My stomach clenched with a pang of homesickness. *I wonder what he's doing right now. And Zorba, and Kenzo, and Enrique. Hell, I even miss Croyden.*

In my mind's eye, I saw Magnus hosting a viewing party of the Hunt in his father's home theater. Servants passed around little sandwiches and petits fours.

"Mr. Crow?" the Mad Mage said, bringing me back to the table.

"Sorry," I said. "Crow is fine. And I know a little about the sciences."

That was an understatement. Growing up, my father had made me read the seminal works of all thirty-two of the Empire's classic scientists. By ten, I'd memorized the periodic table of elements. At twelve, I could build an electrolyzer with my eyes closed.

Perhaps there is some truth to my role as a secret weapon. Why else make sure I was well-versed in so many different disciplines?

But I didn't like to show off. When you were a star athlete *and* you could build your own set of lightball gloves from tin foil, paperclips, and a battery, people tended to hate you on principle. Besides, I'd always found that if you feigned ignorance, experts tended to be less guarded with their knowledge.

The Mad Mage nodded and turned his attention to Geeta. "And you?"

Geeta shook her head. "I would not call myself a scientist. Not like you and Brynn."

Again, the Mad Mage nodded, the braids of his mustache bouncing against his beard. *I wonder if she's telling the truth. Or if she's playing the same game as me?* Although I trusted Geeta, there was still much I didn't know about her past.

"I'll give you the layman's version," the Mad Mage said. "Prior to the Insanity, giants and dwarves were the closest of allies. Perhaps you know what they say about strange bedfellows, hmm? We'd thrown in our lots together, and we lived side-by-side. In fact, at that time, we even ruled from the same castle. You've been there, I think. The one with all the doors? Back then, we called it the Kingdom. It was our name for the land and the castle at its center, a symbol of peace between our people." He lifted his glass and swirled the liquid. "As king, I had a number of rooms in the Kingdom, but my favorite was a laboratory that I shared with Verona, my counterpart among the giants. She was an intellectual talent unlike any other. Brynn comes close, but even Brynn couldn't have matched pawns with Verona in a game of ravens." The Mad Mage glanced at Brynn. "No offense."

"None taken," Brynn said.

The Mad Mage took a sip of his drink, then set the glass back on the table. "Together, Verona and I built many beautiful things. We brought electricity to the Kingdom. Discovered how to use Soul Cores to create sapient artificial intelligence. Eventually, my research led me to explore interdimensional spaces. Other worlds, if you will. Picture it: a door in reality that led to another world. You could head there for breakfast and be back in your kitchen for lunch." He gave a bitter laugh. "Verona warned me of the dangers, yet I ignored her. I thought I had everything under control. But something went wrong. Though I went to other worlds, I never suspected that something might follow me home. That's how the Insanity entered our world. You've heard of it?"

I nodded. The Mad Mage took another sip of his beverage.

"At the beginning, we saw a few cases of giants with strange rashes and runny noses," he continued. "Then the symptoms grew more severe. Giants in the grip of the Insanity experienced dark thoughts. They wanted to hurt things. To kill. As soon as Verona and I realized what was happening, we started working on a cure. We tried every possible solution: biological, technical, magical. The Insanity didn't respond to any of it. By then, it had become a full-blown pandemic. And the giants who suffered the disease were relentless. They didn't only devour their prey. They went cruel. They created ever-worsening methods of hurt and torture. Once they fixated on something, they stopped at nothing to get it."

The Mad Mage finished the liquid in his cup and set it back on the table.

"It was Verona who came up with the solution," he said. "Brilliant Verona, before the Insanity took her, offered us a way out. Using the technology I'd developed, we could create a castle with a thousand doors, a thousand separate escape hatches. Maybe some of them would lead to unpalatable landscapes, but at least it gave my people a chance. A chance to flee. A chance to escape. It wasn't even that difficult, as creating that many rifts in the world doesn't take much. With an understanding of the technique, you could probably do it yourself. But keeping it stable is another story. Once you walk through the door, you want to be able to get back out. And for that, you need a tremendous amount of energy. We racked our brains for an answer, only to discover it was lying here, right below our feet."

The memory of the coils running through the underground caves came back to me. "The subterranean wyrm queen," I said. "You harnessed her power."

The Mad Mage nodded. "From our first journeys into this world, we knew about the subterranean wyrm queen," he said. "She was one of our first discoveries. A nocturnal, oxygen-breathing animal with the genetics of a dragon. She contained three separate electric organs that... well, you don't need to hear specifics. The short version is that she has the ability to discharge tremendous amounts of electricity. Enough for us to open a thousand doors and keep them stable."

Spud jumped in. "How'd you capture her?" he asked. "That thing is huge!" Before the Mad Mage could answer, he continued, "Oh right. You had giants."

"Yes," the Mad Mage said. "At the time, we did. In a week, we'd created a thousand doors to a thousand different worlds and gotten out as many dwarves through as we could. Of course, it was a bittersweet victory—on the fourth day of that week, Verona killed herself. I came into the lab and found that she'd slit her own throat. Sweet, brilliant Verona. Even as she'd fought to save us, she'd known the Insanity was taking her mind. She couldn't bear the thought of hurting her friends. Hurting me. Even though my actions had been responsible for the death of her people."

The room fell silent. After a few seconds, the Mad Mage continued.

"When I first got here, I wanted to die. But I needed to hold myself together. More than ever, my people needed me. So I went about my business making sure the doors remained stable. Because if the doors closed, I didn't know if I could open them again. My people would be permanently scattered across the multiverse.

"The wyrm queen offered the solution. As so often happens in science, the solution to one problem is the genesis of another. Most days, the wyrm queen lay dormant. But every time the doors opened, it sent the queen into a frenzy. Her children would respond in-kind." He shook his head. "What could we do? You can see what a century of exodus has done to our people. We're a fraction of what we once were. If we release the wyrm queen, we give up the dream of reuniting the dwarves. Without her power, the doors slam shut forever."

I sat on the edge of my seat and put my mind to work on a solution. When Brynn stood up, I realized they already had one.

"What do you know of bone?" she asked.

"Bone?" I said.

"Bone." She patted her arm. The real one. "This stuff."

"What's the context?" I asked.

Brynn walked to a nearby table and lifted a club. *Not a club*, I realized as she held it to the light. *Bone. A femur.*

"Bone is technically an organ," Brynn said. She turned the femur in her hand. "It forms the structure of most vertebrate animals. It's lightweight but strong. Hard but flexible. Humans are born with something like three hundred bones, but many fuse together as a person ages, meaning the average human adult has around two hundred. Dwarves are smaller creatures, so they have fewer bones, though the ones they have are thicker. Denser. Ultimately, despite our differences in size, the volume of bone in a human adult is roughly the same as it is in a full-grown dwarf."

She came back to the table and handed me the femur. I took it awkwardly. It was off-white, about a foot and a half long, and rough to the touch.

Why am I holding a bone? Where is this going?

"Before we were arrested, I was working on an energy project for the Thuins," Brynn continued. "Brynn's Spike, I called it. A theoretical device that, if realized, would provide limitless energy."

I handed the bone to Geeta. "And that is good?" Geeta asked.

Brynn gave her a pitying look. "If I'd brought that science to life, I wouldn't be here right now," she said. "I'd have a seat on the Empire Council." She held out her hand and Geeta gave the femur back to her. "The challenge in making this theoretical device was mass-producing a piece called the porous carbon electrode," she said. "It's what makes the device work. Just like you can't have lightball without a lightball, you can't have Brynn's Spike without the porous carbon electrode. That's where bone comes in. Outside of the body, bone has no practical applications beyond the creation of bone ash. 55.82 percent calcium oxide, 42.39 percent phosphorus pentoxide, and 1.79 percent water. But most of the time, bones get buried. I found another use: the microporous structure of bone is *exactly* what's needed to create the porous carbon electrode."

From her Inventory, Brynn pulled a flat white square, maybe six inches by six inches, and set it on the table.

Brynn's Spike (Semi-Fused)

An almost-perfect version of Brynn's Spike. A source of unlimited power.

"Compared to anything else I've ever built, this device has fifty times the discharge capacity with virtually no risk of charge overpotential," Brynn said. "I'd need more research to make an estimate of its longevity, but we've run and refilled this little guy over two hundred times already with no signs of degradation."

Spud whistled. Everyone at the table turned to stare at him.

"That's impressive, right?" he said. "Sorry—from the way you said that, I assumed it was good."

"It's *very* good," the Mad Mage said. "In fact, it's the missing piece in a plan I've been developing to stabilize the doors *without* the need to keep the wyrm queen captive."

"I knew it was good," Spud mumbled into my ear. "Just saying."

Brynn nodded to me. "Your timing was perfect," she said. "If you'd gotten here in another few days, we wouldn't have been around."

"Tomorrow, we take the next step toward a peaceful future for my people," the Mad Mage said. "For the last hundred years, we've been burying our dead in the tunnels beneath the city. We've also been throwing the bodies of dead lamprey and winged imago over the bridges. Between what's under the plateau and what's around it, we have more than enough bone to make a battery that would keep the doors open for the next five hundred years."

I rubbed a hand over the stubble on my scalp. "You want to replace the subterranean wyrm queen with a hyper-efficient battery made from bone," I said. "That's ambitious."

Brynn smiled. "Glad we're on the same page," she said.

"But how are you going to collect the bone?" Geeta asked. "If I understand what you are saying, you will need quite a lot."

"Leave that to us," Brynn said. "I want to maintain *some* element of surprise, or you'll start to doubt my genius."

"We need another day to finish preparations," the Mad Mage said. "Until then, feel free to avail yourself of our facilities. We have a smithy, quiet rooms for resting, and a fully stocked larder. And Jocko has been making good use of our training room. Jocko, would you like to show them?"

I glanced over at Jocko. "Thank you, *pacho*," the Thuin said. "I was going to suggest it myself."

I can't say I liked the devilish smile that spread across his face.

30

While Brynn, the Mad Mage, and Rayne finished their 'preparations,' Jocko brought us to the training room. As we pushed inside, I expected to see a room that looked similar to the gym at the Salvador Valentine Center for Athletics.

Instead, I found myself on the ground level of a six-story coliseum. The floor was made of hard-packed sand. Spread across the sand were boulders and patches of green weeds that looked a bit like dandelion leaves. High stone walls separated the floor from stadium seating that looked down onto the pit.

Dark City (Training Room)

There used to be some pretty heavy-hitting magicians among the dwarves. Most of them are gone, but this enchanted training room remains.

"There's an enchantment on this room," Jocko said as he pointed into the stands. "Anything above the second level of seats isn't real. Go too high and you'll smash your head on the invisible ceiling." He rubbed the back of his head. "Trust me when I tell you that hurts."

I nodded. "So how does it work?" I asked. "Do we spar or something?"

Jocko shook his head. "Not quite," he said. "Follow me." He led us farther into the room, kicking up sand with each step. He stopped at a metal gate that was embedded in the far wall and pulled it open.

"Who'd like to go first?" he asked.

"Pick us!" Spud said as he bounced up and down on my shoulder. "We want to test the magical coliseum first!"

Jocko nodded. "Great," he said. "Geeta, you're with me. Crow and Spud, go stand in the center of the arena."

Geeta followed Jocko into the cave behind the gate, which Jocko closed behind them. Suddenly, I felt very vulnerable.

"Uh, can you give me a clue as to what I'm doing out here?" I asked.

"Training, *pacho*," Jocko said. "I already told you as much. I'll feed you instructions. Start in the center. Over there, by that grassy patch."

Training. I can do that. I've spent a lifetime in training. Then again, I've never trained inside an enchanted coliseum, but I suppose there's a first time for everything.

I turned and walked toward the aforementioned patch. As I did, I flipped the switch on my battery pack, which started up with a hum. Then I pulled Spud from my shoulder and set him to hover above my left hand.

"Quick note," I said to him. "You shouldn't volunteer us for things that might involve our death."

Spud rolled his eyes. "Don't be so dramatic, Crow," he said. "This will be *fun*. Besides, Jocko seems nice. I don't think he'd do anything to hurt us."

I'm not so sure about that, I thought, remembering his devilish grin. But like it or not, I was along for the ride. I got to the patch that Jocko had described and dug a foot into the sand.

"I'm here," I called toward the gate. "What now?"

Geeta and Jocko were hunched over a waist-high podium, both of them focused on something that covered its surface. From where I stood, I couldn't see what they were looking at, but they spoke to each other in hushed voices.

"Jocko, I'm here," I said. "What do you want me to do?"

The Grass King looked up as he pressed one hand against something on the podium's surface. For some reason, his expression was apologetic.

"Remember, the things you see in here are magical constructs," he said. "They'll feel real, but they're not actually going to kill you. Trust me on this one. I can help you get stronger, though I'll need to push you."

From somewhere deep below my feet, the ground started to rumble. Behind me, something screeched. I whirled around, ducking into a low stance and raising Spud in front of me, my eyes scanning the coliseum for an enemy.

The sound had come from a portcullis on the far side of the coliseum that lifted into the air.

Something bad is coming out of there, I thought as I stared into the gaping black tunnel behind the portcullis that led below the stands.

"Remember what I said," Jocko called from behind me. He had to yell so I could hear him over the rumbling. "Nothing here is going to kill you. Good luck!"

The rumbling stopped. As I narrowed my eyes, a shape materialized in the tunnel's depths. I blinked, trying to understand what I was seeing. Then electric light illuminated the darkness, and I found myself staring at the Beast of Ending.

"By the Dregs," I whispered as text popped into my vision.

The Beast of Ending (Simulated Construct)

This isn't the *real* Beast of Ending. It'll still mess up your day. In addition to savaging enemies with its massive claws and teeth, the Beast of Ending can shoot beams of superheated plasma from its eyes.

"Greetings, human," it said, a voice coming through a speaker at its throat. "Greetings, tuber. Shall we fight?"

"Honestly?" I said. "I'd rather not."

Beast didn't seem to hear me. It lumbered into the arena, snuffling as it tossed its head one way and then the other. Behind it, the portcullis closed.

"This isn't great," Spud said. "Okay, one point for you, Crow. I probably shouldn't have volunteered us to go first."

I didn't respond. *Don't show fear*, I thought as I stared Beast down. Of course, that was easier said than done. But I knew how to handle a predator. It was something Valentine had taught me after my first lightball match. Show weakness to a predator and you only made them stronger. If you wanted to survive, you needed to turn the hunter into the hunted.

"I am sorry, human," Beast said. "I am sorry, tuber. I must end both of your lives."

Since I was looking directly into Beast's eyes, I noticed when they started to glow.

"Dive!" Spud shouted, but I'd already started moving. As I scrambled for cover, I activated Spud's flames and sent him shooting toward the metal bear.

"*Arghhhhhh!*" he screamed as he left my hand.

Two beams of superheated plasma cut the air where I'd been standing and immediately turned the sand to glass. I came up on my feet and ducked behind the nearest boulder, pressing my back to the stone and trying to catch my breath.

How long does it take Beast to recharge his plasma beams? Does he even need to recharge? If there isn't some type of refractory period, I'm a goner. Even with cover, I can't outrun continuous plasma blasts. Not for long, anyway.

On the other side of the arena, Spud continued to scream. "Pull me back! It burns, baby! Burns so good! Pull me back!"

I risked a quick peek around the boulder. Even though I hadn't seen Spud hit Beast, I knew I'd landed a direct hit. You don't play lightball at its highest level for a decade without being able to fire precision shots under pressure.

But if Spud had done any damage to the Beast, I couldn't see where. Now the flaming potato rolled around Beast's legs, dodging to avoid getting crushed.

With a thought, I extinguished Spud's flames. I activated my right glove and yanked Spud toward me as Beast launched a new attack. Using its front claws like shovels, the metal bear furiously swiped at Spud, its claws moving more quickly than my eyes could follow. There was flying sand, and then Beast was shoulder deep in a pit of its own making. Had I not pulled Spud toward me, he would've been shredded.

"Thanks for that," Spud said as he landed in my palm. "Any idea how to kill this thing?"

"Not at all," I said. "I was hoping you might have some thoughts."

"But you're the ideas guy," Spud said. "I'm just the face. And the brawn. Pretty much everything *but* the ideas, if we're being honest."

Beast exploded from the pit, spraying clumps of sand and grass that peppered the entire arena. I ducked back behind the boulder, then fell to the ground as something slammed into the other side of the rock.

Did Beast charge me? But no. From the sound of his roar, I could tell that he was still on the other side of the arena. *Plasma beams. There were maybe ten seconds between his first shot and that last one.*

I spit out a mouthful of dirt and climbed to my feet. "For a simulation, this sure feels like the real deal," I said. I needed time to think. As good of a shot as I was, I didn't see any gaps in the creature's armor. Which made my primary weapon pretty much useless.

What else can I do? I can't throw crossbow bolts or jars of pickled vegetables at Beast. Or, I could, but I doubt they'd do anything. Maybe the ham could work as a distraction.

"The club, man," Spud said. "Use Giant's Roar with the Clockwork Guardian's Club!"

It was the one thing that might work. But I'd only use that as a last resort. The only other time I'd used the strategy, I'd been left so weak and achy that I'd wanted to die.

I'd taken too long to make my decision. Spud had just enough time to yell, "Watch out!" before Beast landed directly atop the boulder before me. Jagged slivers of rock peppered my face and a mighty paw slammed into my side. I didn't feel anything break, but I swear my ribcage creaked. I was thrown a good twenty feet across the arena, Spud flying free as I tumbled through the air.

Let Spud get away, at least. I landed with a painful crunch. *Let that sweet potato survive to roast another day.*

I was loopy. Maybe I *had* broken something. But it didn't matter. Beast stood above me, his bulky form blocking out the sky. He roared before standing on his hind legs and beating his chest in triumph. Then his head snapped downward, his jaws wide as he moved for a killing blow.

I curled into myself, expecting to feel the creature's teeth on my neck. My death never came. Instead of ending my life, Beast froze. I lay beneath him, my arms crossed and my knees pulled to my chest, gasping for breath and trying to reconcile my continued life with what seemed like an inevitable demise.

I could hear my heart pounding in my chest. After a while, when it became clear that Beast wasn't going to kill me, I rolled out from under him. Only once I stood did Beast move again, turning around and padding lightly toward the portcullis, which opened to receive him. As I watched him go, I noticed the sheet of glass that'd been formed when Beast's plasma had struck the sand was gone. Even the boulder that Beast had crushed had reverted to its previous form, now standing tall and solid beside me.

Beast trudged into the darkness of the tunnel and the portcullis closed behind him. When he was gone, I turned around. The coliseum was silent. I looked across the arena and saw Spud rolling toward me. Beyond him, Jocko and Geeta had their faces pressed to the iron bars of the gate. Jocko flashed me a thumbs up.

"That was fantastic," he said. "Really tremendous effort. Now let's try again!"

31

As it turned out, using Giant's Roar in the simulation did leave me with the debuff. But it also let me win. After my fourth failed attempt at fighting the Beast of Ending, I finally activated my special skill. When the metal bear came around a boulder, I pulled the Clockwork Guardian's Club from my Inventory and swung with all my might. The club connected with a *crack* that sent vibrations up my arms.

It also knocked the bear's head clean off its shoulders.

"Well done!" Jocko shouted from behind the gate as Beast collapsed to the ground. Where its head had been was now a nest of sparking wires. "That's what I'm talking about!"

You've killed the Beast of Ending (Simulated Construct). Since this wasn't the real Beast of Ending, you won't get any loot. But this was a particularly challenging boss, so good job.

It was the highest compliment I'd received from the dungeon, though my joy was short-lived as my debuff went into effect. It hit me with all the force I'd just used to knock the head from a metal bear, and I nearly collapsed to the ground with exhaustion.

"Man down!" Spud said from my shoulder. "Hold on, ladies and jellybeans. He might blow his lunch!"

I crawled toward the gate. When I reached it, I grabbed the metal with both hands and pulled myself upright. The sand beneath my feet bucked and rolled as if I stood on the prow of a ship.

"Nice going there," Jocko said. "Take a breather. You're fine. You're golden." He turned to Geeta. "It's time for the silent assassin to get her licks. Geeta, hop in there!"

The gate swung open. Geeta moved to help me inside, but Jocko waved her off.

"Leave him," he said. "He needs to learn to take care of himself."

I assured Geeta that I was okay, even if I felt anything but. She shrugged and I struggled into the cave behind the gate, using the wall to steady myself. Once inside, I saw how Jocko had been controlling the simulation: on the face of the podium were a variety of buttons and levers. If I'd had the energy, I might've been more interested. Instead, it took all of my strength to keep my head from cracking against the floor as I collapsed.

Jocko didn't notice, too focused on fiddling with a few dials on the podium. "Ready?" he yelled to Geeta. When she responded in the affirmative, he pressed a button. Through the bars of the gate, I watched the portcullis on the far side of the arena rise.

I passed out. Or I must've, because when I next opened my eyes, Geeta was in the middle of fighting a humanoid monster that looked to be made of solid stone. Based on Jocko's shouts of encouragement, I imagined she was doing fairly well. But I couldn't watch. I closed my eyes and rested in the cool dark of the tunnel, my back to the wall and my head between my knees, trying to keep the contents of my stomach from spilling onto the floor.

Relax. You've been through worse. You'll get through this.

Some time later, Jocko said, "Hey *pacho*, it's your turn again." I realized he was talking to me. I also thought he was kidding, so I ignored him. "Let's go, Crow," Jocko said. "You're gonna fight or you'll die trying."

It took all my willpower to speak. "I can't," I said. "I have to wait a few more hours until I get my strength back."

"That's not correct," Jocko said. "You need to get off your butt. I'm serious. It's a matter of life or death." In one swift motion, he drew his sword and pointed it at me, the angled tip of the blade hovering before my eye. "Get in the ring," he growled.

I didn't actually think he'd kill me, but the look on his face made me pull myself to my feet. I took one step before I stumbled. Jocko let me fall to the ground.

"Up!" he said. "Up and at 'em."

I crawled into the sandy arena. Geeta moved to help me stand, but Jocko batted away her hand.

"Don't you touch him!" he said. "He's training."

"Sorry," Geeta whispered as she walked past me.

I got to the center of the arena and pulled myself to my feet.

"You've seen better days, my friend," Spud said as I set him to hover over my glove. The only way I could stand was by leaning against a rock. "But don't you worry. We'll get through this together. Or you'll die and I'll get a new owner. Hopefully someone who doesn't smell as badly as you."

I've been to some difficult practices, but none harder than the one I faced in the Training Room. My head pounded and my bones ached. Honestly, I was convinced I might keel over and die. In fact, I almost welcomed death. But every time I thought about quitting, Spud whispered encouragement, Geeta offered kind but firm support, or Jocko drew his sword and threatened to fight me himself.

We practiced like that for the entire afternoon. Finally, with Geeta and me both battered and bloody, and my energy at its lowest, I snapped.

Maybe it was because we'd been training for so long. Perhaps the debuff affected me in ways I hadn't anticipated. To this day, I don't know why, exactly, I lost my cool. All I can say is that everyone has a breaking point; after several hours, Jocko had found mine.

"I'm going to kill you!" I said, as he pointed his sword at me for the hundredth time. I knocked the blade away from my throat with a forearm, the edge slicing a clean line where it touched my skin. I towered over Jocko, looking down into his small dark eyes. "You've dragged us into your stupid plot, which we've *agreed* to help with, and now we're fighting ourselves ragged while you sit back here and yell at us?" I yelled. "You're a coward. You're sick! Some Desert Blade!"

"Crow." Geeta's hand came down on my shoulder, but I shrugged her off.

"No," I said. My whole body shook with rage. "I'm not letting him point that sword at me again." I stabbed a finger into Jocko's chest. "If you know so much, why don't *you* get in the ring? Why don't you show us what being a Grass King is all about?"

The cave was silent. Jocko lifted his free hand and moved my index finger away from his chest. Then he slid his sword back into its scabbard.

"Very well," he said. "I suppose that's fair. Even if you can't see it yet, I'm helping you in the long run. But I can understand why you'd want me to take a turn."

He turned on his heel and walked to the podium. When he reached it, he slid levers and turned knobs, then pointed to a green button near the podium's base.

"Geeta, when I give you the signal, press this button," he said. "Get some water, both of you. Take a rest." He nodded at me. "When I'm done in the ring, I expect you to take your turn again."

Jocko was trying to help us, even if he had a funny way of doing it. He opened the gate and walked toward the center of the ring. I looked at the podium, trying to get a sense of his opponent, though none of the buttons, levers, or knobs were labeled in any language I recognized.

"That wasn't very nice, Crow," Spud said. "You could've expressed yourself without all the yelling."

I didn't even have the energy to tell him to shut up.

Jocko had reached the center of the arena. He bounced on the balls of his feet, then bent down and lifted a handful of sand that he rubbed between his palms. He looked over his shoulder to where we were standing.

"Here we go." He clapped his sandy hands. Dust flew into the air. "Now you'll see what a real fight looks like. Geeta, press the button, please."

Geeta followed his instructions. The portcullis lifted and the Beast of Ending once again lumbered out of the darkness.

I shook my head. From what Jocko had said to me during one of Geeta's bouts, he could've chosen to fight any one of a hundred and fifty simulated opponents, at any level, but he'd selected the same one he'd given me.

I understood his point: I was the one who'd called him out. I was the one who'd fought the metal bear several times already, with only a single pyrrhic victory that had left me limp with exhaustion. If Jocko could beat the same opponent on his first try, *and* do it without vomiting, he'd be showing me how far I needed to go to catch up.

Of course, there was always the chance that Jocko would lose. In that case, I'd be the one laughing. If Jocko couldn't beat the Beast of Ending, he wouldn't only lose a battle but his credibility. How could he boss us around if he wasn't any stronger or more talented than us?

No one said anything as we waited for the portcullis to close and the battle to begin. But the portcullis didn't close. Instead, *another* creature emerged from the darkness, and I recognized the sleek mesh and spiked head of Ramzoid. The second Doomsday Construct came to stand beside its brother, one with eyes that glowed blue and the other with eyes that shone yellow.

"That's going to be a slaughter," Spud said. "One man fighting two Doomsday Constructs?"

Yet Jocko wasn't done. With a metallic screech, Metalhawk flew from the tunnel, its claws raking furrows in the sand before it threw out its wings and came to a stop beside the other two Doomsday Constructs. Only then did the portcullis close.

Jocko drew his sword. "Okay, my metal friends," he said. "Now, we dance."

As soon as he finished speaking, all three Doomsday Constructs attacked. Metalhawk triggered its rockets. Beast shot its plasma beams. Ramzoid lowered its arms to the ground and charged, thundering toward Jocko on its knuckles with its head lowered like a mix between a bull and some type of muscular jungle beast.

Before any of the attacks hit Jocko, there was an explosion of leaves around him. When they settled, he was gone. The rockets and plasma struck the space where he'd been, and then Ramzoid careened through the same empty space, tossing its head and throwing up a spray of dust.

"Where'd he go?" Spud asked.

An explosion of leaves appeared behind Metalhawk. Then Jocko's blade punched through the construct's back and out its chest. The creature beat its wings as Jocko sawed up and down. His blade sliced through the armored metal plates like they were made of tin foil. Beast shot another round of plasma beams, but Jocko turned, using Metalhawk's body as a shield. The plasma hit the metal bird, and the force sent a massive armored plate spinning into the stands—then Jocko was gone. The remaining pieces of Metalhawk's body settled to the ground amidst a pile of leaves.

Geeta whistled. "Look at him go," she said.

It was impossible to look away. Jocko was a shadow that I could scarcely follow. Whenever I'd pinned him down, there'd be a shower of leaves and he'd appear somewhere else, his long blade glinting. In moments, he stood back in the center of the arena, his head bowed, his sword sheathed at his waist. The arena around him was littered with pieces of the simulated Doomsday Constructs.

"He really made you eat your words, didn't he, Crow?" Spud said. "Hot diggity! That was awesome."

I couldn't argue. And I couldn't compete with Jocko. At least, not yet. But I could get better. If I wanted to survive, it was a necessity.

I sighed as Jocko jogged over to us. The Grass King hadn't even broken a sweat.

"Where'd you learn to fight like that?" Spud asked as he came through the gate.

"My father taught me," Jocko said. "And I have twenty years of training against the world's best army." He pointed to me. "Now buck up. It's your turn again."

32

The next morning, Jocko, Geeta, Spud, and I had just left the training room when I noticed something sitting outside the door that hadn't been there when we'd entered: a Kinetoscope.

"Have either of you come across one of these in the dungeon before?" I asked Geeta and Jocko, pointing at the machine.

Jocko nodded. "Sure," he said. "The last time I looked through one, I ended up talking to Elvis Madden. You know, the famous TV host? He interviewed me for that show he does about the Hunt. Nice guy."

"Interesting," I said. "Geeta?"

The reptilian shook her head. "I have never seen this thing in my life, inside the dungeon or out of it," she said. She looked from the Kinetoscope to Jocko. "So it is like a phone?" she said. "You use it to make calls? If so, why is it so big? I would think you have phones in the Empire."

Jocko sighed. "You southerners don't understand fashion," he said. "Anyway, I don't have anything to say to Madden. You two can use it if you want, but make sure you're done in an hour. Brynn wanted to be out of here with several days to spare. We'll meet in the laboratory."

"Copy that," I said.

"I do not need to talk to this Madden, either," Geeta said. "So that thing is yours if you want it, Crow."

"Want it?" Spud said from where he sat on my shoulder. "We *obviously* want it. The chance to be on TV? On a real show? Go on ahead, my friends. Crow and I will catch up with you."

Jocko raised an eyebrow at me. Part of me didn't want to use the Kinetoscope, but I remembered Madden's words from our last conversation: 'The next time you see one of these dumb, bulky devices, look through it and I'll help you.' And even though I didn't trust him, I trusted the Empire to serve their own best interests— which meant keeping me alive.

I nodded. I didn't know how the Empire could help me, but I was willing to find out. "I'll use it," I said. "See you guys soon."

"Woo!" Spud said. "Good choice, Crow. I'm gonna be a star!"

As my companions continued down the hallway, I stepped up to the Kinetoscope and set Spud on the surface next to the keyboard. "There's only room for one at the viewfinder," I said to Spud. "The last time I looked through one of these, the Empire kept my face pressed to the machine by engaging a magnet in my ocular implant. So if we do get Madden on the line, I don't want you yelling at me to step away and let you look. Chances are, I won't be able to move."

"That's fine," Spud said. "Will I be able to hear?"

"Most likely," I said. I patted the side of the machine. "The speakers are in here somewhere. And they'll probably be able to hear you, too, so watch what you say."

"I will be the paragon of professionalism," Spud said. "The pinnacle of politeness. The... the... well, I can't think of another appropriate alliteration. But I'll be absolutely charming. You can count on that!"

"Great," I said. "Here we go."

I pressed my face to the viewfinder. Sure enough, a magnet locked onto my eye and I found that I couldn't move. A second later, familiar text appeared on the screen.

Confirming... Live on *Elvis Madden's Hunter Talk* in 3... 2... 1...

"What's happening?" Spud asked. "Let me look! Oh—you can't, can you? We covered that. Then give me a play-by-play. Can you see Elvis Madden? Is he good-looking? Talk to me!"

"I see him," I said as Elvis Madden popped onto the screen.

"Crow!" Madden said, flashing me a smile. "You know the drill. And it sounds like we have Spud this time! Oh, this *will* be fun."

"Hello, Madden," I said.

"Madden!" Spud yelled into my ear. "Can you hear me? Am I coming in? Honestly, sir, it's an absolute pleasure. Once I heard that you host a TV show, you became my idol."

"I can hear you, Spud," Madden said. "I'm going to start the interview, but then my producer wants to bring you in. When we're ready for you, we'll release the magnet so Crow can step back and you can take a peek through the viewfinder. You'll know when it's time because I'll say, 'Where is everyone's favorite potato?' Sound good?"

"It sounds amazing," Spud said. "Thank you, Mr. Madden, sir. This is going to be incredible. I'm going to be on TV!"

"Scene 10C, take one," someone yelled from offscreen. "Action!"

The "Live" icon appeared in the bottom right-hand corner of my screen.

Madden's performative smile grew wider, turning fake and saccharine. It would play well on the screens. "Hello, Crow," he said. "Congratulations on making it this far, and on capturing the attention of the Empire! Or should I say, congratulations Crow *and* Spud. Speaking of, where is everyone's favorite potato?"

"That's my cue!" Spud yelled. "Move, Crow, move!"

There was a click from inside the Kinetoscope, and I stepped away from the machine. Instantly, Spud took my place and pressed his face against the viewfinder.

"Oh my gosh," he said. "This is so cool! There's another world in here. And Mr. Madden! I see you, sir. What an absolute pleasure. Charmed. Simply charmed! Crow, you didn't tell me he was so *handsome.*"

"Spud, the pleasure is all mine," Madden said, his voice coming through the machine's speakers. "Secretly, I was hoping Crow would make it this far, because I've been so excited to speak with *you*. What a team! We've never had anything like it. At this point, you've escaped slimes, conquered the last of the giants, and teamed up with a reptilian from the Emerald Isles, not to mention the Undead Librarian, the Grass King, and the Flight Mechanic. But let's talk about Geeta. What did you think when you got back from Potato Hell and found that Crow had adopted a new companion?"

Dirty move. Before I could say anything, Spud said, "Honestly, Mr. Madden, I was a little disappointed. As the leader of this squad, I like to be consulted on all major decisions. But if you've seen Geeta in action, you know that she's an absolute powerhouse. She's a real addition to the team."

That was a good answer. Maybe Spud *was* made for TV.

"I couldn't agree more," Madden said. "So she's doing well?"

"She's a real trooper, Mr. Madden," Spud said. "Dealt a tough hand and forced into piracy. It's a good thing the Empire takes such a tough stance against enslavement. You'd never see such horror in the civilized cities of the north."

In truth, the Empire had as many enslaved people as the south, but Spud's answer would play well on the screens.

"You're right about that!" Madden said. "Of course, when you talk about piracy, you're talking about Cara Thorne, who once held Geeta and her late partner Silvana on her ship, the *Rancid Pearl*. There's no excuse for any type of piracy, but if it makes you feel any better, Ms. Thorne and her lackeys are having a rough time right now. I can't say any more than that, but hopefully it's welcome news."

"Tremendously welcome, Mr. Madden," Spud said. "Thank you."

"One thing I like about you and Crow is that you make the dungeon look easy," Madden said. "What's your secret?"

"You know, Mr. Madden, I'd chalk it up to chemistry," Spud said. "And when I say 'chemistry,' I'm not talking about starch gelatinization but the kind that develops between a human and a sapient, electromagnetically charged potato when they fight for their lives together in a wild and wacky dungeon. An experience like that brings entities together. You know what I'm saying?"

"Of course!" Madden said. "Now, I know you and Crow have a deadline, but before you go, we want to give the two of you a small gift. Can we bring Crow back?"

"It really was a pleasure, Mr. Madden," Spud said. He moved away from the viewfinder. "Crow!" he said to me. "He wants to talk to you."

I didn't think it'd be productive to remind Spud that I could hear the entire conversation, so I simply pressed my forehead back to the viewfinder.

"Hi again, Crow," Madden said. He flashed me a smile. It was so maddeningly fake, yet I knew the Empire would eat it up. "As I was telling Spud, it's time for you to see the prize you won in the Empire Vote. But before we do, I should say that we must've had quite a bit of engagement from the Crescent, because some people *really* didn't want to see you succeed," Madden said. "I'm talking silly stuff. A pie to the face. More pickled vegetables. Another lamprey to the..." He laughed. "That was quite a scene. And Crow, I hate to say this, but we even had a contingent pushing for some downright dangerous stuff. Can you believe that we almost had to bring back the giant? People really must've been bitter about your record with the Sledgehammers!"

From under the desk, Madden took out a box and set it before him. The box was about the size of the battery pack that was clipped to my belt, made of wood and completely unadorned.

"At the end of the day, though, I'm happy to report that your own city led the charge, with Steel City supporters voting in droves," Madden continued. "I've been hosting this show for a decade now and I'm not sure I've ever seen anything like it. This was a popular one, Crow, and the people have spoken. Without further ado, I'm proud to announce that after the Empire Vote, you are now the owner of..." He trailed off as a panel in the desk slid to one side to reveal a metal chute. Madden placed the box above the chute and it disappeared with a pneumatic *hiss*. Then he turned back to the camera. "A brand-new, sapient electromagnetic tomato with the ability to spit acid!" he said, smiling broadly. "Ladies and gentlemen, please give a warm welcome to Peristopheles Magnesis IV. But you can call him Perry! Watch your shins, Crow."

There was a beep and something banged into my shins.

"Ow," I said. I attempted to see what had hit me but couldn't move.

"Um, Crow?" Spud said, a hint of fear in his voice. "What's going on?"

"We'll let you step back so you can take a peek," Madden said.

There was a click that signaled the release of the magnet and I stepped away from the Kinetoscope to see that a door in the side of the machine had popped open.

So that's what hit me. I pulled the door open to see the box that Madden had sent through the chute in his desk. That thing must've been moving *quickly*.

"I'm proud to say that Perry comes with his own handsome leather bandolier, courtesy of Steel City Leatherworks," Madden said, his voice in my ears even though I could no longer see him. "Get rid of that leather belt pouch and enjoy the upgrade. All yours, courtesy of the Empire! Congratulations again, Spud and Crow. Hashtag Spud Squad. Madden, out."

Cautiously, I removed the box from the space behind the door and set it atop the Kinetoscope. I flipped the gold latch and lifted the lid.

"Crow?" Spud said, peering into the box. "What did he say about another sapient creature? He didn't actually mean that, did he?"

Inside the box was a folded strip of leather. *That must be the bandolier Madden referenced.* I pulled it from the box and dropped it as something that had been hidden beneath the leather rotated to face me.

It was a tomato. Like Spud, it had two wide eyes and a mouth full of teeth. It also had a button nose and a mop of green hair in the shape of a star that I realized was a stem.

"In the name of all that is crispy!" Spud shouted. He jumped toward me and I caught him in one hand. "Kill it, Crow! Kill it!"

Peristopheles Magnesis IV (Perry)

An edible berry of the Solanum lycopersicum, Perry is a close relative of the poisonous belladonna and member of the nightshade family. For that matter, so is Spud! But don't expect the two to get along. While Perry can occasionally be cute and interesting, he also has some serious younger-brother energy. Until he grows into his own, he's destined to piss off everyone by trying *way* too hard. Oh, and the poor guy also has cyclic vomiting syndrome. What's that, you ask? You'll find out soon enough!

The tomato gazed up at me. "Uh, hi," he said shyly. His voice was high and child-like. "I never knew my father. My mother either. But I guess I'm hanging out with you guys now?"

So this is the Empire's gift. How odd.

Spud trembled in my palm. "Crow, I've never asked you for anything," he whispered. "But if I've ever helped you in any way, ever, you can repay me by smashing that thing right now."

"I brought you that bandolier," the tomato said, nodding toward the belt I held in the hand that didn't have Spud. "I don't feel so good."

With that, the tomato opened its mouth and vomited green liquid. Spud screamed at the same time I jumped backward, narrowly avoiding the splash that cascaded over the side of the Kinetoscope. Where the liquid touched the ground, it hissed and bubbled, leaving shallow pits in its wake.

"Are you kidding me?" Spud said. "No way. Compost that thing, Crow. Kill it now. That thing spits acid. We don't want that anywhere near us."

Perry started crying, his glassy eyes brimming with tears. "I'm sorry," he gasped as snot dribbled from his nose. "I can't help myself. It —it happens when I'm stressed."

I moved Spud to my shoulder and looked more closely at Perry. The tomato was roughly the same size as Spud. Since Madden had described him as electromagnetic, I figured that I could probably push and pull him with my gloves.

But should I? On the one hand, a weapon that shot corrosive acid would make me that much more versatile. *But what if Perry really* can't *control himself? That's a huge liability.*

It didn't make sense. As Madden had said, the only thing I trusted about the Empire was that they served their own best interests—and that meant keeping me alive. As long as I lived, millions of Empire citizens would be watching the Hunt.

And if they're trying to help you, why would they send you a weapon you couldn't control? The answer was simple: they wouldn't. Despite what Perry had told me, I was willing to bet his spit-ups weren't random.

I turned on my battery pack and held a hand toward Perry. *This is going to end one of two ways. Either my next move pays off, and Perry becomes a powerful new ally, or millions of Empire citizens die laughing when a sobbing tomato covers me in acid.*

"Don't do it, Crow!" Spud cried as I pulled on the tomato. Perry's eyes widened as he shot into my hand.

"Oh wow… whoa!" Perry said as I set him to hover above my palm. He stopped sniffling and let out a little giggle. "That was fun. Neat trick, sir! And you know what? I'm feeling… I'm feeling *much* better. Like, I don't have to throw up at all! Being around you guys must have that effect on me."

"Ugh," Spud said. "Now *I'm* gonna be sick."

I exhaled with relief. Perry's settled stomach was a good sign. *For now, it doesn't look like I'm in danger of getting splashed by acid. So maybe I do have a read on the Empire? And if I was right about that, I'm wondering if I can control Perry's acid in the same way I use Spud's Hot Potato ability.*

There was only one way to find out. "Hold on, Perry," I said. "I'm going to send you for a little ride."

"Okay!" Perry said cheerfully. "Where are we—whoa!"

I shot him down the hallway. It wasn't a hard shot, but I pushed hard enough to put some distance between us.

Acid. Not a second later, a spray of green liquid erupted from between Perry's lips.

"Ew!" Spud yelled. "We can't keep him. He's going to kill us all!"

But the experiment had proved otherwise. With a pull from my glove, I brought Perry back toward us. I didn't catch him, just in case he was still covered in any of the acid, and he rolled to a stop at my feet.

"I'm sorry," Perry said. The poor guy was crying again. "I don't know what happened. I felt fine, and then I was sick! I want to help you guys. I really do. I can usually control my acid, but sometimes, when I get worked up, it comes out!"

I took a knee beside the sobbing tomato. When I was sure that none of the acid still clung to him, I lifted him up.

"Any chance you feel better now?" I asked.

The tomato looked up at me through red-rimmed eyes. "Actually… yeah. I don't feel nauseous at all."

I smiled as I set him atop the Kinetoscope. *He feels good when he's around us and I can activate his acid with a mental command. That's pretty much what I needed to know.*

Gently, I patted Perry's green stem. "Don't worry about the vomiting. I'm the one who made it happen just now. I can make Spud do something similar. Except instead of spitting acid, he lights on fire."

Perry's eyes darted to Spud, who still sat on my shoulder. "Really? That's awesome!"

"I know it's awesome," Spud said. "I'm the one doing it."

"Don't be rude, Spud," I said. I gave the potato a light flick. To Perry, I said, "You're on our team now, buddy. You can hang out with us."

"No, he most *certainly* can't!"

I lifted the bandolier from where I'd dropped it. It was crafted from dark leather, and the buckle looked to be made of the same silver as the six electromagnetic discs that studded its surface.

"How do I look?" I asked after I'd thrown the bandolier over my left shoulder. I caught the buckle and adjusted it so that it crossed my body and fit snugly over my right hip. "Pretty cool, right?"

"No," Spud said. "You look like an idiot. Take it off!"

Perry looked up at me, his eyes wide. "I think you look really good."

From my shoulder, Spud snorted. "What a suck up. Are you kidding me? Come on, Crow. Leave him here to rot."

I lifted Spud off my shoulder and pressed him to the top disc in my new bandolier. As I expected, when I took my hand away, Spud stayed stuck to the bandolier.

"You can't do this to me," he wailed. "You're the worst friend ever. You and I, we made puns together. I thought that meant something. But it didn't mean… didn't mean…" He trailed off. "Oh, that's actually quite nice. A massaging feature? Wow."

He closed his eyes, and I lifted Perry. Whereas Spud was rough and knobby, Perry's skin was completely smooth. I brought him to my face and the two of us stared at each other, man to tomato.

"Hi Perry," I said quietly. "Welcome to the Spud Squad."

33

When it came time to free the wyrm queen, I stood with Geeta, Jocko, Rayne, Brynn, and the Mad Mage on a stone platform that jutted out from the back side of the fortress. A hundred feet below us, waves crashed against the plateau. Each whitecap gleamed beneath the blue-tinged moon.

Beside me stood Geeta, looking as tense as I felt. Her stiletto was in one scaled hand and she rubbed it nervously against her whetstone.

The timer in the upper right-hand corner of my vision gave us another five days until the Purge. If the Mad Mage and Brynn were correct, we'd be leaving the Dark City within the next few hours.

The two stood nearby, speaking to each other in hushed whispers as they bent over a sheet of vellum. Beside them was a podium like the one in the Training Room, though this one had considerably fewer buttons. As I looked from the Mad Mage and Brynn to Jocko, I couldn't help but notice that the Grass King's right hand rested on the hilt of his sword.

You're fine. Everything is fine. I'd reviewed the engineering behind their plans and it made sense.

Still, it was hard not to worry.

I looked down at my chest, where Spud and Perry slept against my bandolier. Before nodding off, Spud had insisted on the spot closest to my left shoulder—and further insisted that Perry take the one closest to my right hip, which put as much distance between them as possible. I'd told Perry he could take whatever spot he wanted, but he accepted the spot near my hip without complaint. As they slept, Spud snored, each inhale making a sound like wind blowing through the tunnels beneath the fortress. Perry mumbled softly.

"Ratatouille," he said. "Bruschetta. Panzanella."

The only person on the platform who didn't appear tense was Rayne, who crouched on her heels and drew circles in the sawdust that covered the platform. I didn't know whether that was part of a spell or just her way of passing the time. The charms in her dreadlocks tinkled as she moved.

After another few minutes, the Mad Mage and Brynn reached an agreement. The Mad Mage went to the podium and made several adjustments to the dials on its surface. Brynn folded the vellum into quarters and slipped the sheet into the front pocket of her apron.

"Care to check my work?" the Mad Mage asked. Brynn walked over to the podium and looked down at his adjustments. She ran her golden index finger down the wood next to the dials.

"Everything looks good," she said. "Now you won't bring down the fortress. Kidding, obviously. You had it right the first time. But it always pays to double check."

The Mad Mage nodded. "Care to do the honors?"

Brynn shook her head. "These are your people," she said. "Your moment. You do it."

The Mad Mage shrugged and pressed a button. "Sequence initiated," he said.

The ground beneath my feet started to rumble.

"Charges deployed," the Mad Mage said, tapping a dial on the podium. Beside me, Geeta slipped the whetstone back into her Inventory. On my other side, Jocko stared at Brynn, his right hand still on the hilt of his blade.

"Oh, hey there, Crow," Spud said from my chest as he woke up. "Wow, that was a great nap. What's happening?"

The rumbling grew louder. Behind me, soldiers whispered among themselves, but a look from the Mad Mage brought them to silence.

The rumbling stopped.

"Crow?" Spud whispered. "What was that?"

A cry cut the silence, equal parts angry and mournful, followed by a tremendous explosion. Spud spoke again, more loudly this time: "Crow?"

From beneath the edge of the plateau, the subterranean wyrm queen rose into the air. Her head appeared first, then her wings. In the cave, she'd had them folded against her body, but now they lifted her into the air before us. They were easily thirty feet tall and covered with translucent webbing. I took an involuntary step backward.

"Nope," Spud said. "I'm dreaming. Wake up, Spud. You're having a nightmare. Wake up!"

The wyrm queen dove into the water. Her back followed, sinuous carapace unspooling from the cavern and disappearing beneath the inky waves.

She was huge.

When I'd seen her in the chamber below the fortress, I thought I'd understood the full extent of her size, but I realized now that half of her must've been curled into some dark recess.

In that moment, I understood why giants had been necessary to harness her power.

But even with the giants, I still don't understand how they did it.

Below us, the ocean frothed. Beneath the dark waves was something darker still, and I could tell that Geeta saw it, too. It wasn't anything she said, but more of a feeling, a sudden shifting in mood from tension to fear.

Hundreds of winged imago erupted from the water, their pale forms breaking the surface as they buzzed into the sky. If they knew we were watching their escape, they didn't care. They fled the plateau like lightballs shot from a thousand gloves and followed their mother into the distance.

"It's happening," the Mad Mage whispered. "She's free."

When the wyrm queen was about a thousand yards distant, she

rocketed from the ocean and turned to face us, water cascading down her body as she turned and danced in the sky.

"Oh," Geeta said from beside me.

As that sightless face turned toward us, I found myself rooted to the ground. Was it fear? A spell of petrification? Both? I didn't know. Under the wyrm queen's gaze, I didn't only see death: I saw obliteration. Not the end of my body, but my soul. The wyrm queen was ancient. Incomprehensible. How silly we'd been to stand there. The wyrm queen could wipe us off the map with a thought.

If you want to defeat the Empire, you don't need the Doomsday Constructs. You need that.

Rayne stood from her crouch. Stepping forward, she placed herself between our group and the hovering wyrm queen. From the pouch at her side, she removed a book and then opened it between her hands. For the first time, I heard her voice. She spoke in an alien tongue that I didn't recognize, the words polysyllabic and rhythmic.

"*Pittan rua-tak hoven mulkatak,*" she said. "*Biralchatak savachatak menachatak achminatak.*"

The wyrm queen turned and continued her journey toward the horizon. Still, Rayne kept chanting.

"*Yamnatak pirtanatak horvatak,*" she said. "*Shokatak vartanatak netanatak. Thorvatak kamatak murnatak.*"

There was a sound like hail hitting water. *Plink plink. Plink. Plink.* At first, I thought it was my imagination, but then I realized what it was: at Rayne's command, *thousands* of bones had risen from the water. Fibulas, tibias, femurs, and ribs. Ulnas, radii, and skulls. They floated in the air, forming a rectangle that framed the distant wyrm queen like a picture, and then the frame filled in and blocked the queen from view.

So that's how they're gathering the bone they need for the battery.

"*Vohanatak sakatagatak mikatak. Pasanatak mikhatak shimatakamatak takatak hapatak.*"

The bones kept rising. It was as if each one was magnetic. They piled higher and thicker, and higher still. As I watched the Undead Librarian work, I understood how the subterranean wyrm queen had been made: some ancient god had called it into being with a spell like this, a spell that created something grand and impossible.

"Thimatak jokatak dayavatak!"

With a final shout, Rayne slammed her book shut, and the wall of bone crashed into the ocean. It created such a splash that I felt the spray on my face. When I wiped it away, the wyrm queen was gone. The winged imago were gone. I squinted into the distance, but I couldn't even see them as tiny specks on the horizon.

"We did it," the Mad Mage said quietly. "She's gone."

"Thank goodness," Spud said. "I never, *ever* want to see something like that again."

At my right hip, Perry stirred. "Gazpacho. Pico de Gallo. Salmorejo," he mumbled as he woke, yawning and blinking the sleep from his innocent eyes. When he looked around, he saw our group on the platform, every eye on the horizon.

"Oh!" he said. "A party! This looks neat. What'd I miss?"

34

I didn't get any loot for releasing the wyrm queen, because nothing had died. But after running around for what felt like ages, dealing with lampreys, winged imago, and giant metal birds, mere survival was treasure enough for me.

After the spectacle on the platform, Geeta, Jocko, Rayne, and I followed the Mad Mage and Brynn down a series of stone tunnels and into the empty chamber beneath the plateau. Now, there was a huge hole in one wall that looked out over the ocean.

"That hole does wonders for the place," Spud said from his spot on my chest. "Nothing like a little natural light to brighten things up!"

Filen Blackhand entered the cavern from another entrance, two dozen soldiers following behind. Each of them carried a bundle of cables or wire. They crossed the floor and stopped in front of the Mad Mage.

"Reporting for duty, sir," Blackhand said to the Mad Mage, their voice echoing in the chamber. "We brought everything you asked."

"Thank you," the Mad Mage said. He motioned to a spot on the floor. "Start stacking things there. Rayne still needs to get the bone into the cavern. Actually, I believe we should move. It looks like she has already started working."

I followed the Mad Mage's gaze and saw that Rayne stood on a boulder before the hole in the cavern wall. Her book was open in her hands.

"Wise counsel, *pacho*," Jocko murmured from beside me. "It would be a shame to have come this far only to get crushed by a giant battery."

Our group moved to one side of the cavern. When Rayne had dropped the cube of bone she'd raised back into the ocean, I'd figured it was lost. But no: as I watched, the construct rose from the ocean and floated through the opening in the cave wall. It moved as smoothly as a gyrocopter, but without any visible means of propulsion.

That's some powerful magic. The construct settled to the ground in the center of the cavern.

The Mad Mage clapped his hands. "There we go," he said. "Black-hand, I need everyone with copper wire over here. Brynn, start getting the cable ready."

It only took Brynn and the dwarves a few minutes to make the appropriate connections. When they were done, Brynn gave us a thumbs up.

"Ready?" Jocko asked.

"It's done!" the Mad Mage exclaimed. "My friends! The dwarves have been done a great service. Come! Let me see you off."

We walked down the damp, slick path to join the Mad Mage around something I hadn't previously noticed: a door embedded in the floor. It was made from mahogany and had a handle of burnished brass.

The door to the next level. Sure enough, as I looked at it, text appeared in my vision.

Toroth-Gol: Level Three (Dungeon School)

Congratulations! You're about to enter the third level of Toroth-Gol.

"Onward and upward," Spud said from my shoulder.

"Onward and *down*ward," Jocko corrected. He looked at the Mad Mage and pointed at the door. "It's safe to open?"

The Mad Mage clapped his hands. "The device works perfectly," he said. "The door is stable!"

Jocko stepped forward, then crouched down to reach the knob that stuck out of the door like a mushroom. He turned the knob and threw the door open, revealing nothing but blackness behind it. Just a rectangle of pure darkness that sucked in all light.

"And this is safe to go through?" Jocko asked.

The Mad Mage's face fell. "Ah, I'm less certain about that," he said.

"Hmm," Jocko said. He stood and wiped his hands on his pants, then turned to the Mad Mage. "I guess we'll trust the gods on this one, *pacho*." He bowed. "Thank you for your hospitality. And best of luck to you and your people. I'm glad we could play a part in your return."

It was an oddly formal thing to say, but the Mad Mage returned the bow.

"There's still much work to be done," he said. "But the dwarves are no stranger to hard work. If you ever need my people, you can call on me. Make good use of what I gave you."

Jocko nodded as he patted at a bulge in his robes. *I wonder what the Mad Mage gave him?* But before I could consider it further, Jocko turned and jumped into the darkness. Instantly, he was gone.

"Whoa," Spud said. "Where'd he go?"

I might not trust the gods, but I trust Jocko, I thought as Brynn clasped the Mad Mage's arm. They exchanged a few quiet words, and then she followed Jocko into the blackness behind the door. Rayne followed Brynn, and then Geeta. I stood alone with the Mad Mage.

"Mage," I said, meeting his eyes. He stared back, a thin smile on his lips.

"I know it was you who damaged Metalhawk," he said. "And I know you're much smarter than you let on."

I grimaced. "Ah. Yes."

The Mad Mage shrugged. "Get out of here before I call the Beast of Ending."

I nodded and stepped over to the door. "So long!" I closed my eyes and jumped.

THE END OF BOOK I

AFTERWORD

WOW!

You finished this book! If I could make one request: please leave a review on Amazon and Goodreads. As an independent author, I rely on those reviews to survive. If I don't hit my monthly quota, I get sent to Potato Hell.

Also! If you want to be the first to hear about new books and more, join the #SpudSquad mailing list by visiting https://kenny-gould.kit.-com/newsletter

ABOUT THE AUTHOR

Kenny Gould writes science and fantasy fiction. He holds a BA from Duke University, an MFA from Chatham University, and an MBA from NYU Stern. He lives with his wife, two cats, and a very funny dog in sunny Florida.

Connect with him on social at @thekennygould or through his website at kennygould.com.

THE ADVENTURE CONTINUES!

Get *Dungeon School,* Book II in the Toroth-Gol series, for FREE on Kindle Unlimited. Also available in paperback and eBook through Amazon, or as an audiobook through Audible.